The Alchemist's Mind

DAVID MILLER's recent publications include *The Waters of Marah* (2005), *The Dorothy and Benno Stories* (2005), *In the Shop of Nothing: New and Selected Poems* (2007), *Spiritual Letters (Series 1-5)* (2011) (a double CD recording of David Miller reading this same work came out in 2012) and *Black, Grey and White: A Book of Visual Sonnets* (2011). He has compiled *British Poetry Magazines 1914-2000: A History and Bibliography of "Little Magazines"* (with Richard Price, 2006) and edited *The Lariat and Other Writings* by Jaime de Angulo (2009).

The Alchemist's Mind

a book of narrative prose by poets

edited by David Miller

REALITY STREET

Published by
REALITY STREET
63 All Saints Street, Hastings, East Sussex TN34 3BN, UK
www.realitystreet.co.uk

First edition 2012

Typesetting & book design by Ken Edwards

Reality Street Narrative Series No 11

A catalogue record for this book is available from the British Library

ISBN: 978-1-874400-58-5

CONTENTS

Introduction by *David Miller*..7

Barbara Guest: From: *Seeking Air* [Sections 1-11]..........................35

Lee Harwood: The Beginning of the Story 49

Ian Robinson: Delayed Frames...55

Rosmarie Waldrop: A Form of Memory [abridged]
(from *A Form/ of Taking/ It All*)...62

Robert Sheppard: From: The Given [Section 1].............................75

Bernadette Mayer: Farmers Exchange
+ Nathaniel Hawthorne 81

Paul Buck: skiP there is no story speaK to me [extract] 89

Lyn Hejinian: Lola...101

M J Weller: MySpace Opera – Twenty-Three Tales
Slowed Into a Fic-Blogosphere Microfiction
During a Period of Thirty-Three Months 112

Brian Marley: A Perigee Selection....................................120

Johan de Wit: A Dream + Another Dream + And another
Dream + Again another Dream + And again another Dream
+ Still another Dream + Yet another Dream + Yet again
another Dream + And yet again another Dream
+ Once again another Dream + And once again another
Dream + One more Dream 128

John Levy: Goldilocks and the Five Bears....................138

Vahni Capildeo: The Seven Dwarfs and Snow White 143

Paul Haines: Unrecommended Lures 150

Lawrence Fixel: The Graduate...155

Robert Lax: 21 pages...160

Fanny Howe: Even This Confined Landscape
(from *The Lives of a Spirit*)..173

David Miller: True Points 177

Keith Waldrop: Puberty 190

Giles Goodland: Spring 197

bpNichol: The Mouth + The Tonsils + The Lungs: A Draft
(from *Selected Organs: Parts of an Autobiography*) 204

David Rattray: The Spirit of St Louis..211

Guy Birchard: Tom Farr + Vicar of Distance 216

Will Petersen: From: The Mask 223

Tom Lowenstein: From: Whale Hunt Journal 230

Kristin Prevallet: Preface + Eulogy
(from *I, Afterlife: Essay in mourning time*).......................................240

Stephen Watts: Nonno...246

Daphne Marlatt: Journey (from *Zócalo*) 258

Acknowledgements 265

INTRODUCTION

This anthology is intended to highlight the contribution made by poets to narrative prose writing since 1970, emphasising the variety, scope and singularity involved, and signalling that a great deal of the most interesting, unconventional and impressive work in this field, in the UK and North America, has been written by poets.[1]

(i) Aristotle or Otherwise / Business as Usual... or Not

Narrative prose in the UK and North America is, for the most part, not even haunted by the presumed ghosts of "classic" modernism (e.g. James Joyce, William Faulkner, Djuna Barnes, Gertrude Stein, Franz Kafka, Hermann Broch, Andrei Bely, Miguel de Unamuno), let alone informed by an awareness of the living example of these writers, and most certainly doesn't attempt to go *beyond* modernism.[2] It's more as if modernism never existed... except perhaps as something to teach in the academy. Language is mainly seen as a transparent medium, and literature (following on from this) is a largely direct transference of happenings, ideas, emotions, etc, from one mind (the author's) to another (the reader's), only complicated by questions of manner, ingenuity, decoration or embellishment, and order (mostly considered in a fairly rudimentary way, if sometimes "tricky" at the same time). Mimesis hangs behind all this like a moth-eaten curtain, and Aristotle's well-made plot (with its beginning/middle/end) largely reigns supreme, even if a little chronological reshuffling may be indulged in, together with certain other ways of complicating the basic schema.[3] "Character" follows the certainties of conventional psychology, for the most part. We are what we know we are, however terrible that may sometimes be (as with the fictional – and cinematic – obsession with serial killers, for example), and however mistaken we may sometimes be about one another.

The late Edouard Roditi wrote of the present writer's novella, *Tesserae*:

> Traditional notions of plot, character and environment or
> "spectacle", in the Aristotelian sense, are here profoundly mod-
> ified. Perhaps one should even coin new non-Aristotelian terms
> for his fiction and call it amythic, anethic and anoptic, because
> it refrains from the traditional development of plot (*muthos*),
> character (*ethos*) and spectacle (*opsis*), while remaining faithful to
> the Aristotelian concept of diction (*lexis*).... [4]

I don't quote this here to concentrate attention on myself, but
simply for its aptness to the situation many writers have found
themselves in with regard to narrative prose – that is, the need
to find or work towards alternative possibilities. I think this is
important to emphasise. *Even if* we were to grant mainstream
fiction – and memoirs, autobiographies, travel writing are in
much the same situation, *mutatis mutandis* – an agenda and goals
which are legitimate within their own terms, we are still left with
the question of alternatives.[5] For the most part, narrative prose
is a matter of *business as usual*.[6] But not for the writers in this
anthology.

In many cases (though certainly not all, by any means) we
have to move outside the domain of the novel or novel-length
fiction to consider other achievements. And if indeed we are to
look for alternatives to "the usual" in narrative prose, it is
mainly to be found in the work of poets, as I have already indi-
cated.[7] Much of the work in this anthology is either self-con-
tained or comes from relatively small books, although there are
excerpts from longer works, as with Barbara Guest's, Rosmarie
Waldrop's and Giles Goodland's pieces (Goodland's being from
a novel-length work-in-progress). (Some of it doesn't fit easily
into genres, either, or inhabits the space of other genres than
fiction, such as poetry in prose or the memoir.) But regardless
of questions of length, there are certain aspects of these writ-
ings that we can generalise about with some aptness and to
some advantage.

Here are some of the characteristics and concerns involved:

The poet Roy Fisher has referred to "additive form", where

"each section [of a work] was written in an attempt to refer only to what I had already written in that work, and without any drive forward at all."[8] Even if this is not strictly adhered to – and it isn't by Fisher himself in his prose work *The Ship's Orchestra*, the subject of his remarks, due to the way that sections *diverge* from each other – something similar informs the pieces by (eg) Harwood and Sheppard. (Actually, I think Fisher's formulation is slightly misleading, in as much as what I think he is really pointing to is the way that sections are added together, one to another after another after another, without reference to some pre-established and overarching development.) More generally, we can point to a largely non-hierarchical tendency, *vis-à-vis* structure, in a number of the writers here; it can also be said that their work, quite often, resists the tendency to be directed towards an end (or *telos*).[9] However, it should be stressed that we are not talking about an avoidance or dismissal of the notion of structure here, but rather a rethinking of it.

Staying with structure for the time being, we can look at what's variously referred to as juxtaposition, contiguity or contiguous structure, discontinuous structure, and, drawing on comparisons with other art forms, collage, assemblage and montage. At its simplest, this involves one thing (one "piece" of text) placed against, alongside or after another (depending on how you think of this spatially), with the individual "pieces" or elements often of a disparate nature, and sometimes "found" or quoted from other texts. How this may work, in regard to the relationship of discontinuity and continuity, and the way a larger structure is built up from these contiguous "pieces", will differ from writer to writer. Guy Davenport proposed a model for this under the name of *architectonics*: where subjects are arranged "in ideogrammatic form, shaping them with a poetic sense of imagery, allowing themes to recur in patterns, generating significance... by juxtaposition and the intuition of likenesses among dissimilar and unexpected things."[10] The writer in the present anthology who comes closest to this is perhaps Will Petersen, whose prose works interlace journal extracts, excerpts from letters (his own and others'), poems, etc., bringing together memories, observations, narrative strands and reflections on art and theatre, finding connections through imagery and thematic concerns.[11] More generally, I think it's possible to see that much of the work in this anthology can be said to be *constructed or assembled*, in a way that can scarcely be said of more conventional narrative prose. I would instance Rosmarie Waldrop, as a fairly self-evident example, but someone like Robert Lax could also be instanced, though this might not be quite as obvious.[12]

It should be clear from the above that fragmentation, or rather the fragment and its relation to larger textual identities, is an issue or concern here, relevant to a number of writers – including, again, Rosmarie Waldrop, as well as Ian Robinson, M J Weller, David Rattray and others.[13]

Lyn Hejinian and also to some extent other contributors, including Bernadette Mayer and M J Weller, can be seen as playing with the conventions of fiction and narrative, in a way that revisits the notion of metafiction – fiction about fiction, or self-reflexive fiction – in individual ways and to considerable effect.[14] However, while certain writings may incorporate references to aspects of writing and to the writing process, amongst other elements, metafiction as such seems largely spent, where the notion has not been overextended.[15] At the same time, it's clear that all the writers included here show their awareness of how narrative is mediated through literary conventions, rather than being a "transparent" medium.

"The writing itself also becomes important…, in all its elements, and not merely as a *vehicle*", writes LeRoi Jones/Amiri Baraka. He is writing, in the Introduction to his anthology *The Moderns*, about James Joyce, in order to explicate Joyce's influence on William Burroughs and Jack Kerouac. "Samuel Butler's writing is important only so far as it is *about* something", he continues. "Joyce's writing became an event in itself."[16] The notion of a foregrounding of language and a resistance to the idea of language as a "transparent" mode of communication between author and reader, is highly relevant to the work in this anthology, but it should be clear that this is more strongly or radically the case with some writers than others (as indeed it is in Jones/Baraka's book). However, it's my sense that all the writers here are, let us say, intensely *mindful* and *thoughtful* about language, as well as the processes involved in narrative – in their various ways. And I don't think any of them fall into the trap of decontextualising language – treating it as if it somehow existed in a vacuum. (Interestingly, Jones/Baraka is also clear about this in regard to the writers in his anthology.)

Genre has already been touched upon, if only in passing. It is a characteristic of several of the texts here that they either mix genres or inhabit a space that is ambiguous with regard to genre classification. Will Petersen's writing would be characteristic of the former, as I've indicated, whereas Lax, Birchard, Marlatt and Watts might be considered examples of the latter. (Is Lax's "21 pages" fiction, prose poetry or prose meditation? Are Birchard's, Marlatt's and Watts' pieces personal memoirs, prose poetry or examples of travel writing – or all of these? Or possibly fiction – at least in one or two of these cases?) Why would this matter? Because alternative possibilities are being explored; rigid classifications are being loosened... rendered fluid or even beside the point. An opening up can be observed.[17]

Before passing on to some other concerns, I think it is crucial to emphasise that techniques and structures or forms – including almost all of the things discussed above – simply "do variations on the same law" unless subject to "the alchemist's mind [by which] all is changed" (Fanny Howe).[18] Howe has written elsewhere: "If a face does not gaze back at me from the page, there is only paper and wood, the static object empty of divine spark. The human face in repose and in silence is the face I see, when what I have written approximates the unspeakable."[19] Placing these two quotations side by side is instructive, I feel. Texts can be said to come alive, the words of the text can be said to suffer a transformative action, they can be said to make manifest what can't be spoken. Or they can lie dead on the page. While it is important to speak about structures and techniques, it is, in the final analysis, how they are "taken up and used" that makes the difference.[20]

Amongst the texts that are concerned, either directly or more indirectly, with exploring issues of personhood, I would mention those of Guest, Lax, Howe, Buck, Prevallet, Goodland and Keith Waldrop. "No psychology (of the kind that discovers only what it can explain)" (the filmmaker Robert Bresson).[21] If psychology is displaced and "the self" problematised (in the sense of acknowledged as having the nature or status of a problem), this is in terms of an affirmation of the person, not a denial.[22] To problematise means to admit there are problems in definition and knowledge; the very certainties of "the self" as an entity that's rationally "comprehended" in terms of a system of knowledge become problematic. And in doing so within narrative writing, we have the possibility of something breaking through, some awareness and some manifestation or disclosure of the personal that *resists* and remains *radically other* to rational knowledge.

This brings us to the exploration of the alogical or trans-logical within narrative. While this is evident in Lax's or Howe's contemplative approach, it is equally so in the imaginative concerns of Capildeo or Levy.[23] Perhaps trans-logical is more apt for Lax or Howe, and I would suggest that *attention* or *attentiveness* might be considered relevant here.[24] Other contributors can perhaps be seen as working with alogical imaginative concerns, or else we might simply see their work as inhabiting strange or offbeat — often subversive — imaginative spaces. Capildeo and Levy, in the pieces in this anthology, ring the changes on children's stories to bizarre effect; while de Wit, Marley and Weller, in their various ways, inhabit anarchic, wild or delirious/vertiginous imaginative and textual regions. This is also true of an earlier story by Haines, "In Istanbul", where for example he writes:

> I had my shoes shined with a cap pistol and my socks filled
> with honey. No alteration. In the small shop was a tension wire.
> At each end of the wire were teeth of men. All men with cov-

ers on their chests. The floor was cold and covered with rice, onions and eggplant. The tension wire was pulled taut and started to sing. Then it was eased down. Each man, lying on the floor, had the cover of his chest opened and a handful of quarters thrown in for good measure. I was asked to remove my shirt and of course refused.

The story ends:

Soon hands were inside chest covers. The little girl attempted to bite on my face. Getting her off me smeared honey. My right hand locked in the honey of my left wrist. She cried with glee and stepped away. With her toe she opened the cover of my chest and it was more pleasant than I ever thought it could be.[25]

What *on earth* is going on? I could say that I know and don't know, at the same time. But amongst other things, it's an improvisation on certain key terms/things, including feet (shoes /socks/toes), honey, chests... to hilarious and also disturbing effect. "Unrecommended Lures", from later in Haines' life, is more subtly subversive; while lacking in anything cruel or vicious, the text exhibits the deadly agility of an Indian mongoose, as well as its fabled tendency to eject jewels from its mouth. As with (say) Marley, we are quite some distance from satire in any conventional sense.

Imagination, clearly, is important here, especially as it relates to the unforeseen. But this does not necessarily have to do with character, plot or setting (in the sense of strange characters, strange events or actions, strange environments), though of course it can. The imagination works at a fully textual level, right down to the most fundamental elements: the words. In the excerpts from Haines given above, it should be obvious that what is happening is constituted linguistically as much as anything – and I don't mean this in the sense that *any story*, of necessity, uses words. That would be an utterly banal observation (though perhaps some readers, and writers, need to be reminded of it, just the same). Look at the way words interact to mould meaning and also resist any easy interpretation, both between the sentences but also within them. If imagination may well be about *seeing possibilities*, where they haven't been seen before, we must insist on the importance of the words, the arrangement of sentences, the textual structures and so forth. We must look to how a certain word or combination of words sparks possibilities, how the unfamiliar turns upon a juxtaposition of textual elements.... Yes, of course, Capildeo's dwarfs and Levy's bears insist upon their particular imaginative identities, but this rests upon what might be called a *disturbance* amongst words.[26] And *seeing* is not of course anything of a visual nature, or at least not necessarily; it is a matter of *insight*.[27]

Uncertainty: in various ways, I think that the writing in this anthology can be seen as relating itself to uncertainty, and the writers as working with uncertainty. This is as true of the unsettling excerpt from Daphne Marlatt's *Zócalo*, as it is to the searching, the vigilant waiting and the darkness that inform Lax's "21 pages". But at a more basic level, we can point to what occurs when knowledge and certainty break down, and when information, in itself, is seen as inadequate. Or perhaps when we realise that the known and the unknown are in dialogue, a fruitful dialogue, or, if you like, there's an interplay between them... and that this suspends certainty.[28] We may find ourselves in territory where we can say, with the experimental filmmaker Bruce Baillie, "I want everybody really lost, and I want us all to be at home there."[29] We may wish to invoke John Keats' famous letter to his brothers George and Tom (December 1817):

> ...I mean *Negative Capability*, that is when a man is capable of being in uncertainties, Mysteries, doubts, without any irritable reaching after fact & reason – Coleridge, for instance, would let go by a fine isolated verisimilitude caught from the Penetralium of mystery, from being incapable of remaining content with half knowledge.[30]

We may find something similar about what we, as writers, have written to what Jay DeFeo said about her painting *The White Rose* (or *The Rose*, as it was finally called):

> *The White Rose* is a fact painted somewhere on a slow curve
> between destinations.
>   This is all I remember
>   This is all I know.[31]

And it is also what she didn't know... what we don't know... what we are not certain about.

But finally, it is necessary to say that when you leave certainties behind, you have to really write (or paint, or play). No fooling around. You have to *really* write.[32]

But I still need to add something more. Risk-taking can be seen as highly significant, even if it may be entirely in the background of what a writer is concerned with. To take a risk is to play with the possibility of failure; not to take risks leaves us in the region of "business as usual", as well as in what James Agee called "the safe world". However, to set oneself up as *a risk-taker* may have more to do with egoism than anything else, and may result in pretentiousness. (I won't name names in this instance.) I can only say that taking risks as a writer is relevant to all the aspects of writing I have looked at above. And that is how risk-taking should be looked at – not as something *in itself*, but as the necessary attitude required for any of this to happen, for any of these developments in writing to occur.[33]

(ii) A Little More Information

I don't believe it is necessary or even useful to remark on all the contributors (or contributions), but a few may benefit from a little comment....

Will Petersen would probably be regarded by most people who know his work as primarily a visual artist (printmaker, especially), but he wrote poetry throughout his career, as well as being an editor, translator and essayist.[34] Most importantly, for the purpose of this anthology, he was a writer of prose memoirs – or at least, that's the nearest I can come to defining them, with their audacious mix of genres. Petersen's prose pieces, such as "The Mask", revolve around his time spent in Japan, studying to be a Noh actor, often contrasted or at least juxtaposed with his own (or his friends') situation back in the USA.

Again, Lawrence Fixel might be seen by some readers as secondarily a poet, but in fact Fixel probably published more as a poet (if we include prose poetry) than as a fiction writer and thinker, and he published throughout his life in poetry journals and maintained close associations with like-minded poets such as Edouard Roditi, Carl Rakosi and Anthony Rudolf. Although the piece included here is an example of Fixel's singular take on the parable, it might also be seen as a prose poem: Fixel is another writer whose work often resists categorisation. (It should be added that his more philosophical concerns are seldom far from any of his writings. These concerns are most clearly evident in *The Book of Glimmers* (London: Menard Press, 1980).)

Tom Lowenstein's piece is an excerpt from a considerably longer text, relating his experiences on a whale hunt in May 1977. It directly relates to his field work as an anthropologist amongst the Inuit, but also to his concern with Mahayana Buddhism (something that is also evident in a number of his poems). Lowenstein writes: "...mesmerized by constant daylight and fatigue, the mind sometimes drops its psychological habits and enters states of being in which the whale hunt itself seems to become a mere pretext." The rich mixture of wry humour, anthropological observation, personal experience and meditation, together with a poet's sensitivity to language, make this a very valuable contribution, and as a text dealing with the author's encounter with a highly different culture, it bears comparison with Petersen's work, especially.[35]

Stephen Watts' "Nonno" is also part of something larger, though self-contained at the same time. Watts' own comment is sufficiently fascinating to warrant inclusion here almost in full, and without further comment of mine:

These texts... talk, in an immediate sense, of the village in the Alta Val-camonica that my grandfather migrated to London from many years ago, and in a wider sense of language, memory and place. (...) I have lived mostly in London but with a mountain culture inside me and I began to write poetry sensing a second language hidden within. This work addresses issues of mother tongue and grandfather tongue and, I hope, the nature of memory and text – since poetry is my mother tongue and English the language I write it in.[36]

Kristin Prevallet's very moving "essay in mourning time", *I, Afterlife*, written in the wake of her father's suicide, also requires no comment of mine, although I do need to explain something about what appears from it in this anthology (and what doesn't). *I, Afterlife* is a heterogeneous work comprising prose, poetry and visual images. Also, the two prose sections given here do not follow directly on, one from the other, in the original book – in fact, there is a good 26 pages between them. However, I believe they "stand alone" as much as any excerpts from a longer work stand by themselves; I also believe that, with their understated and impressive gravity, this anthology would be poorer without them.

While clearly not autobiography in any conventional sense, Paul Buck's "skiP there is no story speaK to me" tellingly has the first and last letters of his own name inscribed in the title.[37] In a note about this work, Buck wrote: "Since the early nineties I've been thinking, researching, making notes that explore the hidden version of my background, that my mother was Italian. At least five escapades are in progress. Not all will attain completion. Not all will undress themselves. Or be disrobed." Buck's position in UK innovative literature is a fairly anomalous one, in as much as his work relates itself to French transgressive writing, and he also has strong connections to the contemporary visual arts, as well as having written alternative travel books.

(iii) Some of the Things that Aren't Here

Editing this book has involved a certain flexibility, but also a certain strictness, and it has benefited greatly from dialogue with Ken Edwards, who is a very considerable writer of narrative prose but who has chosen not to have his own work included.

This book is not definitive: I don't seriously believe that any anthology of this sort could be. (Where do you stop? Also, do you take on board any criteria upon which writers might *not* be included?) The objective has been to concentrate on poets who write prose narrative, but are not primarily fiction writers (or memoirists, etc.). (So, for example, a novelist who also writes poetry would not be regarded as a suitable inclusion.)

For the most part, poets who have a serious commitment to narrative prose, rather than writing the odd piece, have been prioritised.

Work from 1970 onwards seemed a reasonable starting point, chronologically, given developments in late 20th century / early 21st century writing, and from the point of a manageable selection. However, it did of course mean that a number of excellent writers were excluded. Without even going back to Zukofsky, cummings or Patchen, for example, I have had to do without excerpts from two of the signal books of the 1960s: Tom Raworth's *A Serial Biography* (London: Fulcrum Press, 1969) and Roy Fisher's *The Ship's Orchestra* (London: Fulcrum, 1966).[38] Paul Haines' earlier work was another unfortunate loss, as was Thomas Merton's *Original Child Bomb* ([Norfolk, CT:] New Directions, 1962), an impressive text about the bombing of Hiroshima, imbued with a fierce yet controlled anger.

Emphasis on non-conventional, in many cases innovative or experimental, writing is at the heart of the enterprise, and this of course has involved exclusions.[39] Poets may write narrative prose, and it may be very good within its own terms, but it may also fail to fit the criteria of this anthology.

It has also been regarded as imperative that narrative is at the heart of the matter. Work that only *hints* at narrative has been avoided. (Regretfully in some cases – for example, Peter

Money's *CHE: A novella in three parts* (Buffalo, NY: BlazeVOX [books], 2010), or the prose pieces collected in Roy Fisher's *The Cut Pages* (which were probably all written before 1970, anyway, even if the book didn't come out from Fulcrum Press until 1971).

There was also a decision not to include work by writers who are sufficiently well known and whose work is easily available, that it would seem redundant for them to appear here – eg Robert Creeley, James Schuyler, Iain Sinclair. (In addition, Sinclair has become more a prose writer who also writes poetry.)

Lastly, there are too many contemporary poets who are writing, or have written, prose for anything like an inclusive anthology to be feasible. It would be all-too-easy to imagine alternative selections that might feature, say, Carla Harryman, Ron Silliman, Leslie Scalapino, Peter Redgrove, Brian Louis Pearce, Michael Heller, Martin Anderson or Richard Makin.[40] In some cases, however, these writers would be excluded from the present anthology for the various reasons given above – I won't elaborate, for lack of space, except to instance that Silliman's prose is more to do with anti-narrative or non-narrative than narrative as such. And if being all-inclusive was ruled out, due to its impossibility, it's arguable that the selection is *representative* of the best, liveliest and most significant work available.

(iv) This is Not the Book it was Originally Going to Be

What has turned into *The Alchemist's Mind* began as a somewhat different project. Paul Buck and I had decided to collaborate on an anthology of narrative prose writings by poets, visual artists, filmmakers, composers... even an architect and a design theorist. (John Hejduk and John Chris Jones were the architect and the design theorist, respectively. They were "definites" for me, at least.) The basic objective was very similar – to demonstrate the contributions made to the field of narrative prose writing by practitioners usually associated with other disciplines.[41] The idea was a good one... but we hit various snags, the most important being that the project simply ran away with us... or more precisely, *from* us. We ended up with a list of potential contributors that was far too long, and which also suffered from certain imbalances – in particular, there were more poets than anything else, although admittedly there were also a large number of visual artists.

At this point, Ken Edwards suggested to me that the anthology could usefully be confined to contemporary poets who write narrative prose. I decided that this was in fact the best way forward, and that although it would be a different (if related) project, it would have its own integrity, scope and significance. Paul dropped out to concentrate on other work.

And so, what has developed from this? It's the book that you hold in your hands, *The Alchemist's Mind*, a book that indeed shows what poets have done in the field of narrative prose.

Prepare to be astonished.

David Miller
May 2012

---

1 Even when poets are not writing engaging narrative prose, they may well be writing engagingly about it, and with insight. See for example John Phillips' "That story you always thought..." and "The story...", in *What Shape Sound*, Nottingham: Skysill Press, 2011, pp 65, 87, and Anthony Rudolf, "Zigzag (Teaching Autobiography, 2000-2003)", especially section 6, "The Face beneath the Mask", in *Zigzag: Five Prose/Verse Sequences* (Manchester: Northern House / Carcanet, 2010, pp 56-7).

2 I don't want to explore the murky waters of when or if modernism ended, and how it relates (or doesn't) to postmodernism, but it seems fairly innocuous to suggest that there was a "classic" period of modernism from the 1910s to the 1930s, with predecessors and also with later developments. Later modernist writings especially relevant here would include, amongst others, James Agee's *Let Us Now Praise Famous Men* (1941) (a collaboration with photographer Walker Evans), Hermann Broch's *The Death of Virgil* (1945), Malcolm Lowry's *Under the*

Volcano (1947) and Carlo Emilio Gadda's *That Awful Mess on Via Meru-lana* (1957). And of course Samuel Beckett's later prose writings.

I'd make a point of naming three further writers: Charles Madge, most especially for his extraordinary prose collage "Bourgeois News", and to a lesser extent "Government House" and "Landscape I-IV", in *The Disappearing Castle* (1937); Paul Goodman, whose often audacious fiction was written between the 1930s and 1960, reflecting the influences of Cubism on prose narrative, psychoanalysis/Gestalt psychology/psychotherapy as an exploration leading, in his best work, through the self to self-transcendence, and anarchism, extended from the political *as such* throughout thought and life; and the singular writings of Jaime de Angulo, with their forays into fiction, story-telling and memoir that mix, break and remould genres, and their relationship to his field studies with American Indians. (For de Angulo, see *The Lariat and other writings,* ed. David Miller, Berkeley: Counterpoint, 2009. I've written about Madge and also Goodman, in "Disclosures: Notes on the Poetry of Charles Madge", *Great Works,* No 7, Bishop's Stortford, Herts, 1979, and "Anarchism and Literature: Self-Transcendence in the Writing of Paul Goodman", *Spanner,* [No] 37, London, 1987 [entire issue]. I won't make apologies for such old pieces of mine – believing there is *some* relevant discussion involved, at least. Madge's "Bourgeois News" was reprinted in *Alembic,* No 6, Orpington, Kent, 1977, as a result of my sharing my enthusiasm with the editors. Later "Bourgeois News", "Government House" and "Landscape I-IV" were all reprinted in Madge's *Of Love, Time and Places: Selected Poems,* London: Anvil Press Poetry, 1994.) Why these three, when clearly others might be mentioned, also? Because they don't tend to get a look in in this sort of discussion – and they should. And I think Madge, especially, anticipates in some respects later developments, from William Burroughs and Brion Gysin (*Minutes to Go,* with Sinclair Beiles and Gregory Corso, 1960) and Alan Burns (*Babel,* 1969) to the textual artist Jenny Holzer (*Under a Rock,* 1986) and Antony John (*now than it used to be, but in the past,* 2009) – even if Madge had little if any direct influence.

3 Walter H Sokel's discussion of mimesis or "imitation of nature", in *The Writer in Extremis: Expressionism in Twentieth-Century German Literature,* NY: McGraw-Hill, (1959) 1964, remains relevant in many ways. See p 7 and *passim.* I need to add that we are referring to mimesis as an overall scheme, rather than in regard to specific details. The Aristotelian notion

of narrative with regard to beginning/middle/end is actually not quite as straightforward as it's often made out to be, as Earl Miner points out in his contribution to *To Tell a Story: Narrative Theory and Practice*, by Miner, Paul Alpers, Stanley E Fish and Richard A Lanham, Los Angeles: William Andrews Clark Memorial Library, University of California, 1973. Practitioners often tend to act as if it was, however.

Spatially, any narrative text, no matter how brief, may be said to have some sort of beginning, middle and end – or at least I would hazard that this is the case. (I think this is true even of Fredric Brown's celebrated two-sentence story, "The last man on Earth sat alone in a room. There was a knock on the door...." This piece, which Brown describes as "a sweet little horror story", is cleverly embedded in a longer story, "Knock" (1948), as a story-within-a-story. It can be conveniently found at *koapp.narod.ru/english/fantast/book34.htm*, even if with obvious mistakes; the most recent publication of it in book form would seem to be in *From These Ashes: The Complete Short SF of Fredric Brown*, Framingham, MA: NESFA Press, 2001.) But the Aristotelian model is specific about plot dynamics, in relation to strict causal chains of actions/events. Where the model is actually not irrelevant to narrative prose by innovative poets, it tends to be profoundly or radically modified or rather *shifted* in some way or another, directed/redirected by alternative concerns. (Where there is a divergence from the Aristotelian well-made plot in mainstream narrative literature, it is rarely towards anything more adventurous.)

Needless to say, perhaps, there are some exceptions within the mainstream. E L Doctorow's *City of God* (London: Little, Brown/NY: Random House, 2000), would be one, with its mosaic structure of narrative and other textual elements, and with distinct genres included within the overarching genre of the novel. It is, however, precisely an *exception*. And it should also be noted that Doctorow works towards certain *resolutions* in a way that would be deliberately avoided by many of the writers here, eg Rosmarie Waldrop, Paul Buck or Robert Sheppard.

4 "Foreword: The Non-Aristotelian Poetics of David Miller's Fiction", in: David Miller, *Tesserae*, Exeter: Stride, 1993, [np]. "Tesserae" was later included in my collection *The Waters of Marah*, Exeter: Shearsman Books, 2005.

Edouard Roditi deserves mention here for his own narrative writings, not so much the stories in *The Delights of Turkey* (NY: New Directions, 1977), perhaps, as some of the prose pieces in *Emperor of Midnight* (Los Angeles: Black Sparrow Press, 1974).

5 I fully realise that the notion of a "mainstream" is a contested one, or at least one that's considered problematic. However, if we are talking about *visibility* outside of a relatively small number of readers, other practitioners, critics and academics, then the writers we are celebrating here are definitely not generally known about, let alone in any sense acknowledged or accepted – they are indeed in a marginalised position. However, I cannot subscribe to the notion of a mainstream or dominant literary culture that is monolithic or like a seamless web or a piece of whole cloth (rather, it contains ruptures, fissures, irregularities, even certain contradictions); nor do I believe that there is simply a single alternative – there are, indeed, multiple alternatives, as the work in this anthology helps to show.

In the UK, a lively attempt in the 1960s/early 70s to bring experimentation back into fiction after "classic" modernism largely ran aground when two of the key writers involved, B S Johnson and Ann Quin, died (Johnson and Quin both committing suicide in 1973). Others continued to write in experimental ways, such as Christine Brooke-Rose and the extremely independent Polish expatriate, Stefan Themerson, but they were isolated voices.

In North America, the situation is slightly more complex. This can be pointed up in part by referring to LeRoi Jones/Amiri Baraka's anthology, rather fatuously titled *The Moderns: An Anthology of New Writing in America* (NY: Corinth, 1963) – although of course the title may not have been Baraka's fault. Interestingly, Baraka identifies strong connections between the experimental or alternative fiction writing collected in the book with modernism on the one hand, and with contemporary US poetry on the other. Indeed, as he says, a number of the writers in the anthology are also (or primarily) poets. What needs to be said in this context is that the few writers who achieved any really widespread reputation did so more on the basis of their subject matter than for any other reason – Jack Kerouac, William Burroughs, Hubert Selby, Jr. (The same would be true of a later US writer, Kathy Acker.) This is not of course to say that there weren't other things going on besides the (often notorious) subject matter! But other writers included in the book, such as Paul Metcalf, Russell Edson, Douglas Woolf and Fielding Dawson, have had relatively limited audiences and little impact outside of fairly small circles. (Woolf did receive considerable attention for his novel *Fade Out* (NY: Grove Press, 1959), but his reputation has subsequently slipped into near-oblivion.) In the years since *The Moderns*, there has been work by various writers, including Ron Sukenick, Raymond Federman, Gilbert Sorrentino, Walter Abish, Kathy Acker, Fanny Howe and Dodie Bellamy, that is relevant to this discussion (and Howe is one of the contributors to the present anthology), but the situation remains largely the same.

6 Returning to the question of exceptions, we might ask: *why* do exceptions occur, in the sense of the occasional author who, like Iain Sinclair, achieves a wider impact? In publishing terms, it's often a question of tokenism, such as J H Prynne being taken up by a mainstream publisher like Bloodaxe Books, and also seen as having a token significance. (If Prynne is granted some sort of "significance", other poets who share certain characteristics with Prynne for the most part won't be; and Prynne's "significance" clearly exists in an entirely different poetic universe to the "significance" of, say, Carol Ann Duffy. Also, it is instructive that it is Prynne who's granted this position. Various issues to do with academia have some relevance here, at least – for example, Prynne's own role in Cambridge and as the chief instigator and *éminence grise* of "Cambridge School Poetry", and the way his work cries out for academic exegesis or commentary. Academic outreach, eg articles by academics that appear in non-academic periodicals and papers, may be responsible for awareness of this poetry filtering down somewhat... but to *what* extent and effect is not entirely clear.) Subject-matter, shock value and personal/public image can also play a role, of course, singly or more likely together, and here we are often in the territory of the cult writer. Also, occasionally a writer may begin as fairly conventional and become more unconventional, without his or her reputation *necessarily* declining. (A blind eye can be very useful for a critic at times. At times, also, one guesses there is a genuine response, against the odds and against the grain of mainstream criticism.) And we can perhaps also refer to, in certain cases at least, the *comparative* extent of experimentation/innovation/etc involved, in relation to a measure of acceptability. (Almost all of these issues would be relevant to a discussion of Jack Kerouac's writings.) I don't mean to denigrate readers here – I'm more concerned with the way that writers are *sold* to them.

As an instance of how writers are sold to readers, I have in front of me Ben Okri's *The Famished Road* (London: Vintage, (1991) 1992). On the back cover, we are told by a reviewer, Linda Grant, that Okri is "incapable of writing a boring sentence". If only I had a pound coin for every boring sentence in this 500-page novel.... Put alongside Ruskin, Melville or Faulkner – I am deliberately using historically accepted examples – it should be obvious just how boring Okri's sentences are, for the most part. Possibly an even more misleading job of product description can be cited, involving the current Poet Laureate, Carol Ann Duffy, being lauded for having a "razor-sharp technique". I don't remember the reviewer's name, but he or she clearly had a very limited knowledge of contemporary poetry and no knowledge at all of razors. I think we have to ask ourselves why such work is being served up as the embodiment of excellence, and thus acting as a model for how "good" writing can be, while anything more adventurous is in danger of being cast into oblivion. (However, while asserting this, I must again return you to the question of exceptions... as discussed above.)

I admit that this discussion is necessarily a limited one, for obvious reasons, and can't do complete justice to the complexity of the situation involved, with the business of publishing supported, augmented and in some respects or instances complicated or even challenged by the role(s) of critics and academics, on the one hand, and the non-business (for the larger part) of small presses and little magazines and the role(s) of (different) critics and academics in relation to them, on the other. (For some sense of what's involved with little magazines and to a lesser extent small presses, and the way they tend to champion and disseminate the sort of work in this anthology, please see David Miller and Richard Price, *British Poetry Magazines 1914-2000: A History and Bibliography of "Little Magazines"*, London: The British Library, 2006.)

7 This is not of course to deny that novel-length fiction has indeed been written by innovative poets, including Gilbert Sorrentino, Ron Loewinsohn, Robert Creeley, Iain Sinclair, Fanny Howe and Ken Edwards. I should also mention the UK poet Douglas Oliver, whose novel *The Harmless Building* (London: Ferry Press, 1973) appeared, interestingly enough, in the year of B S Johnson's and Ann Quin's deaths.

8 Jed Rasula and Mike Erwin, "An Interview with Roy Fisher", in: *Roy Fisher, Nineteen Poems and an Interview*, Pennsett, Staffordshire: Grosseteste, 1975, p 14.

Stanley E Fish makes some apposite remarks in his contribution to

To Tell a Story: Narrative Theory and Practice (*op cit*, p. 67): "...the axis on which semantic units are combined into a meaning that is only available at the end of a chain becomes instead a succession of equivalent spaces in which independent and *immediately* available meanings are free to interact with each other, unconstrained by the subordinating and distinguishing logic of syntax and discourse. Sequence is no longer causal but additive; it no longer processes a meaning but provides an area in which meanings separately constituted are displayed and equated." This gives us another interpretation of the notion of additive structure; but I should be fair here and admit that Fish is writing about the 17th century preacher/writer Lancelot Andrewes.

9 This is true, even if sometimes they may *play* with a movement towards an end – a teleological movement, in a limited sense – as in Harwood's treatment of the wizard figure in "The beginning of the story".

10 Davenport, "The House that Jack Built", in: *The Geography of the Imagination: Forty Essays,* San Francisco: North Point Press, 1981, p 45. He is actually writing about John Ruskin's *Fors Clavigera* (published serially between 1871 and 1887), but elsewhere in the book he refers the notion of architectonic form to Bely, Broch, Dos Passos and Paul Metcalf, amongst others. See especially pp 316-18. Also see my essay, "Post-modernist Fiction: A Discussion of Guy Davenport", *Parallax: a journal of literature & art*, vol 1, no 3, Wellington, NZ, 1983, where I look at notions of contiguity/contiguous structure and architectonics.

11 Admittedly the excerpt from Petersen's "The Mask" shows this far less than the work as a whole does. Unable to include a significantly larger excerpt, it was necessary to decide upon something that stood on its own reasonably well. I am not apologising – I am, however, recommending that readers seek out Petersen's books, as hard as they tend to be to find, and also that publishers consider reprinting his valuable and distinctive work.

12 See my essay "Robert Lax's *21 pages*", in: David Miller and Nicholas Zurbrugg (eds), *The ABCs of Robert Lax*, Exeter: Stride, 1999.
  Constructing or *assembling* is less to do with *a way of telling* a story than with a narrative emerging from the process concerned. We are not talking about something that's written as an Aristotelian linear narra-

tive and then the constituents shuffled into a different order or pattern for a novel effect. The narrative *as such* tends to come out of the act and process of construction. The emphasis needs to be on the fact that one is not simply trying to tell a story in a novel way, when the story could easily have been written in a more conventional "manner"... that is not what is going on at all.

One other thing perhaps needs to be said here. An emphasis on structure does not preclude a concern with emotion – if we look to J S Bach's music we should surely see that this is the case. It should also be self-evident from the writings assembled here, where an opposition between emotion and structure would be falsely dichotomic and a misinterpretation.

13 This is more evident later on in Rattray's diaristic piece than in the beginning.

For a discussion of working with fragments in literature, see my review of Olivia Dresher's anthology *In Pieces: An Anthology of Fragmentary Writing* (Seattle: Impassio Press, 2006), in *Stride* (*www.stridemagazine.co.uk/2006/Sept2006/fragments.MILLER.htm*). I remark upon a concern with the fragmentary in relation to "Avoiding the continuous, the systematic and the closed, while exploring the power of compressed language and a range of *possibilities* of meaning" amongst certain writers, as well as "with a dialogue of *some kind* between fragment and whole, discontinuity and continuity." (That this is true of journal writers, for example, can be shown in the way "the writer is aware – to some extent at least – of that which precedes what is now being written", rather than the individual bits and pieces being totally and uniformly discrete. Tom Lowenstein's journal excerpt would be a case in point.) I also point out that some writers "have tended to involve themselves with contiguous structure by explicitly composing with fragments – putting one distinct thing directly alongside another and another and another, but not as separated entries (and, by the way, in an *exploration* of meaning, not as an intended negation of meaning)." I should also have said that there is an exploration of structure involved, not a negation of it.

14 To take Hejinian's piece – Hejinian both plays with *and* subverts conventions, leaving us (enjoyably) we know not where, while exploring various narrative possibilities and treating us to pithy sayings along the way. The verve and inventiveness of her writing are telling.

15 Tex Avery was playing with fictional and cartoon conventions in quite audacious ways in his banned animations, *Red Hot Riding Hood* (1943) and *Swing Shift Cinderella* (1945) – although it must be emphasised that the films were geared purely and simply towards entertainment. (As retellings of classic children's stories, Vahni Capildeo's and John Levy's pieces in this anthology take us into much stranger territory.) The use of *metafictional conventions* – and I think it can be put that way – in recent popular culture is now common currency and more and more part of "business as usual".

Looking back, it seems to me that much of what is referred to as metafiction, in terms of fiction writing, either pretended not to take itself seriously while taking itself very seriously, or else took itself very seriously when there was little basis for it. In the latter category, I would put an example of "weak" metafiction – metafiction that doesn't really have the courage of its convictions – such as John Fowles' *The French Lieutenant's Woman* (London: Jonathan Cape, 1969), a tedious and gimmicky book if ever there was one. However, I was probably wrong to be so dismissive of metafiction in general when I wrote the essay "Post-Modernist Fiction: A Discussion of Guy Davenport" (*op cit*). I won't bother to quote from it here – anyone really interested can surely track it down.

16 Introduction, *The Moderns, op cit,* p xv.

17 This is not exactly a new phenomenon – for example, George Borrow's extraordinary books *Lavengro: The Scholar – The Gypsy – The Priest* (1851) and its sequel *The Romany Rye* (1857) are "good examples... of largely unclassifiable imaginative prose. If one points out that Borrow refuses to resolve the ambiguity of *Lavengro* and *The Romany Rye*'s status as fiction or autobiography, one has done little to identify the strangeness of these books. Borrow himself, in denying that *Lavengro* is 'what is generally called autobiography' [notice the use of the word 'generally'!], says it is 'a dream' and 'a philological book, a poem if you choose to call it so'." (David Miller, "Interrelation, Symbiosis, Overlap", in: *Art and Disclosure: Seven Essays*, Exeter: Stride, 1998, p 15. The quotations from Borrow come from the "Appendix" to *The Romany Rye*, London: Dent, 1969, pp 367, 368. Within the texts themselves, Borrow refuses to give his narrator a proper name at all, so that if he isn't "George", neither is he "not-George"! Or to put it another way, he could be "George", but then again he might not.)

It might be worth adding a comment here with regard to precursors. It is commonplace to refer to Lawrence Sterne in connection with the ancestry of experimental fiction/prose narrative, but reference might also be made to Borrow, James Hogg and Thomas De Quincey... and possibly Charles M Doughty. (If we were discussing German literature, E T A Hoffmann, Friedrich Schlegel and Achim von Arnim would need to be mentioned; and so on.) The question may arise: are contemporary writers (and other creative workers) simply repeating what certain earlier figures have done? No; of course not. Even if we were to affirm the idea that "nothing's new under the sun", we would need to modify it in certain ways as well as interpret it carefully. Surely Schoenberg's twelve-tone compositions, Ad Reinhardt's "black" paintings and Eugen Gomringer's "constellations" (Concrete poems) all came as unexpected arrivals to almost everyone (and the "almost" would refer primarily to those closely connected with the creators in question), despite precursors. In other words, the existence of precursors hardly prevented their work from having the effectiveness of the unexpected, and very intensely or strongly so. The relationship of present to past in writing and the other arts is, or should be, active rather than passive, involving renewal, extension, redevelopment and re-invention, change and transformation, consciously or not, rather than simple repetition. If the notion of a dialogue between present and past writing (and so forth) is important, and I think it is, this distinction between active and passive is crucial.

18 See Howe's piece "Even This Confined Landscape", included in the present volume.

19 Howe, "Well Over Void", *Five Fingers Review*, [no] 10, San Francisco, 1991, p 80.

20 I am borrowing this phrase from Hans-Georg Gadamer: "For in speaking, there always remains the possibility of cancelling the objectifying tendency of language, just as Hegel cancels the logic of understanding, Heidegger the language of metaphysics, the Orientals the diversity of realms of being, and the poet everything given. But to cancel [*aufheben*] means to take up and use." (*Philosophical Hermeneutics*, tr and ed David E Linge, Berkeley and Los Angeles: University of California Press, 1977, p 240.) (If only all poets cancelled "everything given"!)

How are techniques and forms or structures being used, and what is it they are being used towards? What is the *fundamental orientation* involved (the phrase is *suggested*, at least, by Frank Samperi's writings, as well as Simone Weil's)? I remember an especially fatuous argument that used to be advanced, namely that because advertising had taken on or adapted certain literary techniques (primarily far-fetched metaphors, eg a gold cigarette pack as an Egyptian pyramid), advertising had somehow replaced poetry or else proven that the experimental could be absorbed into the commercial. Clearly this is specious on more than one level. First, we need to look at what exactly is supposed to be taken over by advertising (the example I've given above doesn't go beyond Martian School poetry); but secondly, and more importantly, there is the question of what is being achieved (or attempted). Advertising is oriented towards persuasion, manipulation, the sale of goods, making money; any techniques or strategies involved are part of an arsenal of rhetoric. Poetry challenges the reader, opens up, explores and discloses the unfamiliar, while at the same time remaining resolutely resistant to any interpretation or explanation that would simply empty it out. (However, I can't speak for all poetry or narrative prose by poets, obviously.)

21 Bresson, *Notes on Cinematography*, tr Jonathan Griffin, NY: Urizen Books, 1975, p 39.

22 A theoretical/conceptual critique or even denial of "the self," in relation to its having a reality outside of being a cultural, social and linguistic construct, is one thing. To deny personhood, however, is to support, tacitly or not, the subjugation of the individual and the denial or erasure of his or her rights, colluding, tacitly or not, with totalitarian /Fascist leanings. How we try to define personhood (and within what context) is admittedly a difficult and complex matter and, I'm suggesting, it will always fail. The very failure needs to be seen as significant here, and the effort towards that failure is one that is purposefully and necessarily renewable. Does personhood indeed underlie our entire field of experience, underlie our sense of our physicality and others', and underlie our human rights, and yet remain resistant, excessive or transcendent to what can be established in rational, systematic and epistemic terms? Is it still disclosed, manifested or shown to us? Can we still speak about it and feel that our speaking is justified and can be

useful? Yes. And it should be obvious I am not simply referring to a
lexical shift from "self" to "person". Nor some metaphysical essence.

23 I would strongly recommend other prose writings by Capildeo and
Levy, especially Capildeo's extraordinary "Person Animal Figure", pub-
lished as a booklet by Landfill Press in Norwich (2005) and included in
her collection *Undraining Sea* (Norwich: Egg Box Publishing, 2009),
and the work in Levy's *A Mind's Cargo Shifting: Fictions* (Lawrence, KS:
First Intensity Press, 2011).

24 "Attentiveness is the rarest and purest form of generosity" (Simone
Weil, quoted in Jacques Cabaud, *Simone Weil: A Fellowship in Love*, NY:
Channel Press, 1964, p 251). (The phrase occurs in a letter to the poet
Joë Bousquet.) If the philosopher Nicholas Malebranche said that
attention "is the natural prayer of the soul", Weil echoed this, con-
sciously or not, when she wrote that "Attention, taken to its highest
degree, is the same thing as prayer. It presupposes faith and love".
(Weil, *Gravity and Grace*, tr Emma Crawford and Mario von der Ruhr,
London/NY: Routledge, 2002, p 117. The Malebranche quotation is
known to many of us, and certainly to me, from Paul Celan's famous
speech "The Meridian" (1960), in: Celan, *Collected Prose,* tr Rosmarie
Waldrop, NY: Routledge, 2003, p 50.) (No space here for going into
Weil's fierce critique of the imagination in relation to her espousal of
attention.) See my essay "Robert Lax's *21 pages*", *op cit*, where I speak of
attention or attentiveness in relation to a contemplative or meditative
approach. Attention is what persists, obdurately, and penetrates and
uncovers... disinterestedly, and by *staying with* its subject, rather than by
some act of force. Attention is faithful to what it attends to. It aspires
to a form of lucidity, no matter how complex (and without ignoring
this complexity or trying to falsely simplify it). It is an absorption into
things, but a thoughtful one.

25 Haines, *Secret Carnival Workers*, ed Stuart Broomer and Emily
Haines, [np]: H Pal Productions, 2007, p 8.

26 A disturbance, in this sense, does not have to be accompanied by
trumpet fanfares and drum rolls; it can even work beneath the surface
of our awareness.

27 "In-sight": the visual emphasis seems to be there in our language. "Vision", in the sense of the awareness and/or making manifest of the spiritual, is a term that might be considered relevant to some of our writers, but again we have to emphasise that "vision" should not be equated, necessarily, with something of a visual nature. We can point, for example, to the importance of *oral* modes in various religious or spiritual traditions, as well as to the famous instance of God *speaking* out of the whirlwind in Judaism; we can point to the mystical significance of *the letters of the Hebrew alphabet* in Cabbalism; and so forth.

28 Not only the known and the unknown, but the visible and invisible and the said and the unsaid/the sayable and unsayable, may be said to be in a dialogic relationship. (I am following Hans-Georg Gadamer here.) This is something I have discussed in, for example, *Art and Disclosure: Seven Essays*, *op cit*; see especially pp 12-13, 42-43.

29 Quoted in P Adams Sitney, *Visionary Film: The American Avant-Garde 1943-1978*, Oxford: OUP, 1979, p 169. Baillie doesn't leave it there, but what I've quoted is sufficient for my purpose in this Introduction.

30 Keats, *Letters of John Keats*, ed Robert Gittings, London: OUP, 1970, p 43. I've tried to say a little about this in relation to negative theology (as parallel instances of an emphasis on uncertainty and unknowing) in "The Dark Path: Notes for/from/about Fanny Howe", *Five Fingers Review*, [no] 17, Berkeley, 1998.

31 DeFeo, quoted at the beginning of *Jay DeFeo and "The Rose"*, ed Jane Green and Leah Levy, Berkeley: University of California Press/NY: Whitney Museum of American Art, 2003. DeFeo was writing in 1965; *The Rose* was begun in 1958 and abandoned in 1966 – though in a state that could be considered "finished" – at least, as much as could be the case with a painting that made nonsense of the entire notion.

32 I am paraphrasing the musician Albert Ayler: "You have to really play your instrument to escape from notes to sounds. You have to really play. No kidding around" (quoted by Robert Ostermann in his article "The Angry Men who Make the New Music (they don't call it jazz)", *National Observer*, June 7, 1965).

33 For Agee, see his book (and Walker Evans'), *Let Us Now Praise Famous Men: Three Tenant Families*, London: Panther Books, 1969, p 15.

Many of the issues I have addressed in this section are also discussed, interestingly enough, in an interview with the experimental filmmaker Leslie Thornton. For the sake of comparison – a comparison that extends across art forms – I recommend that readers have a look at this: "An Interview with Leslie Thornton" by Irene Borger (1998), *www.egs.edu/faculty/leslie-thornton/articles/an-interview-with-leslie-thornton/*. A few of Thornton's films can be seen on UbuWeb: *www.ubuweb.com/film/thornton.html*.

34 Petersen was associated with Gary Snyder, Cid Corman and Frank Samperi, especially. He worked with Corman on the second series of the latter's legendary magazine *Origin*, and later edited his own magazine of poetry and printmaking, *Plucked Chicken*. Jack Kerouac based one of the characters in his novel *The Dharma Bums* (1958) on Petersen.

35 In as much as Lowenstein's text involves a journey, it can be usefully compared to Daphne Marlatt's piece, as well as to the contributions by Watts and Birchard. In all these pieces there is a dialogue between location and dis-location, in terms of physical and mental space, even if the journey involved is perhaps familiar as well as unfamiliar. (More evident in some of the texts than others, admittedly – and I should also add that the journey in Marlatt's piece is not into familiar territory in any sense, even if the presence of the protagonist's boyfriend mitigates this to some extent.)

36 Included as a prefatory note to "Nonno", in *Modern Poetry in Translation*, Third Series, No 11, Oxford, 2009.

37 While mentioning the autobiographical, we have in this volume bpNichol's splendidly unusual, startling and funny re-invention of the autobiographical mode.

38 I have of course mentioned James Agee before. It's possible that Agee is best known as a novelist and scriptwriter, but he was definitely a poet, and furthermore his highly unconventional prose work *Let Us Now Praise Famous Men* is as much a huge documentary prose poem as it's anything else. I think *Let Us Praise Famous Men* is instructive in this

regard, as in others: what indeed is it? Agee wrote it about three poor
white tenant families in rural Alabama, and his (and photographer
Walker Evans') experiences staying with them; interestingly, the edition
I have is published by Panther in its Panther Modern Society series,
giving the impression of a sociological study. But that scarcely pre-
pares one for Agee's phenomenological readings or accounts of physi-
cal things/environments, so long, detailed and relentlessly *attentive* as to
become near-hallucinatory – let alone preparing one, for example, for
two pages composed solely of single words, or passages from other
writings (Blake's, and The Bible) collaged into his own text, or, indeed,
the anger that Agee displays in the book towards what he calls the
"safe world" ("Every fury on earth has been absorbed in time, as art,
as religion, or as authority in one form or another. The deadliest blow
the enemy of the human soul can strike is to do fury honor. Swift,
Blake, Beethoven, Christ, Joyce, Kafka, name me a one who has not
thus been castrated.'"). (*Let Us Now Praise Famous Men, op cit*, pp 15, 14
For the passage of single words, see pp 415-17.) Add to this Agee's
insistence that Walker Evans' wonderful photographs included in the
book "are not illustrative. They, and the text, are coequal, mutually
independent, and fully collaborative" (*ibid*, p xv), and we are also in the
territory of text and image/image and text (and Evans' name in fact
appears on equal terms with Agee's on the cover and title-page).
(Agee's criticism and foreswearing of the imagination in the Preamble
to Book Two of *LUNPFM* bears putting alongside Simone Weil's
attack on this same subject, which I've referred to above; and, alas, as
with Weil's comments, there isn't room for discussion here.) For an
instance of how Agee's prose is relevant to more recent writing, I
would ask the reader to compare bpNichol's "Still" (included in *The
Alphabet Game: a bpNichol reader*, ed Darren Wershler-Henry and Lori
Emerson, Toronto: Coach House Books, 2007, pp 220-25).

39 While continuing to use the terms "innovative" and "experimental"
as shorthand for certain tendencies in writing, I prefer the word
"exploratory", as a related term, but with a slightly different emphasis,
ie the desire to explore modes of language, thought, feeling and imagi-
nation, and to discover and disclose aspects of existence and experi-
ence – beyond the merely familiar and conventional. I put this slightly
differently in "Interrelation, Symbiosis, Overlap", where I referred to
"the desire to explore modes of thought, feeling and imagination,

within or in terms of the possibilities of a material medium [etc]" (*Art and Disclosure: Seven Essays*, *op cit*, p 16). I was thinking of "medium" as referring to eg words or paint marks or sounds or physical movements, and not as a synonym for "vehicle" in the sense of something you jump into to get from A to B, metaphorically speaking.

A term I think should be resisted is "avant-garde", as outdated or, if used to refer to contemporary figures, ahistorical; as well as clannish; and underpinned by naive ideas about how the artist relates to society as a whole, in an historical perspective. The "avant-garde" is a useful term for discussing certain developments in the arts in the early part of the 20th century (eg Dadaism and Futurism), but arguably has little application to what's happened since, except in the limited sense of a recycling of certain formal and gestural modes. Why? First, primarily because of its absurd concern with a *tabula rasa* – a concern embraced more wholeheartedly by some adherents of the avant-garde than others. This concern may have helped with certain ways of working in the arts, through acting as if the past might as well not have existed, but it was also limiting, of necessity – given that a *tabula rasa* is not actually possible, even if it were really desirable in the first place. Second, with its often mutually exclusive clusters of groups and movements, the avant-garde presented a fragmented front while theorists have falsely pushed the idea of avant-gardism as some sort of united front of activity and ideology. Last, the idea that the avant-garde artist is projecting into the future while "the rest" of humankind slowly follows him or her, gradually catching up (of course while they're doing so, other artists are meanwhile projecting even further), is at the very least an overstatement, but in some respects it's more a travesty of the complexity of the historical process involved. (Kandinsky's upward-advancing pyramid, with the avant-garde artist at the apex, is paradigmatic for this particular sort of thinking about "progress". For some comments on "progress" or "advances" in the arts, see my essay "Interrelation, Symbiosis, Overlap", in A*rt and Disclosure: Seven Essays*, *op cit*, p 17. I should add that I'm emphasising a "strong" model of avant-gardism, where the model is firing on all cylinders, so to speak.) Futurism may have lost its teeth, but this has more to do with its age than with anything else, and of course the fact that the powerful machinery of the art museums promotes it – the very institutions the Futurists would have liked to see demolished; while Gertrude Stein's *Tender Buttons* (1914) is apt to prove as puzzling to the general reader today as when it first appeared – more resistant to ageing but in no wise something that humankind "as a whole" has "caught up with", which in the Kandinsky model means *occupying the space* once occupied by the avant-garde artist or writer. James Agee makes the point that when writers and artists find large scale acceptance, it can be in terms of their work being trivialised and rendered safe rather than anything else (*Let Us Now Praise Famous Men*, *op cit*, p 13 especially). Agee was not expressly thinking about the avant-garde, and I suspect he was being deliberately negative in some respects, in order to emphasise what he felt he and Walker Evans were up against with their particular project; but at the same time, between this position and the Kandinsky model of artistic progress and its reception, there seems little in common. (Incidentally, *how* do these respective processes take place; *who*, following on from the artists who create the work in the first place, is responsible for these processes, and why; and *who* actually constitutes either "the rest" of humankind or the recipients of a trivialised and safe version of what might otherwise prove profound and dangerous?)

Again, with regard to the work in this anthology, let us speak first and foremost of alternative possibilities rather than anything more restrictive in definition.

40 Actually, Leslie Scalapino was someone Ken Edwards and I both thought about including, but we failed to secure any work. Other writers whose work I failed to secure would include Carlyle Reedy, Gad Hollander and Philip Jenkins.

41 A little of this interdisciplinary emphasis survives in the inclusion of Will Petersen, quite clearly, and also in Tom Lowenstein's, in as much as Lowenstein is an anthropologist who writes narrative prose (as well as a poet who writes narrative prose). But I can also point to *related* interdisciplinary concerns, in M J Weller's work as a cartoonist, Brian Marley's as a photographer and music critic, Keith Waldrop's as a collagist, Barbara Guest's as an art critic, Paul Haines' as a librettist, music critic and video-maker, Ian Robinson's as an artist specialising in drawings, and my own endeavours in visual art and music.

BARBARA GUEST
from Seeking Air

I

I began to know you somewhat when you introduced me to your friends. That is, I began to see you outside myself. I was permitted to witness those aspects of your person which were not private. The public view, as a painting seen at an exhibition, is so important. You know how often I have repeated that a painting varies in values when seen in the studio, at a gallery, or in a museum. How often I have been enchanted with the work of a painter when it was showed at the studio, brushes in hand, the cup of cold coffee on the table and here and there the evidence of a struggle in the crumpled sketch paper or the postcard tacked on the wall or the notebook open to the three scrawled lines, written no doubt in the early morning. And the variation at the exhibition of this same painting, its statement lost among the personalities.

And didn't we enjoy that museum in Siena? Despite your cold and runny nose, the missing tissue. Especially keen to us was the landscape outside the window corresponding so exactly to the painting on the wall. We were quite unable to " judge" the value of the paintings themselves. They might have been rather ordinary, as indeed, I remember many of them to have been. Here for an agreeable time was no element of art "triumphing" or "improving" nature. Nature and art were in such similitude due to the exact degree of their presentation; due that is to the light reaching into the room, to the color of the ground and to the distance of the hills, each of which appeared in the painting.

And so it was with you, Miriam, when you said in that voice which is so like the color of your hair: "This is Robert. This is Celestine."

Robert I did not like immediately. I resented his having known of your existence longer than I. Then he is handsome and I am not. An old-fashioned attitude of mine. It seems no longer one makes the choice of deciding if a person is handsome. Like so many disappearing conveniences which have been replaced by other conveniences, the aesthetic of the human face has been withdrawn. Now one says, "He has an interesting face" or more likely, "He looks like his sister," or again, "How virile," or again, "I like a nose slightly out of joint." Note that one never mentions, as ethics also are changing, "a corrupt mouth."

Do you suppose people still say, "He wears his heart on his sleeve"? I know very well that a few romantic exchanges still persist. Just the other day someone said to me, "How Doris has changed. Her eyes are so dark and sunken. She has cried too much." And it was true. The life of Doris was beginning to disintegrate, or rather she was in the middle of that era in her life when a decision needed to be made which she sought to postpone through constant tears, tears that successfully hid what she could not bear to see. I know also that Annette was chastised because her face was becoming too "full."

Actually the plumpness of her cheek line gave it a mature beauty. But it was not the aesthetics of her face which were questioned. No one, I reiterate, cares much about the proportions of beauty. What exactly was meant was the moral comment that Annette had been drinking too much and this incontinence was betrayed by her face. Nearly always our comments are relative to the presence of the superlative. One can permit the comparative, indeed that is what success is based on, but the superlative is disastrous.

There is something a little superlative about Celestine. Can I guess it is because she loves Robert too much? I noticed she was unable to concentrate on our conversation. I wasn't altogether flattered that it seemed a matter of indifference to her whether or not she was introduced to me. Celestine likes you. But I don't think she approves of you. She is given (part of her superlativeness) to conclusions. From a few "chance" remarks, such as, "Miriam you should go out more," I gather she has concluded you live too much the life of a spinster. How ridiculous this is we both know. Celestine really does admire an intense love. You can tell this by the way she dresses. There are so many open spaces in her clothing and then they are flattened out. In order to vary her ensembles she adds a bit too much. It is like her apartment where we went afterwards. I like it when she uses primary colors, but she does not understand dark corners. There is too much eloquence in her window dressing. You see how given one is to criticism of a superlative sort of person? I hope I didn't show my distaste for the way she made our supper.

It wasn't the food, it was the preparation. Those "let's have" and "put in another can" and "one should always use" I objected to. Robert was pleased with the meal and she appeared to enjoy our conversation which might have been about the sunrise for all I know. It was only when he began to tell us of his trip to Asia that I woke up. I was reminded of a trip I had made on the Nile which reminded me of my mother's earrings which reminded me of the garbage which used to collect under her window in our summer house which reminded me of my sister Jennifer's bicycle I used to borrow on a glowing morning which reminded me of you who have always reminded me of Jennifer.

And so I began to relax in the company of your friends, because they were part of you. I knew that after a few hours I should see you alone and then I would see you differently, then you would be part of me, but I did want to postpone your separation from your friends so that I might study you more octagonally; you were still only rectangular to me and I wished to seize the opportunities of our supper party. Now you are more like a pebble. Your sides do not match; you are neither round nor square, yet you are beginning to have a promising shape.

I almost came upon it in the dark. When we were alone at my apartment. You were lying on the sofa and your head fell slightly to the left. Your skin was a dark green. Your eyelids were that natural grey and your hands slightly yellowed, a spot of moisture above your lip. You were speaking of revolutions and the shortening of the span between medieval and modern. Your

laughter occasionally broke into black lines, the spaces contra-
vening between thought and speech. Your long upper thigh was
stretched tensely toward an object I could not see, but which I
understood to be just out of my reach. It was the posture of the
lion in the cage whose paw gropes outside the bars for a lump
of raw meat. I snapped open the lock and opened the cage. I
hoped to discover under that mild manner of yours the ferocity
which I had noticed when you bit into a piece of cake that
evening in St Augustine.

Miriam. You have been given the perfect name. There are
two vowels and three consonants.

2

The next morning after you had left I was neatening your traces.
You do leave behind you an extraordinary disorder. That was
what I thought when first I knew you. Now I recognize your
assortments. There is a lucidity in your placing of personal
objects. On one table the hairpins. On another the powder.
Here is a half-eaten pear. In the bathroom the soap has slipped
to the floor. A lipstick lies on an ash tray in the middle of the
bed. And yet there is "order, clarity, lucidity." And there is a
purity in your design, like a Matisse painting of "Studio." It took
me a long time to learn this.

At first I was scandalized, as was my mother with my adoles-
cent room. I can see her stooping over a garment, questioning
me why I live so differently from her and father. Following her
eye to the lawn I would think of the linen closet with those ele-
gant shapes of towels and sheets and wonder, indeed, why my
own closet, my bed which I thought of as my splendid tent,
should be so messy. Later when I owned my own apartment I
became obsessively neat. I missed my mother.

I wanted to tell you about my return to my parents' house. It was last summer when you had gone off on what you call your "assignments." I know they are not assignations, but this business life of yours is so disparate to me; your life in what is known as "outside our world" is so cloudy to me that I cannot fictionalize Miriam meeting a strange person, Miriam asking this person an intimate question, Miriam writing down what is said in her notebook. You have showed me this notebook. To me it is only filled with diagrams of train schedules which explain to me where you will be in one hour when I shall need you.

3

Last summer I went to the country to look at our old house. My parents had always been so unfortunate in business dealings that it had become impossible for them to find a tenant for the house. Going over my objections they still could not find someone to buy the house.

I seldom visit this house, but it was a dry summer, a hot summer. I knew that the house by the sea with its furniture shrouded in sheets would be cool, even chilly. When I opened its windows the sea air would blow through it, pushing out the smell of mothballs and old mattresses. The tap water after the first rush of rusty water would be clear, cold, cold. I could walk to the ocean and bathe each day, returning to that old outside shower under which I used to stand letting the sand and salt water wash off me, the shower water running into the slightly browned grass around the drain. I used to think of myself as a gazelle at a watering spot! Later, many brave animals who had come to the water hole briefly to drink.

In those days I was always changing myself into an animal. When I was a unicorn it was in the parlor near the watercolor picture of Mélisande. I remember that she was looking sadly into a pool where her gold ring had been dropped. I was angry

with her because she had betrayed me with King Pélleas. I had
confused my centuries; any lady in court dress would hold the
head of a unicorn in her lap. For Mélisande the unicorn could
only be a myth about which she had read, who had once
appeared in another country. You know that I remedied that
error in my book which is now translated into several languages.

4

There is a dog who lives near our property. There is always a dog,
but this spaniel I could see watching me from across the lawn. As
I went from room to room opening the windows I would see him
racing back and forth in front of his house. At night when I
would climb the stairs, crossing the landing, going from room to
room turning on the lights, I would hear him howl. Finally the
watchful presence of this animal to whom I had made no over-
tures, but who so concerned himself with the movements of my
life, began to disturb me. I decided that inasmuch as he was the
only species of life in that community who was aware of my
identity, that is, the peculiarities of my personal habits, I might
very well make overtures toward him. Keep in mind I had been
staying in the house, talking to no one, going each day to the sea
for a swim, and returning to a shrouded house to cook my meal,
to reminisce, and go to bed. I was aware that after I had retired he
would come to my house, poke into the garbage, roam about the
grounds and sniff at the porch. Yet never in the day time.

One morning after my swim, when I was showering and
recalling my lost animal identities, I saw him sitting halfway up
on the lawn. I whistled. How long it had been since I had whis-
tled! It was such a dusty noise, yet he heard it. There he was
bounding toward me. To shorten this, Miriam, we became
friends. Whereas formerly my tracks had been from the sea to
the house, now he began to accompany me about the grounds.

He knew those old paths better than I. He took me to the barn, then to the carriage house. It was there I made my discovery the consequence of which has set me on an entirely new train of metaphysical enquiry. The results of which can only be antithetical ro those of my colleagues. Yet what are colleagues? Enemies!

The grass was rougher, tougher in certain clods. These clods stood out against the clean, thin, fresh slips of grass. They were coarse-grained and the clods were in the shape of a horse's hoof. These were the same tracks that had been made by my grandfather's carriage horses. They were the tracks the horses had made when we children rode over the lawn to the fury of our elders. What a cautious hoarder is nature; how sly and penurious, how reproductive, how unforgetful. She likes to hear the same old opera over and over. Nothing new about her. Reflect that I was led to these conclusions, only a fraction of which I have stated here, by a dog.

I shall not bore you any longer with these reminders. Long Island is not Balbec, any more than Balbec is Combray. Any more than I would use a bathing machine.

5

Dinner at my apartment. An evening with a New Zealander.

I received a telephone call from young Tom Powell saying he was passing through this city. He was bringing a herd of cattle to New Zealand from Ireland! Tom is the brother of Sheila, a delightful girl who was the governess of the children of friends with whom I had stayed in London. "Gouvernante" was really the term the hotel people liked to bestow upon her, the hotel where she and the child would have dinner. Actually she came from that indispensable British agency, Universal Aunts. Sheila had accompanied a family of Americans when they travelled to

France, Italy and Greece. The good humor and manners of this girl (23) were compelling. If she indulged herself in moods this indulgence certainly took place privately. She was fond of her young wards. She was pleased with the countries she visited. (Liking Italy less, a bit overwhelmed by France, an admirer of Greek ruins.) Her geographical and presumably cultural educarion completed she wished to return ro New Zealand. We had been surprised at her decision, thinking she might marry a Welshman, a farmer, who had grown up near the border, quite near the spot her family had emigrated from. However, such is the pull of her island that Sheila desired to return to it.

I have photographs of her wedding which took place at Waipawa. There stands the wedding party in front of the white wooden church. They are properly arrayed in taffetas and borrowed formal dress. On the wedding group shines that white clean New Zealand light, the envier of shadows. It is an English wedding. An Episcopal style church. Bless Sheila, she will have children named Diana, Rosemary and Guy.

Arrival of Miriam. Her first New Zealander. She helps with the table. She is in a friendly humor. Arrival of Tom.

He is tall, well formed, blond and healthy-cheeked. His hair is cut in a bang across his forehead. This once might have signalled the country bumpkin, now it is a modulated version of the current long hair. Fresh from a British barber. Its original cut modified somewhat by his recent stay in Ireland. A ruffling of the locks into authenticity.

Tom delights us. He is simple, direct (as was Sheila), he appears to have none of the traces of inferiority toward more cosmopolitan places as would his contemporary from this country. We were both rather overcome by this person. Later in the evening a wee bit bored.

His most important remark, or so I thought, aside from his description of loading the cattle onto an airplane in Ireland, was made when he told us of visiting Westminster Abbey on Commonwealth Day. The remark was: "You know we used to sing those old Episcopal hymns in our little church. I never quite understood what they meant, although I would sing along. Then we sang the hymns, the same ones in the Abbey. A great throng there was and a large choir. Suddenly I understood about England's fair and green land. I knew about the Lord being a Shepherd, because I had tended sheep, but I hadn't before realized the sheep in the hymns were thousands of people, not just wooly bleating animals."

I think Miriam liked best his telling us of visiting the minister in Shropshire. Miriam.was teary-eyed when Tom told us the minister was the last of his branch of the Powells, and further was preaching the last Powellized sermon. Would Tom return to hear another sermon so that another Powell would sit in the congregation? That he wouldn't.

I forgot to say Tom brought flowers. Red and white carnations for Christmas.

A well-articulated man who carried himself well. Large flushed hands.

6

At the movies with Miriam. Another Italian import. I fell to thinking about a review I had read of a book called *The Case for Spelling Reforrn*. The question was: is there a case for spelling reform? Henry Sweet, "the greatest of all Engrish philololgists", thought so. The book was written by Mont Follick. This kept me occupied through three quarters of the film. I then cast a few shadows toward the Shavian alphabet. I finished the last episode of the movie with a Shavian denouement in mind. Follick believed that the adjective "subtile" was derived from "the days when the Roman philosophers used to wander up and down under the lime trees trying to emulate each other with clever arguments and phrases, often splitting hairs over very fine differences, so *subtilis* was born – lime tree being *tilia* in Latin."

7

Things have fallen out and things have fallen in.

H G WELLS

Miriam we are going to Minna's. Ah this is when you put your hand in mine. We are going to pass through the corridors – of my past. Then stairs. First up to the rooms. We push the bell. Someone nearby says, "They wouldn't let me into the bar of the Seven Seas." We are in a hallway. Miriam. I touch you. You who have never known the years of these rooms. I feel your heavy dress. We go up the stairs. There it is.

This is the water's music. I am walking by the water. I am telling you my sister, you are syllables. You are the music dropped on leaves. I am saying there is the funeral of Lenin. If you wish to listen. I am saying we are living at the top of the house and there the chords make such a sound the steeple sweeps sideways against the sky. And then we begin.

8

It is six A.M. in Los Angeles. The hour of first light. A beginning of a day which has no changes, remaining all seasons, a boy with his wheel.

Ah Miriam, we are lying together on such a low bed. Not at all like our old bed. It is really a pallet. The light from the ceiling hurts my eyelids and I think of morning's cool haze. So dark at first then a faint light, then the roses strewn; yet hesitant, some-how careful, as if the roses were floating into day which carried a handful of cards, a bright deck hidden in the palm.

Searching you. The light on your face. The yellow.

Miriam, where are we?

Your skin. Dowsed with light.

Except that Miriam we are in New York and you have promised that there will be no deaths. Before I tell you a few extraordinary tales.

It is night. I have told you about the jewel robbery about the man "who didn't care" and about the bedrooms filled with watches. You have told me how you froze in your black winter coat (like Roman cherries that coat). Even if the fur did rough up the edges and make you fear that "snow will never settle here."

Morgan!

I am listening. My real dreams hurt you. Stabs of joy.

9

It's laudanum time.

A wisp of green sunset falls across the chaise.

The papa of Elizabeth is pacing his study floor.

The dog thumps his tail.

The book of poems quietly turns its leaves.

Robert rounds the corner, his boots chumping in the watery snow.

The heavy eyelids of Elizabeth stoop lower into the smile at the mouth's bend which is slightly plumper with patience.

The Jamaica bananas with their soft round toes.

I like astrakan sunsets on the rug. And "gaudy melon flowers." And the firm bite of exile.

Robert has arrived. He has brought a present. It is called *The Care of Books in a Tropical Climate.*

It is the last Christmas on Wimpole Street. They are going to the land of Ruddigore.

Miriam exits with a flick of the fingernail. Ta.

10

I have changed to the new typewriter with the large type. Sadly, tenderly I put the old one in the closet. And I confess only to you, Miriam, how near I was to tears. The letters I have written to you on the old typewriter. The hours I have spent in front of it seeking your image, or trying to reclaim your image from the alphabet that settled over your face. The sentence that would describe with its careful punctuation (and its momentous pauses while I lit a cigarette) my exact feeling for you and the tonal area of our solutions.

Now space enlarges in front of me. The proportions are attenuated. There is more prose on the roller. I must maintain my former techniques at the same time as I move stealthily into the new structure whose windows are still dark.

I am only beginning to "touch" it. And I have been seven years "touching" your face.

11

And I returned to "Dark's" exegesis. Which if ever finished I shall deliver No. 3 in the series of "Evenings Of and About Literarure." Transforming the wild evenings of Alaska into something less raw, translating the kayak noise into black clefs, white floes into Dark. Don't tremble Miriam when I put the bandage over your eyes; we shall only slide into the underground. And we can read standing up the gold emblems of Dark. A nest of swallows clinging to the sooty bridge. Dusk into Dark. Night imagery or scenery, symmetry of night thought. From a broad vision, like balsam on the ah – hair.

LEE HARWOOD
The beginning of the story

1

The castle was built on a small hill overlooking the river. Probably it once commanded the whole valley – chose who could pass through the valley, who could come up river in boats, who could cross the river at the nearby ford. Now it stands empty and the surrounding lands are once more scrub and forest. The castle, after all, was only built by men and manned by men. And now it is just one more feature of the landscape, though maybe more passive than most.

2

Parting the leaves you look out onto a sunny meadow that slopes down to a small wood with a stream the other side.

A thick wood bordered the meadow with the beech trees' branches trailing the ground. The leaves of one tree slowly parted and a face appeared.

3

Blue objects flashed before the eyes of the face. As though a giant blue boulder dominated the foreground, and all else was only a haze. A rounded blue cylinder rising out of the earth, or descending from the heavens. There were obviously many explanations and interpretations for all these stunning phenomena.

4

Late in the morning on a mild and sunny autumn day I was in the kitchen. First I made a delicious chocolate blancmange, then prepared a bowl of stewed pears made even more fragrant by a touch of ground ginger added to the boiling syrup before introducing the segments of pear. The quiet happiness one feels with such domestic duties is perhaps one of the greatest joys of having a home.

The choice of dishes prepared will obviously signify something to a person looking for such things. Whether he's right or wrong is of little importance to me.

5

Threading its way along the valley was a string of pack horses. One could just make out the small figures of the accompanying traders.

Up here overlooking the valley...

Perhaps they're not traders, or not all traders. Perhaps one of them is a magician. How to imagine his clothes? that is if he dresses differerently from his companions.

And whether he should be a wizard rather than a magician? And whether, rather than these people merely being on a journey or trading, there are more serious and more exotic matters in hand? Threats of dragons? Threats of invasions by harsh forces, or worse?? Threats of the moon disappearing, of tides growing wild and ravaging the shores, flooding the valleys?

6

The wind moans about the houses and the last yellowing leaves are stripped from the trees. The birds become more obvious and seemingly more active in their continual search for food.

Trim the wisteria, tie up the jasmine and honeysuckle, re-stake the chrysanthemums, beware the gales. Trim the house, all ship-shape. The winter almost upon us.

7

In his pouch the wizard had a small silver box. The box was beautifully engraved with curious designs and the suggested figures of birds, otters, foxes and wild boar. There was no apparent way of opening the box, though it could be opened by the wizard. Inside was a small flint blade and a flower that never faded.

8

A quiet and mild day in early winter. The sunlight in no way clear or bright but somehow there. The garden below my window is all wetness. The last damp yellowing leaves hang from the wisteria. A single half-dead pink rose is the only colour in the flower bed other than the dull browns and greens of the dying leaves surrounding it. On such mornings a similar lethargy fills us.

9

One clear night the wizard stood alone in a small meadow beside the river. The moon was almost full and clearly lit the whole landscape. He placed the silver box on the grass and stepped back a few paces. The box then slowly opened as though of its own accord and, once open, a bright silver light burnt over the whole surface of the box, inside and out. And at the same moment as the silver box opened a blue cylinder of light slowly appeared hovering a few feet above the box. The blue light, at first faint, as the box's own light was, gradually generated more and more power until it was a near-dazzling throbbing humming block of BLUE.

All this happened in silence, though somehow you sensed at the edge of your hearing a small and delicate music almost like the tinkling of glass wind chimes.

After a time that no one could measure or remember the blue cylinder of light began to fade until in the end it was the faintest of outlines, and then disappeared completely. And at the same time the silver box's light also faded and died, leaving the box an almost indistinguishable dark object set in the pale moon-lit grass.

10

A great sadness fills us.

Questions

i)

Does the man go mad?
Does he even commit suicide? (hence a well-rounded drama) or
continue a life of quiet suburban despair? (so a well-rounded
'Modern' drama)

ii)

Is the wizard murdered soon after this event?
or several years later?
or does he lose his powers? slowly or quickly?
or, the reverse, does he go on to become truly prosperous and
renowned for his skills, living to a fine old age?

iii)

Late on a summer evening we find ourselves in the leafy subur-
ban streets of some small town whose name we don't as yet
know. There is a velvet darkness that brushes our lips and
cheeks with great sensuality. This darkness is only broken by the
vague pyramids of white light around the rare street lamps, and
the opaque yellow glow from some curtained windows where
people are still about. The silence hisses and crackles, it is so
near complete.

iv)

Shrieks of anguish are muffled in blankets.

v)

Do we pour chocolate blancmange over the wise wizard?
explaining to him the while that it is a symbolic gesture attacking

all he stands for, but that he shouldn't take it personally?

vi)

Are we denied peace?
Not the peace of answers, set ideas, and realised hopes, (stagnation), but the peace to do things we want to do for ourselves. To push on, unhindered by jobs, exhaustion, and 'the treacle of fears and evasions'!!??

vii)

The man closes his book. Out of his window he knows and sees the seasons change. His guarded optimism is justified by events.

viii)

Shrieking statues are suddenly muffled in the public gardens by council workmen. The flowers join in the horrified chorus. 'WHY ME? WHO ME? NOT ME?'

IAN ROBINSON
Delayed Frames

…no sugar thanks, I said. Yes, it was almost late. A warm day, not bright. The sea was calm. From my new room, the sunset was… Yesterday we visited the funfair. Order had become a very fragile vessel. Relatively meaningless. Five hundred million years ago there was no such thing as a backbone. The dunes were crowned with small shards of grass. I left the umbrella behind. Last Thursday was cold. A mile away the Elizabethan town rose up on a knoll. Once the sea had washed right up to it. The boat seated twelve people. We watched the shore grow smaller. Larks whistled in the air above the dunes.

Yesterday we glimpsed the hills. Once there were only worms twitching in shallow seas. It was annoying to think this. Far out fish were leaping. Nearing the beach we caught sight of something white moving behind a dune. The tramp was walking down the street. Other fossils lay on the bottom level. The island reared up over the horizon. Later I painted a picture of the tiny cove. Leaning against the wooden door I listened. Difficulties were overcome. I held my breath. The rocks stretched away into the mist. When I looked up it was all over. We saw a tangle of bare limbs. How are you today?

Some of them formed chains, others isolated beads. There was no harbour. We sat down to watch. That was how life was. Today we drove to the cathedral. A thin landing stage waited under straight black cliffs. Altogether there were three of them. He wore huge balloon-like trousers. There was life even in the simplest sponge. Gulls circled overhead. The scene resembled the annual mating of toads. It was an evolutionary dead-end. Heading into the wind, the boat tossed up and down. All three of them were linked together. In a month's time we shall be back in town. The blue clay contained many fossils.

At 5.00a.m. the birds started to sing. There was no way to avoid the boredom. I felt a sharp pain in my neck. Comb jellies wriggled on seabeds. I was glad to leave the mainland and my father behind. Two men were wrapped round the woman. Unluckily for some it was winter. Tall breakers rolled in from the Atlantic. Parts of her emerged occasionally from the heaving mass. They were held up with string. Some swam by using their cilia. We stepped out on to the slippery wood of the landing-stage. The whole package continualy moved, twisted, intertwined. He held out his hand. We have them too. From the strip of shingle we climbed stone steps to the cliff top.

Several times the woman lifted her head. Ballon, mein Herr? he asked. Everything was an interdependent complex, I was excited by the newness of it all. Her mouth was open. We tried to take no notice. Life on earth was complicated enough. Everything became very green. The wallpaper was new last year. Her buttocks raised thernselves out of the ruck. It was nearly evening. The Picardy third is a well-worn device. A road led off between grassy banks. Somehow this was not important. The sunlight highlighted the twin opaque ovals. It was setting at the end of the street. So were most things. After ten minutes we reached four small cottages.

One rolled on top of her. Millions of years before there were only gasses and volcanoes. They were built in a hollow. No one noticed that it was already evening. His hips began to pump. You gave him a coin. The world was only methane, ammonia, hydrogen, steam and fire. The tallest was called the Marengo Tavern. Nothing was that simple. The other moved underneath her. It lay in his open palm. You could buy everything there from stamps and raincoats to food and china dogs. Arms rose up and pulled her down He regarded it with some surprise. Could Christopher Dresser have taught Gertrude Jekyll in the 1860s?

They were pirates who had used the island as a base. Then she submerged between them both. He turned round and walked away. Anything was possible. We bought postcards of the landscape. I couldn't remember when. All three rolled sideways. The balloon surged above his head. It was still light. But there were difficulties. I walked off on my own. It was possible to observe how their buttocks moved in and out on her. The sunset happened after he had gone. Sharp stones dug into our feet. I found my way to a cliff edge. No trace of the violin remained in the room. Her moans drifted across the dunes to us. The chains broke up and formed other chains.

Piromanishvili painted the actress Margarita many times. Far below a line of rocky buttresses rose up from the sea. Perhaps one day it will all be easier. Finally the man on top finished and rolled off on to the sandy grass. His paintings were like contemporary ikons. The chert covered the shores of Lake Superior. I held my breath. It was an evolutionary dead-end. The prow of the boat rose and fell in sharp jerks. Living things emerged from the sea-beds. Two men were wrapped round her. The world was young then. The sea was dark green. The other twisted round on her. She was always full-face and two dimensional.

Every afternoon I sat on the same bench. White foam shot upwards continually from the foot of the rocks. Her legs entwined his head You couldn't help looking at her eyes. A grey squirrel accepted a piece of my sandwich. Above was a dark grey sky. There were dissolute evenings at No 29B. For an instant we made out his red upright penis. It was love at first sight. Couples with linked arms walked past. The edge of the island stetched away into the mist. Then it disappeared into her mouth. The noise was deafening. This image never left him although she did. I could hear the shouts of the coxen on the river. I took photographs of the sea.

Eventually her head stopped moving. Each day the squirrel joined me. It was about three miles long. They lay quite still. As the bus crossed the causeway I saw the black swans floating on the water. For a month it was the most important relationship I had. After three hours we went back down to the boat. The third man had apparently gone to sleep. One day there was no one there. We appreciated the distance. The swans drifted in and out of the mist. The sky grew darker. We walked off to the sandy sea shore. I couldn't use that bench again. It had been a long day. Half an hour out we were caught by a sudden storm.

By the Creagorry Hotel men were digging a large hole. There was no sign of them when we came back. The sun filtered down through the dense leaves. For a long time I remembered those two ovals. People were being sick into the wind. There was only a deep depression in the sand behind the dune. The bus was four hours late. An unnatural silence filled the clearing. I avoided the trails of slime. My back was up against a tree. Her mouth was wide open. Every thing depended on something else. We tried to take no notice. I was excited by the newness of it all. The walls closed in. Artificial yet necessary.

The island disappeared behind a curtain of rain. The fox stared at me from the bushes. It was time to go. I waited. The sky was far above. The headlights bored into the darkness. Clouds touched the water. All day I had hardly talked to anyone. The door stayed locked. The postcards were bent at the corners. It was 5.30p.m. when we reached the mainland. In slow motion we continued the the ritual for three hours. Several times she raised her head. The sunlight travelled round the clearing. You couldn't help looking at her eyes. The fox took the food from my hand. Later I painted a picture of the tiny cove. I put my ear to the wood and listened.

Difficulties were overcome. The curtains moved. I held my breath. When I looked up it was all over. So many corners. Outside the clouds had lifted slightly. The rocks faded away into a mist. She was always full-face and in a two-dimensional pose. Every afternoon I sat on the same bench. He covered her with his body. Above us was a charcoal coloured sky. It was love at first sight. Pieces of rotten wood lined the shore. Yesterday we visited the funfair. The blue clay of the cliff face was full of fossils. At 5.00a.m. there was a scream. Birds sang. There was no way to avoid the boredom. I felt a sharp pain in my neck.

The balloon surged above his head. Tall breakers rolled in from the Atlantic. They were both breathing hard. Unluckily for some it was winter. Finally we waited for a sign. They were all linked together. A pattern began to emerge. No one noticed that it was already evening. Each afternoon there were larks above the field. The sunset from my new room is... The sea was calm. It had been a warm day, not bright. I photographed the waves. The black swans were floating on the water. At last the complexities proved insoluble. Her mouth was open. I couldn't describe it. Yes, it was almost late. Sweating I waited for the pain to stop. Did you leave the umbrella behind? Life was like that. No, I said, no sugar for me, thanks...

ROSMARIE WALDROP
A Form of Memory *[abridged]*

Physical Description of Motion

Alexander von Humboldt shipped out on the mail boat "Pizarro" with sextants, quadrants, scales, compasses, telescopes, microscopes, hygrometer, baromenter, eudimeter, thermometer, chronometer, magnetometer, a Leiden bottle, *lunettes d'épreuves* and a botanist, Aimé Bonpland.

Before him, using the newly improved astrolabe to determine the ship's position, Columbus had thrown his coin not as a mere adventurer, but with a plan.

The mistress drew the switch through her left hand and smiled at each of us in turn.

"Stress" is used for metrical stress whereas "accent" is reserved for the emphasis demanded by language.

All landmarks disappeared, and the sea horizon extended all the way round the sky.

Even before Columbus, the earth turned on its axis to divide the day from night and afford a convenient means of measuring time.

Alexander von Humboldt knew that Columbus' inspiration "from the heart" had been a flock of parrots flying toward the southwest, a word with level stress where the accent falls with equal emphasis on both syllables. Birds, said Alexander von Humboldt. All land is discovered by birds. He lifted his field glasses, but could see nothing but an expanse of water apparently boundless.

The mistress slightly lifted a knee and let her foot touch the ground with the tip of her toes which formed a straight line with the shinbone. Only then did she slowly lower her heel. Her full, round, delicate knee stretched at the moment the heel came down.

In spite of the successful Egyptian campaign, Napoleon could not take the fortress of Akkon or reduce the bulge of the equatorial regions.

Alexander von Humboldt talked twice as fast as Napoleon, and in mixed German, French, Spanish and English. He reserved Hewbrew for intimate letters. No wonder there were rumors. (See Henriette Herz.)

Reference

Humboldt, Alexander, Baron von (1769-1859), German naturalist and scientific explorer.

Physical Description of Motion, Continued

The action of a muscle is to contract, or shorten in length, and thus the two structures to which it is attached are brought closer together.

We had to hitch up our skirts to the hips and walk so slowly that I could have run around the whole house for every single step. If we put down a foot too quickly the mistress' switch was on our calves.

Enter Beethoven: I shall take fate by the throat.

Alexander von Humboldt had fallen in love with a young officer, Reinhard von Haeften, notwithstanding the rumors about Henriette Herz.

Metaphor implies a relationship between two terms which are thus brought together in the muscle.

The hips were the center from which all walking was willed and directed. We must not feel the ground under our feet. We must not feel our feet. We must feel nothing but our hips. We must think with our hips.

Montezuma received the messengers in the House of the Serpent and ordered two captives to be painted with chalk. Like metaphor, this required an eye for resemblance and clear skies. The two captives were then sacrificed before the messengers' eyes, their breasts torn open, and the messengers sprinkled with their blood. This was done because the messengers had seen the gods.

Reference

1799-1804, Alexander von Humboldt and Aimé Bonpland undertook their famous expedition to South America which led them to Teneriffe, Venezuela (the Orinoco-Casiquiare region), Columbia, Ecuador (ascent of Mt Chimborazo) and Mexico.

Connections

When Columbus set foot on the new world, the two hemispheres which God had cast asunder were reunited and began to become alike.

Our running had to be as if we were carried by a cool wind. Our heels were not to touch the ground. This was to give us beautiful legs.

Montezuma sent captives to the Spaniards because they might be gods and wish to drink blood.

It was not the tidal wave that advanced westerly, only its form.

Eyewitness Report

Cortés took off his helmet and stroked his beard.

A vast twilight zone, nearly 1500 miles wide, was slipping around the earth as the latter turned on its axis.

Aimé Bonpland sat under a tree. His hands were resting a book on his knees. He was memorizing Linnaeus' *Species Plantarum.*

The Creoles aspired to a larger participation in the government, whereas the incumbent Viceroy hoped that patriotism would supersede the desire for social reform.

The Aztec harlots bathed frequently, a heathenish idiosyncracy to Father Sahagún.

No part of Alexander von Humboldt's body felt altogether comfortable. His face and neck were burned. The skin was flaking off. He was unable to shave. Every exposed part of his body was bitten by insects. Some had even found their way inside his clothes.

Volcanoes

Alexander von Humboldt was seized by a sudden desire to climb the Teneriffe. Increasing cold seeped through his light tropical clothing even though the steep mountain side caught the rays of the sun at a less oblique angle. Alexander von Humboldt paused to examine the stones and catch his breath. Sulphurous fumes burned holes into his jacket, and his hands got stiff at 2° Celsius.

Physical Description of Motion, Continued

The Indians had never entered the cave of the guacharos, or "oil birds," farther than the first chamber. Beyond, in the dark, lived the souls of ancestors along with the birds.

Alexander von Humboldt insisted on wading on through the birdlime and the biting smoke of their torches. With effort he unstuck his sole, lifted his knee and let his foot touch the viscous mass with his toe. He did not always lower his heel, but simply straightened his knee and lifted the other foot.

Three girls and three boys we were in our room and shy with one another. One night, the mistress pulled my covers off and carried me naked out of the house. In the garden, she put me into a small box which exactly fitted my size, and closed the lid.

Alexander von Humboldt found strange formations of subterranean plants which grew, pale and ghostly, in the dark cave. The Indians looked at the deformed plants with fear and could not be persuaded to penetrate any farther into the cave.

Napoleon asked: "What is the matter?"

The prosody allowed for liberties, but Alexander von Humboldt ducked to avoid the stalactites.

Now and then, when one of the Indian guides raised his torch, Alexander von Humboldt and Aimé Bonpland could get a glimpse of a momentarily blinded bird. They fired into the dark vault, in the direction of the loudest screams.

I remember nothing further until I saw daylight come through the holes in my box. Then my little coffin was put upright and opened. I felt dizzy as I stepped out into the light.

The two specimens Aimé Bonpland killed proved the guacharo to be indeed an unknown species. It was the size of a crow, with a wingspan of 1.13 meters and an enormous beak. Between their legs the young birds had a thick lump of edible fat.

"What a battlefield this would make," said Napoleon.

Reference

Bonpland, Aimé (1773-1858), French botanist and Alexander von Humboldt's companion on their famous expedition to South America (1799-1804).

Physical Description of Sexual Intercourse

The explorer travels over the beloved body, but nowhere does he find an end or edge.

When Columbus set foot on the Bahamas, the two worlds which God had cast asunder were reunited and began to become alike.

The moon unusually large and near. At times, the sea rises into the light and becomes incomprehensible.

The contract is definite when the man steps into the woman's shoe. As long as the foot still hovers above the shoe, his body may still turn on its own axis, which takes about twenty-four hours.

What does my body want?

Reference

Haeften, Reinhard von (1773-?)

Volcanoes, Continued

Alexander von Humboldt was seized by a sudden desire to climb a volcano, mountain or at least staircase.

Three years later, representatives of aspiring emancipators in both New Spain and New Granada arrived in London to solicit arms and munitions in exchange for discrepancies of longitude.

Physical Description of Sexual Intercourse, Continued

"Aimé," said Alexander von Humboldt.
Aimé Bonpland recited the *Species Plantarum* by Linnaeus.

Reference

Humboldt's services to geology were mainly based on his attentive study of the volcanoes of the New World. He showed that they fell into linear groups, presumably corresponding with vast subterranean fissures.

Elegy

At last they came. Their horses carried them on their backs wherever they wished. They came in battle array, as conquerors, and the dust rose in whirlwinds on the road.

No part of Alexander von Humboldt's body felt altogether

comfortable. His face and neck were burned. The skin was flaking off. He was unable to shave. Every exposed part of his body was bitten by insects. Some had even found their way inside his clothes.

A line from which unstressed syllables have been dropped is called truncated.

Then the slaughter began: knife strokes and sword strokes and death. The people of Cholula had not foreseen it, had not suspected it. They faced the Spaniards without weapons, without their swords or their shields.

Alexander von Humboldt examined the Great Cholulan Pyramid with leisure and his usual care.

Even before his hearing deteriorated, Beethoven was downcast and distressed.

In 1519, Patlahuatzin touched his hands to the ground and to his forehead. A few minutes later the Cholultecas had flayed his arms to the elbows and cut his hands at the wrists so that they dangled.

Among the attempst to refer all that is unstable in the sensuous world to a single principle, the theory of gravitation is the most comprehensive and the richest in cosmic results.

Poetry

Alexander von Humboldt wanted to write an epithalamium for Reinhard von Haeften's wedding.

His voluntary muscles included many parallel striated fibers, bound together by connective tissue. Their opposite ends were fastened to the separate bones by extensions of the connective tissue.

Alexander von Humboldt could not find any feminine rhymes. He returned to the study of volcanoes, arranging them in linear groups indicating vast subterranean fissures.

Food

The incumbent Viceroy hoped to profit by catering to the Creoles.

The man from the Rio Negro declared that the meat of the manimodas monkey was only slightly inferior to human flesh.

I am not hungry, said Alexander von Humboldt.

Volcanoes, Continued

Comparing local times all the way round the globe, the Cabildos deposed the Spanish authorities and created provincial juntas.

Beethoven proposed marriage to Therese von Malfatti.

I am still not hungry, said Alexander von Humboldt.

While New Spain, like Venezuela, New Granada and Chile, was the scene of bloody combat, we must picture Beethoven in a turbulent emotional condition.

A volcano, properly so called, exists only where a permanent connection is established between the interior of the earth and the atmosphere, and the orgasm continues for long periods of time.

News from the mother country bent the motion of light rays out of their course which caused the Creoles to aspire to larger participation in the government.

When one of us said "I" she meant her body. Her body from head to toe. We felt ourselves more in our calves than in our eyes. I don't remember what anyone said. I remember how each girl walked.

This involved the action of muscle, which is to contract, or shorten in length. Thus the two structures to which it is attached are brought closer together.

The insurgents were unconcerned with the eccentricity of the earth's orbit. They desired immediate freedom from oppression.

Physical Description of Sexual Intercourse, Continued

A virgin had best be offered to a passing stranger whose centrifugal force lessens his attraction. If there are no strangers, the husband must wrap his finger in a white cloth which is torn into bloody bits and distributed to the priests. This does not cause pain to the husband.

On Friday afternoon, at 3:45, Beethoven requested that Frau Nanette Streicher mend his socks.

A refrain is not unusual.

Napoleon surveyed the locality with a profound air.

The interior remained unfamiliar to Alexander von Humboldt.

Physical Description of Motion, Continued

In my new class I was made to walk on my hands. Two older girls took hold of my legs. My hair hung down to the floor, my skirt fell over the belt down over my neck. Thus, legs high in the air I walked across the stone floor.

The simultaneous contraction of many fibers caused Montezuma's biceps to shorten and bulge, as he lifted his hand in greeting. Since his striated muscles were under conscious control this gesture was considered voluntary.

What does my body want?

That same year the equinoxes traveled westward about fifty and one quarter inches.

Physical Description of Sexual Intercourse, Continued

As the explorer approaches the beloved he recites a poem, preferably using frequent enjambment. The beloved prepares herself for the encounter by having the explorer's coat of arms tattooed on her belly. Ropes are to be kept near in case of need. The couple now throw off ballast, hoist the flag and launch full speed ahead into the water.

Variant

The beloved prepares himself for the encounter by having the explorer's coat of arms tattooed on his belly.

Repeat

Ropes are to be kept near in case of need.

Physical Description of Sexual Intercourse, Continued

Alexander von Humboldt did not trust the soundings of naviga-
tors who had voyaged there before him and with such apparent
ease.

This Is To Say

The only effective defense against the insects was to wave one's
arms and slap one's body.

Volcanoes, Concluded

"Alexander von Humboldt is a spy," said Napoleon.

Physical Description of Motion, Concluded

They hanged Macuilxochitl in Coyoacan. They also hanged
Pozotzin, the King of Culhuacan. And they fed the Keeper of
the Black House to their dogs. And three wise men of Ehecatl
were devoured by their dogs. They had come to surrender. They
arrived bearing their painted sheets of paper. There were four of
them, and only one escaped. The other three were overtaken,
there in Coyoacan.

In 1859, Alexander von Humboldt felt weak and feverish. He
remained flat in bed, and his horizon, meridian and prime verti-
cal stayed in a constant and definite position. His thought was in
the last fraction of its diurnal arc, preparing to leave the horizon.

*Slowly, slowly we walked through the streets, seeming to glide above the ground.
A procession of girls in long white gowns. Slowly we lifted our knees and let*

our feet touch the ground with the tip of our toes. We walked as if carried by a cool wind. On both sides of the street, crowds of people were cheering, showering us with flowers. I saw a procession of boys, also in white gowns, approach from the other side as we mounted the temple steps toward the priest in the white robe, toward the great black stone, toward the flaming sun.

Physical Description of Sexual Intercourse, Concluded

When the explorer does not encounter any object, his mind spirals off into space.

Flesh which is object for no subject becomes disturbing and uncommunicable.

Rigor mortis is due to coagulation of myosinogen and paramyosinogen by fibrin ferment, forming a cloth of myosin. Sarcolactic acid and acid potassium phosphate are also generated in considerable quantity after death, and probably aid in the process of coagulation.

———————————

Note: there are quotations from Konrad Bayer's *Der Kopf des Vitus Bering*, Miguel Leon-Portilla's *The Broken Spears*. and Frank Wedekind's *Mine-Haha*.

ROBERT SHEPPARD
The Given: Part I (*from* Out of Time)

I don't remember going to the Granada in Portland Road, Hove, don't recall the film on show, and don't remember, on the same day, seeing a play, or its plot, or its title. A frame set up, years later, by others. Outside of it there are voices, whispering. Empty landing, tall doors never shut, banging in any wind. The attic, its sloped tar-hair padding, muting all street sounds. On one page, attempts at painting, soaked blots, dried solid. Across the folio, *words*. A carpet of *Daily Herald*s for the blackened man to hump sacks upon through the house to the bunker at the back, in the garden. Coal dust on the doorframe, where the hood catches it. Chorusing thanks over pie-chart fractions. Crawl into the hole under the stairs where browned instructions from the Blitz still hang. Regard a patch called the Egg Field. A gold clock turns under a glass dome. A wasp pullover bobs with a ball by the airbrick. A bedroom, narrowing to this world. Chained from picture rails, oval portraits of tinted babies. Silk slung over banisters. A dozen or so knapped flints pushed into the earth: a Roman road straight across the horses' field, the wheat, the ridge of the Downs. Timbers, pram-wheels, string, scattered around the garden. I don't remember the day I passed cleanliness, the day I drew a pictogram of a body with a blade through it. In the back room, a treadle invites feet that will never reach its gentle whine from the leather dip of the creaking chair. I don't remember riding the trams at Knokke. I don't remember walking the boxer dog Tina. The nude calendar's metal spine will not bend enough for complete concealment. Recaptured on the landing, door swung wide. I don't remember the deaths of Giacometti, Hans Hofmann, Jean Arp. The enemy is always pure machine with flashing lights and monotones. Nazis machine-gun the cheese crates and screaming POWs leap up to their deaths. The pebbly beach beneath the power station will do. An aluminium bowl of wasted food before which feeding is practised with moral intensity. The cool of the wooden hut, a scent of ice-cream that is not ice-cream. Witnessed, it sinks. I don't remember the thunderstorm I watched from my window, lightning flashes over Southwick, flickering, striking ground. After the toad in the witness box, real policemen arrive to investigate stolen buttons, the wrecked foreign car. Tall cream hallway to a room of drums, the shining vibraphone. I don't remember Radio Morse or the term "key jockey". Rubber gristle in the mouth for hours, or spat in the toilet, airless gully, escape. I don't remember taking that photograph to use the rest of the film. I don't remember getting Mum's shopping, the day I bought John Lee Hooker's "Dimples". I can't remember what I don't remember. I don't remember crossing the Forth Bridge. I don't remember what code I used. The sound of boots on the floorboards, a fragrance of leather and whitewash. The rustling of the bluebell wood, the urine-inducing silence. Dozens of pink stamps, carefully cut from envelopes, franked "Natal 1899". A gutted fish on a board: a pantry smell that is the coldness of fish itself. It sits on the window-sill, along with another, whose vitreous leaks from its cracked shell. I don't remember trying to buy *This is Blues* and finding the record sleeve contained only cardboard. I don't remember tracking Radio 260 through the streets of Southwick, the "common" English of the DJs, the warning that they'd cut up rough if we found them. Outside of it there are voices, evaluating. I don't remember whether I understood that in bringing Apollo 13 back to earth, they would have countered the rising carbon dioxide levels by use of a filter containing lithium hydroxide. The desire to write is the desire to write. I don't remember reading *The Day of the Triffids*. I don't remember watching colour TV. The red blue and white Daz packet, separating red, blue, and white, expanding along the melting body. Magnification without limit. Men ski the wallpaper. I don't remember seeing Portslade on the radar screen, don't remember the visit to HMS Collingwood. Inside the cupboard there are scribbled weather-charts. I don't remember writing a list of stories I'd written. I don't remember being shot at by somebody from a van. I don't remember the good programme about Lenin on the radio. I don't remember debating nuclear warfare in English. I don't remember Kathy getting too close for comfort. I don't remember the day Frank Sinatra retired. I remember the Ruby wine at the Romans, the way the barman would loll his tongue from the side of his mouth as he poured the soupy chemical liquid into Tony's bottles. I don't remember Doll and Arthur's caravan at Selsey. I don't remember witnessing Hitler's last will and testament. I don't remember arguing about Fats Waller. I don't remember trying to define a book. I don't remember writing a history of the avant-garde. I don't remember recording Son House off the radio. I don't remember thinking the prints of Blake ugly when I saw them at the British Museum. I don't remember when I started writing poetry. I don't remember getting a harmonica with Green Shield stamps. Or sea and sand with nothing familiar, perhaps a tent of evangelists.

I don't remember David's bottled fish. I don't remember Emerson Lake and Palmer playing a tribute to Hendrix, a week after his death. I don't remember typing "Time and Place" in Miss Starkey's flat though I still remember the typeface, the thickness of paper. I don't remember reading *Go Down Moses*. I don't remember calling Sarah "my beautiful scruff". Why don't I remember her face streaked with tears? I don't remember eating a photograph of Jennie. I don't remember the Maoist in my novel. I don't remember Ann Starkey's reactions to my novel but I do remember the *words* that describe her reactions to it. I don't remember singing "Jerusalem" on the way back from the Cardiff Stock Exchange. I don't remember the marketing man who called for a halt to economic growth. I don't remember the TV programme on Stalin. I don't remember seeing a band called Vomit. I don't remember her sighing as I kissed her. I don't remember tea and scones before retiring for sherry, the daughter of the house languidly asking why people *have* to write *such* personal poetry. I don't remember writing to Bob Cobbing. I don't remember feeling illiterate. I don't remember the barrow full of bloodied pigs' heads at Smithfield Market. I don't remember playing my tape of *The Waste Land* to an empty room. I don't remember when poems became a currency. I don't remember a girl called Annie flashing her tits on Toby's houseboat. I don't remember my guts hurting when Linda sat on my lap. Helen didn't remember saying, "Is it from Dennis?" I don't remember writing a poem about Bill Butler's bookshop. I don't remember Dad's 50th birthday. I don't remember finishing *Ulysses* at 4.40 pm on Wednesday 3 July 1974.

I don't remember the night that was not particularly memorable. I don't remember a band called White Noise. I don't remember buying Barry MacSweeney's poem about Jim Morrison. I don't remember being in a queue at the Occupied Hamburger Bar. I don't remember the Scottish woman who helped me at Metal Box. I don't remember sitting in Southwick Rest Garden to read Wilfred Owen. I don't remember dancing with a girl with a big nose whose brother was a surrealist. I don't remember walking to St Faiths on a crisp sunny Sunday morning. I don't remember Evelyn. I don't remember that I bought *Bomb Culture* the day I saw Country Joe and The Fish, the doped-up auditorium, the girl in front on downers. I don't remember the girl who was raped in the States telling me, "I've never seen a poet dancing." I don't remember Tony arriving at 15 Oakapple Road with a letter from Henri Chopin. I don't remember that Jemma thought herself the greatest poetess since Sappho. I don't remember my provisional *Notes on Literature*. I don't remember the German sailor dead drunk on the steps of the Crown and Anchor. I don't remember turning up at Saturn Studios to find them locked, John Purdy losing his job on the spot, before we went in to record "The Lover". I don't remember smoking bum-deal dope and listening to Zappa with John Kemp. I don't remember, when I asked him what he thought of Lee Harwood's writing, Anthony Thwaite replying, "Rubbish!" I don't remember going to a concert that didn't happen, in a hall that doesn't exist, with a friend who'd gone home last Wednesday. I don't remember playing John Kemp the concrete poetry LP. I don't remember seeing X J Kennedy and thinking the sonnet is where professors go to die. I don't remember the clever-dick who wanted to know why the Newhaven-Dieppe crossings were more expensive than the Dover-Calais ones. I don't remember what happened to Dorcas or Tamsin Vaughan-Williams. I don't remember Hilary. I wouldn't remember a man saying of Zappa: "As an artist he has to produce things that aren't art." I don't remember seeing *The Tears of Petra Von Kant* or reading *The Prime of Miss Jean Brodie*. I don't remember arguing with Bob Hodge about the applicability of Kuhn's paradigms to literary history. I don't remember squinting at the smallest penknife in the world. I don't remember David Gascoyne reading "Hölderlin's Madness". I don't remember seeing the Doctors of Madness again, not getting it the second time, that blue-haired zeitgeister Kid Strange. I don't remember Jemma fainting on me, with visions of a dead friend. I don't remember reading *Lud Heat* in the swelter of '76. I don't remember Flatfoot at The Alhambra. I don't remember Roger Chapman falling off stage or Trev carrying a broken bottle in case we were attacked again. I don't remember the nice girl from the Joyce and Beckett seminar who sat with me for a few minutes in the bar. I don't remember the disco to celebrate Franco's death. I don't remember the gazebo, don't remember having a blow with Helen in the gazebo, but the Steve Hillage ticket proves that some version of this evening happened. I don't remember that the conversation had been about the death of John Purdy. I don't remember laughing at the statue of the past Mayor of Brighton, with Tony, Tony Lopez and Lee Harwood. I don't remember Dad suggesting journalism and me saying it's a mug's game. I don't remember David Plante lecturing on his masturbatory writing technique. I don't remember complaining that George Barker may have been big in the 1930s, but.... I don't remember ceasing to exist at the party as I became the complete novelist. I don't remember jumbling the verses of "Travelling Riverside Blues", our first gig. I don't remember that Bob Cobbing still wore knitted ties. I don't remember Jeff Nuttall saying, "This place is death!" as we cabbed it through Norwich. I don't remember William Empson had wind.

I don't remember meeting John James and feel vertiginous loss of internal pressure as negative objects throw positive shadows over events I'm not now sure occurred in ways I thought they had only yesterday. I don't remember his laughter was a sneeze of irritation. I don't remember pitching the authority of the text as the subject of itself against the authority of self. I don't recall being willing to accept obscurity. I don't remember doubting that Tim's girlfriend existed. I don't remember Alec the Cowboy at the Penny Farthing Club in Ulverston. I disremember wanting to reach so deep inside that she'd have to let go. I do not remember singing Nick Drake's "Time Has Told Me". I don't remember the biggest slagheap in the world. I don't remember what happened to Rita Nightingale, sentenced to 20 years in Thailand. I don't remember declining the role of lead singer in The Painkillers at the benefit for Satan's Slaves in the backroom lock-in after the gig at the Wheatsheaf. I don't remember climbing Chanctonbury Ring, the moon rising ensanguined over the charmed hills, the drink at the George and Dragon with Mick and Val and Tony after.

I don't remember making love, suddenly, dangerously, after going out to vote and getting a soaking. I don't remember seeing Elton Dean at one venue under the vaults of King Street, and Stéphane Grappelli at the Theatre, hours later. I don't remember seeing *Last Year at Marienbad* and recalling the last time I saw it, with Trev and Martine, the year before. I don't remember not meeting Peter Stacey because the clocks had gone back and I don't remember us discussing six basic vowel sounds pitched from a fundamental. I don't remember Mum turning 50, but I called it "the threshold of old age". I don't remember offering my spare bed to Paul Stewart who vowed to emigrate if Thatcher had won by the morning.

BERNADETTE MAYER
Farmers Exchange
for Russell Banks

I went in for some soil. The guy looked at me, I had the baby too, and he said after a long while, "pottin serl?" They had nice petunias out front. I said yes pottin soil. I need alot of it. He said how much. I said I dont know how much, what sizes are the bags. He showed me the small bag maybe a mere five pounds or less. Then I got to see the twenty pound bag which also looked small to me but I said I'd take it & come back for more if I needed it. Then the other guy said well it's cheaper this way in the bigger bags. So I said ok I'll take the forty pound bag. So the bag got taken out & he threw it in a wheelbarrow displayed out front & then I asked if I could pay for it & did they have any basil seeds. The first guy was lookin in a book, he said I'm lookin in a book to see what it cost but out in the car my children were screamin, I could hear them from there though I took a look & saw Lewis was calmly readin The Times anyway & not freaked out. Then he said I'm sure we've got some basil round here somewhere but I dont know where, he was still readin his book of prices. Then he said well I guess the serl'll have a price marked right on it. It was 3.98. A nice young couple was backin up their pickup to the veranda of the exchange. She had on a Henniker t-shirt & they were havin what I would call a real conversation with the other guy, not like the one I'd had. And they were gettin millions of things put in their truck. I wanted to take a catalogue & git some seeds but where kin I put them tomater plants anyway since what's his face has took all the good garden space, fenced around, I'd rather eat the weeds, it's a helluva lot cheaper'n plantin & what if the volcanic ash in the sky causes alot of June-July frosts'n stuff like in 1813, the year without a summer, remember the sunflowers in Worthington & the guy in the Senior Citizens crafts store in Conquered who said, the old people have all these things they can do but the young people who need em cant do em so we sell em to em.

Then we saw the ex-minor-league baseball player's wife strugglin along Main with two of her kids & she & I'd give each other wan sort of smiles & then we saw her husband, the pharmacist now, runnin the little league game, then I thought of the woman with the German name like "Till Eulenspiegel" who's the secretary, or one of them, to the Vice President for Academic Affairs or whatever he calls himself at the college & how she said to me, you're young yet, no use staying around here, I wanted to travel all over when I was younger & now I'm too old to sit in a car, it's dull here, you dont get to see anything. But then I had a dream that a combination of Bob Holman / Bob Rosenthal / Greg Masters & others had become in NY a paranoid schizophrenic lunatic & he darts in & out among the poles & struts saying Beware the Rastaman's fortuitous relation with the chokecherry nature of the chakras! He even put an ad in the Poetry Project newsletter to that effect. We try & comfort him, realizin it's just our age, it's a dim kind of brain damage, it's inevitable, more so than the Love Canal on Canal Street & who knows besides alligators what's under them pavements. And then some man told me rich people wrap their heads in plastic to keep from gettin old. In real life Marie'd put the plastic bubble blower into her vagina & said it stung and then I read in the papers Terry Furlow had died in a car crash in his Mercedes Benz full of alcohol bottles, weird kinds of cigarettes & a furry white powder & I thought about the woman who'd moved from Boscawen to Penacook, just her & the kids she said, we overheard her conversin with another woman at the Conquered Clinic & when the other woman said to her well what happened to yer husband, she kind of leered kind of happy at it all & said, extenuatin circumstance, you know. It's thunderstormin, full moon & Raphael sent me a postcard of two frescoed haloed mourners by Aretino Spinello who died a long time ago.

Nathaniel Hawthorne
Conclusion

After a while, enough time had gone by for people to arrange their sentences about the scene that I have described & then there was more than one version of what had been seen on the scaffold.

And most of them testified, most of them said they had seen a scarlet letter on the breast of the priest. And it was the same one the *she* wore but this one was printed, was imbedded in the flesh of the man. And where it came from was all that was left to talk about & all this was done in a logical way. Some of the ones who were talking said that the priest, the same day she first wore her letter, began to wear his, or at least wear his into himself – something about penance, a method of penance, or many methods, some kind of strange torture, the presence of the letter in the flesh. And some of the ones who were talking, these others said that the sign of the letter had not been produced until much later, when the old shaman & lover of the dead had made it appear, in an amazing regression, through the use of magic words & poisonous drugs. And others again – & these were the ones who knew the priest best, understood his lability & studied psychoanalysis – they whispered their belief that the insistence of the letter in the mind of the priest caused it to grow steadily outward, finally manifesting the judgement of memory in the own body of the man by the visible presence of the letter. You can choose among these theories. We have talked all we can about meaning & we'd gladly, now that it's played its part, erase the print of the letter from our own brain. We've thought too much about it, it's become too distinct.

But it's odd, anyway, that some of the people who saw this whole scene & said that they never looked away, some denied that there was any mark at all on the breast of the priest, as if he were a baby. And, according to these people, his dying words never said, they didnt imply any, even the slightest connection, for him, with the guilt for which she had worn the letter. And according to these same people, the priest, conscious that he was dying, & conscious also that his sainthood had been preserved, has shown his desire, by dying in the arms of someone openly guilty to express to the world how worthless & stupid the ideas, of right & wrong are. And so he was an angel. After spending his life in the way that he had, he had made his death some sort of lesson for his audience, that, in any view that encompasses everything, we are really all the same. And it was to teach them, somehow, that the best readers & writers were just so far above any others as to see the little you need to know to get rid of any idea of value at all. Without arguing such an amazing truth, we have to consider this version of his story as just an example of that enraged faith with which a man's friends will sometimes defend him, when proofs, clear as the sun on the character of the letter, establish him a false one & just as confused as anyone else.

The authority we've been using – an old manuscript drawn up from people's verbal testimony – says all these things, & some of these people had known her & other ones had just heard the story from her own contemporaries. A moral becomes a pressure at this point – the priest's experience leads nowhere. This is the only moral we will make a sentence out of: it's Poe's "My Heart Laid Bare," again, it's "Show freely to the world, somehow, if not the worst & the truth is not just the worst, but anyway, show something from which we can infer the worst, deal with the worst, or maybe, just show, something, anything."

Nothing was more amazing than the change that happened, almost immediately after the priest's death, in the looks & attitude of an old shaman. All his strength & energy, all his conceptual & intellectual force, his power seemed to desert him almost completely; in fact he withered, he withered up, he shrivelled away, he was vanishing, he was vanishing into thin air, he was going up in smoke, he was ceasing to be, almost vanishing from sight, like an uprooted tree that leaves many branches behind, that leaves not a branch behind. This fantastic man had made the whole center of his life the study & systematic exercise of revenge through transference; and when, by its complete triumph & consummation in the total reorganization of the employment of faculties in the mind of the priest, when that, in this case evil principle was left with no more material to work on, nothing to support him or it, when, in short, there was no more devil's work on earth for him to do, all that was left for the dehumanized man was to find himself a new master of his own, another shaman, & work for him & get paid. But toward all these shadow people, these introjections we've just begun to understand – all the others & even the shaman himself – we might just as well feel an attitude of beneficent neutrality, a simple fascination. It's a curious subject of observation in any inquiry or analysis, whether hatred & love are the same in the end. Each, when it's pushed that far, supposes an incredible intimacy & heart-knowledge; each renders one person dependent on another for both food & fame, existing in a state of symbiosis; the passions of the lover & the passions of the one who hates create an anxiety of the same force when the subject is withdrawn, the anxiety of separation, loss of the possibility of mutuality. So, looked at this way, love & hatred seem the same, except that one happens to be seen in the light of desire for strength in a stronger existence, and the other is a lurid distortion of this, as the repetition of a dead desire, In some other world, the old curer & the priest – mutual victims as they have been – may, without knowing it, have found what they made of their hatred changed into love, their stock of baser metals transmuted into gold, & may in fact have discovered, these mutual victims, the elixir of perpetual youth.

But forgetting all this, there is some information you should have. When the old doctor died, which he did within the year, his rescue fantasies did not cease, and by his last will & testament, of which some of the ones who were mentioned before were executors, he left an enormous amount of property, both here & in England, to Pearl, the daughter of Hester Prynne.

So the elf-child, child-wife, the demon offspring, as some people, even up to that point, continued to call her, became the richest heiress of her day in the new spirit. Pretty predictably, this circumstance changed everbody's mind; and, had the mother & child stayed here, the demon child, after adolescence, might have mingled her wild blood with the blood of the most puritanical of them all. But, in no time after the doctor's death, the bearer of the scarlet letter disappeared, and the child along with her. For years, though every once in a while some vague story would find its way across the sea – like a shapeless object carved with the initial letter of some name – still no real word was heard. And the story of the scarlet letter was a history. But its magic never lost power, and kept the scaffold where the priest died awful & the house by the sea where the others had lived, this was invested with magic. Near this spot, one afternoon, some children were playing, when they saw a tall woman in a gray robe come up to the door of the house by the sea. In all those years it had never once been opened; but either she unlocked it, or the decaying wood & iron fell at the touch of her hand, or, or she went as a shadow through any impediment – but, in any event, she went in.

She stopped in the doorway & turned partly around – maybe, the idea of going alone & so changed into the space of an old life & an intense one, was more than even she could bear. But her hesitation only lasted long enough to show the color of the letter on her breast as a point of light.

So she had returned, she had resumed, something about guilt. And if the child was still alive, she must have been a woman by now. No one knew, or ever learned for sure, whether the elf-child had survived or in what direction a wildness like hers could go in the world. But, for the rest of Hester's life, there were indications that the recluse of the scarlet letter was the object of love & interest from some inhabitant of another world. Letters came, with armorial seals upon them, but they were bearings unknown to English heraldry. And in the house there were such amazing things that no one could ever use them

& only incredible wealth could provide them, & love imagine them. There were small books too, ornamented books, designed books, bespeaking a continual remembrance, that must have been made in editions of only one. And once Hester was seen embroidering clothes for a baby & she was using all the colors, she was using so many colors that any baby would have been a whole scandal appearing in these clothes in our monochrome community.

In the end, the gossip of the day was – and the man who made investigations a century later believed – and one of his recent successors in office believes – and I believe – that Pearl was not alive, but rich & happy & would have been glad to share that whole life with her mother.

But there was something else for Hester Prynne to do here, in New England, and not in that unknown region where Pearl was living now. Here had been the origins of her desire; here its completion & its distortion & the working out of that; her real work was still to be done & it had to be done here. She had returned, she had resumed – and freely, for even the sternest authority of that iron period would never have imposed it – resumed the outward symbol of what this whole story has been telling. She never abandoned it again, it was always visible. But, in the lapse of the years that made up her life, the scarlet letter ceased to be a stigma which attracted the world's abnormal scorn & bitterness at a broken taboo, and became a type of something to be looked at & studied, sometimes with awe, an amazing sign of something about the future, or the progression of time itself, the insistence of the letter in the unconscious. Some people worshipped it, in a peculiar way. And, as Hester Prynne had an investment in understanding human behavior, people began to know this & brought all their troubles & confusions, and sought her as a counsellor, as one who had herself gone through an amazing struggle. Women especially – in the continually recurring instances of wounded, wasted, wronged, misplaced, or erring & unaccepted love – or with the incredible burden of love withheld because it was unvalued or not sought out – came to her house by the sea, demanding why they were so unhappy & what was the cure! Hester comforted & counselled them with the methods she knew. She assured them, too, of her firm belief, that, at some brighter period, when the world should have grown ripe for it, when people understood enough, a new truth would be revealed, in order to establish the whole relation between man & woman on a surer ground of mutual happiness. Earlier in life, Hester had imagined that she herself might be the destined prophetess of this sexual & psychological revolution, but she had long since recognized the impossibility that any mission such as this should be done by one woman, especially one burdened with what she still considered a lifelong sorrow, a lifelong guilt. The angel of the coming revelation must be woman indeed, but direct & wise, and not through grief; and this at least was her fantasy: she would be showing how love & sex should make us happy or sublime by the creation of a true science in a life successful to such a end!

So said Hester Prynne, and glanced her sad eyes downward at the scarlet letter. And, after many years a new grave was delved, near an old & sunken one, in that burial-ground beside which King's Chapel has since been built. It was near that old & sunken grave, yet with a space between, as if the dust of the two sleepers had no right to mingle. Yet one tombstone served for both. All around, there were monuments carved with armorial bearings; and on this simple slab of slate – as the curious investigator may still discern, and perplex himself with the purport – there appeared the semblance of an engraved escutcheon. It bore a device, a herald's wording of which might serve for a motto & brief description of our now concluded legend; so sombre is it, & relieved only by one ever-glowing point of light gloomier than the shadow: –

"ON A FIELD, SABLE, THE LETTER A, GULES."

PAUL BUCK
skiP there is no story speaK to me [extract]
in pursuit of the Italian Project

Since the early nineties I've been thinking, researching, making notes that explore the hidden version of my background, that my mother was Italian. At least five escapades are in progress. Not all will attain completion. Not all will undress themselves. Or be disrobed.

January 2010

> *Leave. Don't leave. How to put it. Declaring the opposites in alternation in order to invent what you are thinking.*
> *Mathieu Bénézet*

(A:) *every day I hear direction*
Be the one to speak words of dismay, for scarcely had they finished slipping their tease to pass their time cruelly than the amusement switched away from gender.

"I too was born an invalid," I was informed. "My mother was Italian."

We were told to stay outside the room. We were too kind to give chocolates and books. We could visit another time. Not today. He wanted to be alone. It wasn't our fault. The rooms were too small. And besides…

"But if I have to leave…" he managed to say. His thoughts were surrounded by dark outlines. At last, the thirst of the unconcerned, the undecided area of timidity, that enrapture that was love, not only the grace of her look.

At the desk, across from the fireplace, he was turning his back on his imaginings. He withdrew the note from his pocket. He read:

She seemed to be unable to manage because she

showed sadness, she was not smiling enough, not
content to share her indignancy and admiration, to
say exactly when she needed to gain her place.
She bit her lip. She was right to reflect, to play the
memory game.

I shall give it to you, without a word of warning. I'll give it willingly. She turned her back on him and went to the door.

She had turned her back on childhood too, now was the break, her intentions were to signify it, the cold face admonished him, her usual affectionate tone had slipped away. Blinded by frustration, a cry came to his throat as he fell headlong into despair.

They made their way in silence to a position overlooking the Forum. He could see her slight breasts crushed in the top, the sliding glances, the longing eyes…

He was not a solid block of salt, or marble. Again, he could feel his desires stir as they moved into the meadows. An expanse of unbroken fields, a solid green. She had worn her red skirt intentionally, she was leaning on his suspicions. She was a corrupt girl. He had been warned. As long as it suited him. "Does it suit you?" You can stay with her, and yet, he couldn't help.

"I've closed the door," he said.

"Am I supposed to be pleased?"

"Yes, for you're finding the flat askew."

She started, for she heard the lift move off beside her, and she hadn't seen it was occupied.

"That's why I shut the door."

One side after the other, and we were made to talk.

"Why shouldn't we talk about it?" he asked. It seemed as if his remark was to be overshadowed by the complete surrender of his promises. For the first time it seemed as if he accepted her friend's presence as the reason for his feelings. It was so cold. The night sky that summer was open.

(B:) the inevitable crumbling of hesitance

What could she have dispelled? She was not missing anything, I can assure you. She assured me. I thought I was looking at her as a child when she was in fact already in her fifties. Happier times though occurred when she was still young. She assured me. I sensed she had been in the midst of an argument when I arrived. I was ready to reply. I pretended to forget what I wanted to say, with the utmost discretion. I thought. Then the girl opened the door and a gust of cold air struck me hard in the face. She opened the door and a gust of cold air struck us hard in the face. I came to resent the intrusion. I was too deep in the sofa. Stay there. You can stay there. I made myself comfortable. No point in humiliating yourself. Like that. Like what? I was rich in virtues, there could be no grabbing the lesson. To be present. To feel lovely. She added that somewhere else would even be tiresome if we intended to pour ourselves through our tenderness. That's just it, I am without passion. I can do nothing for you but uncork my thoughts, let them pop out and hastily retreat. In order not to consent and then not without some disgust, for she had lost her sense of direction. There was also the furthest end of what she said.

Every now and then he asked the girl what she was feeling. It was clearly a question for forgetting, of forgetting, for the past was a cruelty that told me not to pursue it. Not to look for trouble. She cried, with a forced welling of tears. With a gaiety that goaded the others. Or with a mischief that came to her, that laughed. A vague uncertainty that showed she lacked confidence or the steadiness of slicing the squeals from beneath her shoes. From beneath the heels that danced to the tune. Is this the tune? We danced on, edging towards the darkness.

Twitching with impatience, nerves that could be seen beneath the very boredom that you know how to be as impulsive as she is. But you're not going to speak seriously. He insisted, think first. And then there was silence. And then there was the throwing of objects and clothes in all directions, pulling themselves into what she had now doubted.

It was her brown chestnut hair, the fine calm of her brow and the slim waist that had been tried, and forced with the insertion of her hand. Into the same blackness, into what she had fallen into, the sleep that the self has, that she was truly within her room and not how she could be sat down on the bed, in the half darkness. She added that there was a raising of her voice. Please, do it. Look at your eyes. There was a pavement, there was a loss. Lost to the view. Sunshine become a fuss, the receding of the shadows into the course that answered his motions, rather an uncertain, a certainty that he had taken such affection towards her, that had crumbled her breath, lumps that formed, where there was no stopping, gently, going down as if to say within.

Drive that thought. Go faster, lower the window, abort the big wheels where I can lay a finger on what is reflected in their eyes, their mouths. One with the device and the virtues that helped others to be a sign of progress, in relation to what you know, she continued, still staring at him, her eyes with that need to feel. And I haven't any happiness, the fault is not entirely mine. I don't know how to reach for air, that irresistible decision, that assurance of the absurd, a passion like a fast boy, a passion for loose living. No, she had him by the arm.

Do you mean it?

I told you there was no silence. She didn't talk like that because she had a wardrobe that could be cared for, a comb for her hair, then she would be married. He whispered to her while she fleshed out her shoulders, while she had the width of flabbiness that bared arms, that afternoon that really happened, and yet not at all.

(C:) abandoned by instinct, we conceive of exception

Success, he announced.

There was an audience – the woman and his faults.

And one fault was his accursed politeness. What had just begun? Why was he after his thirst? What was he pursuing? What could he gain from the severity of showing her the depth of his feelings?

Black and it dimmed.

As if others were meddling with his whole charm.

And what did she think?

That when she saw him, she slowed, she slaughtered a vodka.

Expect that.

When?

Confronting with glass, the bottle in her hand. Impassively. A conscious courage.

Whereas he was strongly attracted to her, the one he had already fallen in love with.

Whose fault was it to be accepted?

He must find the night itself, must be kissed by her. He still hoped she might accept him.

A different effect. He did not share his path with her.

And yet he was the only one to smell the fear. And to look with a smile, to propose what was suggested, to thwart not by error.

The first time, in this room, I had longed for her. She withdrew one of the lace thin garments, the same blunders, that he had often sworn not to repeat. The result being that he would be involved in more blunders, in the end being unable to endure it any longer, to turn around or take his eyes off the argument.

For his secret life he was registering fascination, any traces of richness, the steps where she knew that lunch was to be served.

Time to accommodate both her and her friend, hugs that quickly turned to rough caresses, cries that screened with an attentive eye.

She saw that he was now what he was almost played out to be. Although he was the restraint in the gaze, an eye for the gallery that served to be ready for informing, a theme that all would be what she was, a reply to pre-empt, to trail her feet into her soft leather shoes with the crowd stretching their necks and poking at former times, the alterations at the far end were not for touching.

(D:) distance the words, she is with desire

He felt her body lying so close to him. Beside her was a naked man.

He was rowing now, and his motion was sat facing him.

"Will you let me play too?" she asked. He wore clothes that had been hung from a peg. His shoes sat on the floor like gum stuck to his look. Here was the shoulder where it all began. He made faces and stubbed out his cigarette.

Man was nothing without a woman and he felt the white hot blaze of the sun encircle him and he said, "yes, what harm can I do?"

He repeated himself, he turned to her, sitting a little apart now, eating a pastry. He wanted to feel he could be almost like her, would have liked to say whether he was more attracted or frightened by her presence.

It wasn't the most urgent aim, but it was right to feel himself, for if there were other women there, then there was the possibility of an evening of consummated sex.

You pretend to talk for a bit, but there is no door. There it's the porch, the gate, but nothing is locked and her body is there and turns on the current at the mains. Such a meal, there was always somebody waiting to stand for a second, to hear the sounds, to feel the shapes, to dissolve into the flesh and obscure the point of honour of that lyrical pleasance. At first he had tried to make her perform, to draw her into the cupboard that was full of old crumpled clothes.

That was where they found the blood-stained garments and the real truth of the young girl who had said she had not been out. That occurred at the table, her head hanging heavy with shame. There was a drowsiness about him, beneath his laughing face, from beneath which she was prevented from dominating, from being merely the shortness of breath.

But when the lights went off again, he walked through the state of agitation and anguish like a swirling of lovers clutching at themselves, their arms feeling as if they had reached the door of his room where he was standing facing her. He asked quietly what was it that his mother's obtuseness and assurance had aroused in her. She pushed it away because she knew I was going to see it on her smile. There was no soap that could remove it. I sponged her full of moments of fragrance. She asked if I'd been very ill, if she hadn't supposed that I'd noticed that beneath the redness of her lipstick she might not be happy.

It was her mother who interrupted. Each time I woke I found the day had peaked and the more I looked the more I felt I was never going to get to the bottom of what I sought.

(E:) such an inversion, health or the rights to intervene

...in the air, in the folds of the curtain, the memory that was thrown at me.

...leaving my legs exposed, legs as the magnified hurt, for walking was distraught, and every perhaps had too much trepidation, too much delight. And I found the tears. I wanted you to be rich with the realization that curiosity resided. I wanted to see the house, there was nothing else to be found outside in the bare and gleaming expanse.

There was the entrance.

Before you get married, you have to have eaten with me, at the same table, and you will receive gifts, money enough from the mention of her, forcing me to become like her.

"Please forgive me," he said. "But I receive so much pleasure from laughter, and though I joked with him, there were many others who could be cross with me."

And immediately he asked if I would stand his presence.

He wanted to be serene. I told him in an underhand way that what I wanted was a mixture of reason and some other form of marriage that might come to be useful.

We went out to meet her. When she was late, our friends were carried away, as if they were my desire.

And that fault was as if fidelity had thought she would probably be offended by the request to regain money.

I laid my clothes where I wanted to go.

Not to be busy with yes, I answered, too quickly. Not to see her open the shutters and start to tidy the room.

One evening she said she would like to sleep with me.

If it was too early I would slip out again, go out to find what I should feel deeply about. I was attracted, but I tried to hide. All I could do was lend some colour and strength. Only once, she told me. But it was an expression of her distance.

I laughed again. "Of course, there are two. Of course, I'm sure."

She didn't mean to offend, not you, not the flying man, not the vanished. I repeated, "the vanished, not the vanished."

She was looking at him, facing him now, with her palm, my hands, they are longer and larger. And still warm.

"Don't you find it difficult to imagine what a person, what your lover felt, what she loved? Again. Even more than before."

"Say it again."

"White gloves and stockings."

The lover chose her man. He was in his forties. He was not so tall, he had curly hair. She was freed from herself. She moved away, she pulled away and went on walking. "Did you hear what she said, what that young woman said?"

I asked her again.

"What was he like?" I asked. And at the same time I made my way so that I had to be understood.

Before she was left in such a way that every way she turned she came to terms with the numerous ways, my casting stone across the village square. This was a new thought, a new sentence to bear. Let's wait a while. "Do you still think about going to confession?"

There was a trace of cunning in his calculation. To say to them I'd love to. I'll love you. I don't like it beside the glass. The glass is enough to make me feel I ought to be offended. I am offended. I am flattered. But this sense of impetuousness is nothing but a politeness. My fear is that I know that like everybody else, that confession is only a spiritual dismay, a distress that has its opening like a story that has no response. At that moment the door flung open.

"No," she said. "You cannot pull yourself together. The table has been cleared. Now and not later."

But at that moment, it pierced me, pierced me to my heart. "To you," I muttered.

And the groan that it occasioned was such that there was an indication of a rising, the searing heat that spoke to me between the houses, as I clenched my chest and walked back to the village square. "Which was the house? I haven't been here in years, I remember so little."

I hurled myself at the afternoon. It has been taken, it has taken a while for her to finish rummaging through her drawers to find the time. I remained lost.

Lost in thought, I moved the sheets on the desk. It didn't matter to me whether I did or did not assume an air of indifference. After I had put several questions about my concerns and interests, it was merely a counting, a mechanism that the days were my suitcase.

I noticed she shared what I was drinking.

We made love the next day.

I began to find the way that this love, which could be tragic as well as ecstatic, had come into me. Revolving in my chair, I shake less than my head. As if to say that she did not accept it was a matter of concern.

"Is it cold now?" I said. "I'll pour a fresh cup."

(F:) of the flesh, of relation to self, of submission
"Just a few then."
My wife has always been its singer.
"The lone singer…"
"…was roused." And I fell over backwards.
"How long after kissing her… How long?"
There was a furious and real duplicity, a treachery. But I accept that it had been accumulating, a mass of specifics that the love I felt for my wife was strengthened by my physical exhaustion. That threaded through all that fortune I might perhaps have recognized in what had happened. So that in order to dress, her hair had to be sat down in her chair. "I'll be there."

Thus he read about the lesson of importance, of the fault that others found with the bare gains.

And there was the exercise book that contained the story. It seemed to be in front of me but in fact it was what I now found private and locked away. I was extremely grateful that my wife, for the way she now… the way she then settled in silence. Into the silence of the horses tied up, tired.

I am strong now. I had told her on the way back that perhaps I was too fatigued. I opened it and set the book down on the chair. "At the moment it's not suitable to read." "That's true," I responded, remembering the incident when she came to tell me that diplomacy was better as we went into the room, sure that I should find my writing had wrecked my ambition to accept my strength as a music, and I could not help smiling again as we went into the room and I discovered when I read it over that as the composers of the day were in the habit of saying nothing more, I said nothing more, all I did was stroke her hand.

(G:) soliloquy in a way out, escaping… dissolving
She was completely invisible beneath the enormous blanket of answers, because they do harm you, "didn't you tell me that before?"

Playing at the snake, he wanted to be punished, but always came his remorse, before. And at the same time better than his

"No, I don't, because I've my pride, such as my Italian restlessness."

He thrust his foot forward, roughly, away from her, and added, quite slowly, that besides there was the carelessness to be moved up the path and "Yes, the lino that was revealed, waiting all these years for an answer, had come with a smile, had come from Rome, though not quite certain of the date," or the meaning of why now.

Then the words of this process were displayed.

Then the pleasure was for him to peruse from that consciousness what he had broken, what had stopped in the midst of the hunger, the irritation of the proof, apart from anything else the authentic nature that his quest for redemption had a normality. There could be only that anonymous letter and yet, immediately he was thinking, as he knew well that the involvement was a fresh territory, and that at this hour the chuckling had to stop, the desert had to be marvelled at and go down well.

Places remained open until after midnight. And we watched the night life run up and down the creepers. One moment casting a hasty glance at the black spiders as we went down to greet the visitors, she in her rustling silk, me entering the lift with a burst of forgiveness. "It's the greatest possible solemnity I'm offering you."

And I felt so much better. But perhaps I ought not to have her in my face. And with her elbow she was gone, going, interpreted as looking down at the same sheet of paper, much more than me, here, but if you need anything then make sure, yes, of course, you can say no, but no says yes, don't come up, just tell me to set off in that direction, to carry what was asked of him, to engage me in a burst more closely than in the amorous embrace, and then to be heard, in any case let's eat, let's dine together, there's an if, as if to conceal the emotion, almost, going over and finding the size, the almost excessive brightness that has been accompanied by the greeting.

It was as though there was an almost, an almostness, quite the opposite perhaps, a line that had been managed, a whatever to a whomever, that could have been thought through. So it's true she exclaimed with a flurry of her hands, an affliction that she had, in profile no less, no less precise and no less absurd for there was another arrival, because I know that it isn't true that what followed would lead to the dance.

"What could it be," she murmured. She was panting. In tears. Burst into tears. That's why she went today. You can see that there was the cause of her uttering no, nothing would not have been possible, she thought.

He went further along the passage until he found the half-closed door. It was larger than he thought. He approached the group inside surrounded by improvised chairs, some of them coloured red. One small one had occupied their flat and he realized that he would have a small problem with the degree of its largeness.

LYN HEJINIAN
Lola

The dog on its leash knows the secret of freedom.
This is promising, says Lola.
Fanfare and ridiculous light.
Chapter One.

Chapter One

Chapters admit events, chapters worlds apart, chapters in a mood, mid-air, in plumes.

Sam comes along with binoculars, cash, gloves, a bridle, and a net, he says, there's a bird – with a rat! – and there are payers.

There are didacts, a killer, one polymath, a mother, a Russian gymnast, occasional passersby and idle salespeople, a juggler, a man with a sore throat, and a sorrowful child with cold hands and a three-legged dog on a leash, and all of these are players.

The sisters Hertha!

Drew!

Nina!

Abdul Tommy Ahmed!

Trish O'Reilly!

Kurt Krakauer!

Ludmilla Kaipa!

And Sue!

Chapter Two

Maggie Fornetti walks by quickly in her left hand holding an iPod adjusting her headphones with her right.

Askari Nate Martin's calm strikes Maggie Fornetti as hostile.

He can imagine her going off to some weird place no one's ever heard of and coming back with an exotic wolfish sort of cat or rodent to exhibit before some startled audience forming a circle around the thing.

Askari Nate Martin is troubled, Maggie pretends not to see him hoping he will greet her, he nods indifferently and passes by unhappily.

Maggie tends to listen to pieces of music until she can no longer hear anything of them except her responses to her experiences of them which are often more of things or thoughts that occur while she's listening than of the pieces exactly, she thinks, in pieces.

When causes can't be repeated, you infer them from effects.

Chapter on the Side of One, Two, Three

Every child early on should be taught to apologize, says Sally Dover.

According to Sally Dover the goal of education is improvement, the goal of self-education self-improvement, and she asks Jeanie's mother Minnie Jones, How systematic are Jeanie's efforts to improve?

How systematic are yours? Minnie asks in return indignantly, don't be defensive, Sally Dover quips, are you crazy! Minnie declares, and the exchange of bad pleasantries comes to an end.

Three must wait for one to be subtracted to be two.

Children must be very patient in order to be educated.

Jeanie while being patient picks her nose.

Just down the way Helen is plucking hairs from her chin as she addresses them impatiently, you'll no longer inhabit this continent.

Helen has fine handwriting and she displays it to herself in a green and black hardcover notebook in letters addressed to herself, Dear Helen, Quindlan is afraid.

Lola cycles past a telephone pole studded with staples.

Two little girls in pigtails snarl and paw the air and are jerked back onto their chairs.

Chapter One

Sid is a young Marine, Quindlan is a player, Mrs Lee is climbing the stairs and in the grocery bag she holds in her arms are a starfish, a potato, a bottle of syrup, a map of Minnesota, a misspelled word, a sample of satin, and an ominous owl, a scream.

Then along comes Chapter Two for which everyone must practice constantly and with it comes Chapter 3.

Chapter 3 and Chapter Two

The apple in fall comes to rest near a man with his fortune rolled up in a ball that he caught on a dare as it bounced off a car, the door slightly ajar, a strange smell in the air.

The lovers tumble to the side of spontaneity without wondering what it's for, what it can do, and declare it "an un-in-ter-rup-ted round of pleasure!"

Along comes a juggler with a treasure hiding jars in the air made bright by the sun in the eyes of the lover, a beholder.

A small cop tumbles into view, happening onto the scene without a clue as if at fate's request to find a guy left high and dry whom he can arrest.

Symptomatically belligerently Quindlan asks, What's dubious about Fritos?

Did you know that cats that purr don't roar and cats that roar don't purr? Maggie Fornetti asks Askari Nate Martin, who thinks perhaps he's being grilled.

Helen says paranoia is archaic, Maggie says, full of old surprises.

Askari Nate Martin notes that conversations in real life rarely move directly from A (derived from elements of the theme being developed) to B (derived from completely different elements using completely different talents) but still the conversations give birth to the image in which the matter is most clearly embodied.

The juggler juggles with jugs that have been prepared, the tumbler is him or herself prepared.

The result will produce in the payers a complete image but of something bearing little relation to the bigger theme.

Chapter Two

Askari Nate Martin, when inspired by love, takes note with a silent nod intended to point out things that he loves to the one he loves as his love but Maggie Fornetti when it comes to love wants more than a nod, more than shadowboxing, Take that! and that! and that! she says to herself sarcastically dismally.

A strong wind is blowing rings around them, hardly noticeable at first, shadows flit, leaves pretending to dance with themselves flirt with the shadows, but now shadows and leaves are dodging, ducking, seeking refuge behind each other, done with dancing and then with batting at each other, they would gladly drag whole trees after them to escape the wind.

I'm not sheltered in arms, Maggie Fornetti thinks to herself involuntarily, touching her hip bones through her coat pockets.

Pleasantly aware of appearing thoughtful, watching Maggie thinks of Nate investigating, going on with only what he calls Piece A and Piece B.

Askari Nate Martin is making Maggie Fornetti anxious, his maneuvers provoke anxiety (desire), in an effort to alleviate her anxiety she thinks she should throw herself into his path.

Piece C, she says to him, connects them – it comes between them, not after.

What to See in Chapter Three

Faces everywhere.

Faces bend to the soft valley without emotion except that of ended joy.

The young Marine Sid thinks, he can't see beyond faces, there's nothing behind them, he thinks, he thinks of loud stormy nights and grasses, the sand and dead mice, the battle-field, the population, a lost purse, a dark vehicle.

The young Marine keeps his words in his cheek, he thinks, he's nothing himself but a face at the doorstep with nothing behind him but trees perhaps hiding the sky, why would trees go to such extremes as to hide the sky, in the forest they are trooped with their fellows.

That one feels oneself to be an unworthy person doesn't warrant one's opting out of being human altogether.

The young Marine thinks, nothing follows.

Sid the young Marine has crimson circles on his cheeks like permanent marks of embarrassment or of excitement too long sustained.

Chapter for Fun

Frankie is romping and Fredo is watching, then vice versa.

Chapters intensify everything, chapters express "intensifica-tion," Frankie, says Fredo.

Fredo likes the way hurdles come and go, Frankie feels a slight dilation.

Frankie jumps over a sawhorse like sunlight just coming over treetops and shining into a field showing its clover.

Lion or lamb, says Fredo, Frankie says, lamb, Fredo puts up his hand, what we do by chance one day may soon become a habit.

The life of a weed is not an embarrassment, says Frankie.

Chapter Two or Three

Education should provide us with more than merely material for justifying our opinions, says Maggie.

Our crimes, you mean, says Nate.

Chapter Three

Come on, Graciela, Jeanie Jones whimpers.

A twig snaps, a car accelerates toward the ocean.

From somewhere in the shrubbery at the edge of the parking lot the singing of the mockingbird unfolds as in a dream continuing day and night – free of fate, since no matter how much seems to happen, nothing actually does.

Period – so there – it's over – fini – the end – come all.

Chapter One

Welcome, there will be interruptions, that can't be helped, we're occupants of a tent now pitched, there are always many players and help is not always on their side.

Lola's on a bike, Helen is a largeness, Bill tumbles backward and jumps to his feet pointing to the parking lot, Nina says she wishes it were a field in which she could pasture a trick cow, you can't train cows says Bill, but Nina remains spontaneously reasonable, on some days she wakes to play placards and on others to play the flute politically and she says, Look, I'm telling you what I saw not what I know, that comes tellingly second.

Players all have second things poignantly in mind.

That's just what I said to my mother the day I was born, says Jeanie.

A juggler attempts to seize everything at the very instant he lets it go, the juggler says the field doesn't leave us, we leave it.

For all the years that my wife will live after me, though I'm dead I'll long to be with her, says Bill.

Lola cycles past.

Graciela Parker is missing.

Chapter Around

The last of the fog is no more than light just visible in the breeze, the sun is up to the trees.

To see it no mere illusion to see that Lola will see! – but she makes only a brief appearance at this time to say irritably that it takes her time to appear.

There are branches no thicker than wires in hand to dance in the lights of what's to come.

There's a little scab on the skin over the clavicle of a man on the beach.

Dang! says a child Lola thinks to call Maria when she wins at Bingo.

Dang! says a general others generally think to call when he wins a war.

Circles, scenes, and conjunctions – no peace.

What a circus!

Chapter One

I'm called Sharl, says Charles to Frankie, and this is my wife, Doe-rah.

Eagerly Frankie says his name is Frankie but my real name, he says as if he'd only just this moment received it, is France! – and am I right to guess that you're from France – too, as it were?

From Lyons in the West, says Charles, yes.

This is Fredo, Frankie says.

Olla, Fredo says.

The sun is drifting like a tourist through a country market overhead.

We have arrived to escape Lyons, Dora says – everything is dead there, living every day.

Living every day for the person living it should not be a negligible part of a long biographical act, says Fredo to his surprise.

We cannot know the name, says Dora drawing her shawl closer to her chest, of what, Charles asks irritably, of living every day, Dora says.

Then let's call it a circus and admit rings, says Frankie, each as different from another as the minute before noon is from the minute after, which is when, having parted from Frankie and Fredo, Charles and Dora find Graciela Parker lying as if asleep among the poppies Dora's thought to pick from the yard at the edge of the parking lot among the tall gray weeds.

It's against the law to pick those, hey! Helen is shouting, as Dora whimpers, shudders, and screams.

Later she will remember the moment at random as one she would never justly foresee, mournfully, angrily.

Nearby a kid is standing on the rear bumper of Charles and Dora's red rented Dodge scratching OLLEH into the rear window glass.

Lola goes by, fleetingly.

Lola – voilà!

Chapter Aside

We want to piss in brilliant colors, say Montgomery, Bill, and Drew.

Chapter One

Welcome back, players and payers, all coming along, paraders are shapers – shapers, snipers, and chumps.

The paid must participate more than the payers, the paid invent events, they aren't permitted to invent history.

The paid soldier on, suddenly it seems their appearances occur without cause, the payers catch them under spotlight with peripheries obscured, payers are always intimate with the loss of their time as well as their money, experience's ghost.

There is for every payer some one act that is the image of his secret or the secret of his coming out of order.

The fog is coming in again and out for a walk in a sundress Ludmilla encounters it and is shaken like a bee dying on a windowsill or an ant defending its anthill, she says aggressively quivering at the checkout stand setting down shampoo and potatoes, fuck, Montgomery is impervious to her abrupt unsmiling pleasantries.

You always get what you pay for, Fredo tells Charles behind Ludmilla and behind him are Helen, Sam, Donald Dover, Trish O'Reilly, and Quindlan.

Helen smiles, mouth open with just the tips of her teeth bared, as if preparing to give life a well-meaning, amorous nip.

Shall we follow?

Boldly!

Chapter One Introduces Chapter Three

A crime has occurred in Chapter Three, maybe more than one, that's for Askari Nate Martin to discover, but in Chapter Two Maggie Fornetti considers bicycling past the police station in the hopes of encountering, as if by chance, Askari Nate Martin.

She dismounts.

It is explicable but not necessary that Quindlan happens to take a snapshot of Maggie at just this moment.

Quindlan explains that the photographer's interest is not sincere but neither is it patronizing, it's momentary, random, reactive, he catches Maggie Fornetti with Askari Nate Martin.

Maggie Fornetti is far too human to care for art or is she far too human not to care for art, she knows she can't have it both ways and would like to ask Quindlan what he thinks.

She has a picture that she studies with great delicacy and a violin that she plays without melancholy and no one's bad opinion, she vows, will keep her from satisfying her curiosity, but she is highly susceptible to opinions, these are, to her regret, what she is too often curious about.

Maggie Fornetti must have had a pleasant childhood, she understands very little about human nature.

Chapter Three and Two

Askari Nate Martin's secret is that he believes that every crime is committed in the name of love, every love invents a crime to carry out and does so.

Someone should ask Nate, then, if there is happiness in getting away with it, but he has no inquisitor.

What he knows of crime and what he knows of love are much the same, says Carolina-Francesca to whom Maggie is confiding.

The enormous ego of the melancholic Askari Nate Martin is composed of remnants, the sum total his accumulated losses.

In a notebook he expertly sketches multiple horizons, clowns, rivers, spiders, and shifting poles.

In fall the golden orb spiders proliferate, but in May its broken webs are less easy to locate.

It's evening, and Quindlan is taking out the garbage, but as if it were luggage, as if it had angles, as if it came from a bunker, as if it had been composed by Vivaldi.

Sid was never a fire eater, Sue eagerly says to Askari Nate Martin, who knows there are many ways to keep someone from playing.

Chapter Two

All gets subsumed back into the structure of which they're parts of the day, the crime, the town, the war, and this.

For a few minutes there walking with Askari Nate Martin without speaking Maggie Fornetti feels she is being for once completely understood.

Wait, Maggie Fornetti says, there's a foxtail in your sweater, Nate hesitates, pauses, Maggie lifts the back of his green sweater with her left hand at the ribbing and pushes the foxtail through with her right, see?, they continue and see Sid coming out of the shadow of Drew's shop hefting a green backpack onto his shoulders.

Sid's a sweet guy, says Maggie, with secrets, Nate says, they hold him back.

Chapter One

If this were a novel, on the first page it would have begun and on the last it would be done, but something or someone always comes along.

The chapters do but are never done.

Chapters Three and Two and One.

Chapter To View

A novelist is no more a scientist than a snake charmer is a herpetologist or a tightrope walker is an engineer or a cook is a chemist or a voting booth is a sanctuary or a confession is an autobiography or the folding of the nomad's hammock is a surrender of territory.

A goldfish is no more a guard dog than a divorcée's guilt is a balancing rod in the hands of the tightrope walker making his or her way from the Arctic to Antarctica or vice versa.

Go, little pebble, go shoe, go accountants in trances, go missionaries distributing rice to saxophone players on tour in the Sierras, go naked.

The lion in its cage knows that life's a preposterous catchall.
I'll sleep here tonight, says Nate Martin.
Sawdust and circular reason.
Chapter Three done, Chapter Two, Chapter One.

M J WELLER
MySpace Opera – Twenty-Three Tales
Slowed Into a Fic-Blogosphere Microfiction
During a Period of Thirty-Three Months

Wednesday, March 14, 2007

Gates's "Cartoon Kid" tag came from drawing graffiti in high-risk locations. The upper blocks of Sinkmoor were covered in colourful and obscene squiggles. Like his father, Gates was the artistic type.

from "Addingcombe Calling Inspector Pannifer" – Slow Science Fictions no.3

Monday, May 28, 2007

On the first page of the graphic novel Hussain Elmaz is reading in a Zone Four Kid Doctor Clinic thrift shop. Hussain Elmaz – fictional character of the novel – drives Rebecca Schwaffer, Elaine Clark, Peter Piggott into parking space of a nondescript Whitehall building.

from "Graphic Novel" – Slow Science Fictions no.4

Friday, June 15, 2007

Dylan Wilson sat in front of the screen in his room at Brightside Road Catford. Zone Four.

His mother was out and it was the second weekend in a row Hannah had only returned to her room in Margaret Cooper's house to quickly drop books off and dash off again. Hannah no longer resembled a student activist. She was a girl dressed for clubbing and this made her even more desirable to the Professor's son.

from "Hannah Watts" – Slow Science Fictions no.2

Saturday, June 30, 2007

My name is Mick Weller.

I live in 3World in 4Time which sounds confusing but it isn't.

I have several near-clones who are not too different from me. They include Mike Weller the poet and M J Weller the writer. And a Michael Weller who lives in Penge, southeast London. And a Mike Weller who lives in parallel reality "Addingcombe". Mike in Addingcombe is occasionally nicknamed Mick.

Friday, July 27, 2007

Other students were on their feet, shouting and protesting. Wilson had not seen anything like it before in his long career. He realised there had been growing tensions on the streets in the previous weeks.

from "David Wilson's Sinking Heart" - Slow Science Fictions no.5

Friday, July 27, 2007

For Cliff, *2001: A Space Odyssey*, Robert Heinlein, Isaac Asimov, Marvel and DC comic book superheroes fleshed out details of how he would appear in his unique destiny. Costumed Commander of the Cosmic Squad leading young twenty-first century cosmic crusading Invincibles.

from "Cliff of Albion" – Slow Science Fictions no.6

Wednesday, August 22, 2007

Frederick Burrell saw a figure standing in the shop's back-room. Although shadowy it gave out more life than Choat. Marginally. The outline was close to disintegration.

from "Frederick Burrell Possessed" – Slow Science Fictions no.7

Tuesday, October 09, 2007

(...now where's that old 1930s Mogilowski story *The Battle for Heaven* I can sample thinks Weller... ah, yes, here it is... reprinted in *Space Opera* number four...)

from "A Voice Inside" – Slow Science Fictions no. 8

Wednesday, November 07, 2007

One summer evening, sleeping on the steps of Block One, Sinkmoor, Addingcombe, Surrey – Billy had a fantastic dream.

He dreamed he caught a tram from Addingcombe to a place named "Beckenham Road". The dream-place was just like Addingcombe but jumbled about a bit. Billy couldn't quite work out where he was.

from "Billy Crombie and the Crock of Shit by M Y Jolly" – Slow Science Fictions no.9

Sunday, January 13, 2008

"I am great. Call myself Mick Weller now. I'm on Facebook and at *MySpace Opera* dot com if you want to be my online friend, Doc."

"Groovy, Mick. Can I call you Mick, Mick?"

from "Character Avatars" – Slow Science Fictions no. 10

Friday, January 25, 2008

Gatch invented a variety of techniques to suggest the esoteric dialogue of dreams and telepathic communications. These included crossed out, hatched-over words, or lettering shaded by squiggles, along with combinations of all these techniques. The intention is to read such words nullimagely - or - nullimaginatively, to be more precise.

from "Ultimate Legend" – Mike Weller's Space Opera no.1

Wednesday, February 13, 2008

Alpha Zee, in social reality years sometime after 2000, designed a virtual world – Unicorn – underwritten by EarthCo Entertainment. Zee's Unicorn Contemporary Games had moved to San Francisco and expanded into an online metaverse of dramatic space opera.

from "Convenient Truth" – Slow Science Fictions no. 11

Tuesday, March 18, 2008

M'wboe cups Michelle's head and turns it towards the back-street scene. "That girl in the picture is G'wboe. My twin sister. The-Girl-With-Blanked-Out-Eyes. Watch her move. Twist little sister! Twist!! Twist!!!"

from "G'wboe or, the Woman-With-Blanked-Out-Eyes" – Slow Science Fictions no. 12

Friday, April 11, 2008

The art of science fiction is to make the science *appear* convincing. I had my writer character Mike Weller create 3World in 4Time in this light.

from "Lucky for Some" – Slow Science Fictions no. 13

Saturday, April 26, 2008

"We should have a carnival to celebrate winning the battle of Lewisham," Lucky said to Jinkerman. "Get sound systems into the park. All the punk and reggae bands together, man."

"The party can organise it," Jinkerman said.

"No. *I* organise the *party*. You dig what I am saying, Mister Jinkerman? Or should I say Pin-Eyed Ferryman? You can't fool Lucky Francis, man."

from "Hope Not Hape" – Slow Science Fictions no.14

Friday, August 08, 2008

Michael J Weller typed the slow fiction, writing Michelle and Madeline. His characters, Lucy, Becky and Elaine looked up at the present author, pathing him nullimaginative character-synapses.

"What do you know? A girl's thing. Don't go there, Mickie Dripping, there's a good boy..."

from "Tomorrow People Mixdown" – Slow Science Fictions no. 15

Friday, August 08, 2008

"These are bad weather times," said the King. "It began near Croydon when the Crystal Palace on Sydenham Hill burned to the ground. The best efforts of our firemen failed to save Paxton's splendid monument to the Great Exhibition of the British Empire from ultimate destruction."

from "From Eduard Mogilowski's Old Typewriter" – Slow Science Fictions no. 17

Thursday, September 25, 2008

Don't bother, young Wilson said in a subvoice and closed the door. His Cosmic Crusaders concentration broken, he went to the fridge to consume a cling-filmed slice of cheesecake.

from "2001: After Space Opera" – Slow Science Fictions no. 18

Sunday, October 12, 2008

Pin-Eyed Ferryman observed Poitier's dark porcelain features, facial make-up – blue mascara, light lipstick. His full, very feminine upper figure suggested implants.

"Hi, man," Poitier said, greeting Ferryman. Poitier remained seated on a leather chair. Slender legs crossed.

from "It's the Power, Man" – Slow Science Fictions no. 19

Monday, November 24, 2008

Five hundred years had passed by. No Guardian had been selected to represent the Enlightenment or the Modern Age.

from "War in Heaven" – Slow Science Fictions no. 20

Friday, January 30, 2009

"So much is changing in Addingcombe, Dorothy," said Ian Beaumont, "If American President Sam Poitier and Michelle turn up in Addingcombe for their marriage blessing, how will St Edward's avoid the hooh-hah? I welcome their wish. I am happy to extol blessing upon them, but I have concerns with the publicity issue."

from "The Marriage of Heaven and Hell" – Slow Science Fictions no. 21

Thursday, October 01, 2009

"Fourteen, fifteen, sixteen, seventeen, eighteen, nineteen, twenty, twenty-one, twenty-two Guardians of Life and Civilisation? Am I bid more kid cartoons?"

from "#22 Kid Cartoons Parts I & II"

Saturday, October 10, 2009

In his heart of hearts he knew he'd found the girl of his dreams in Michelle. But was it all just a crazy dream like an old Gene Kelly and Cyd Charisse singing and dancing *Brigadoon* movie without the music? He'd searched Google Earth Addingcombe a hundred times and not once did it throw up a result.

from "Now Here's a Tale with a Happy Ending"

BRIAN MARLEY
A Perigee Selection

There he is, mopping his face theatrically, using a handkerchief as big as a tablecloth, the gleam of sidereal light on his brow. No, he's way over there by a stand of pines, the scallywag, addressing a goat – a nanny, I believe – in a most cordial manner. During a 28-day period almost one thousand sightings were logged. Their veracity has been established by the use of a polygraph. Occasionally, while rummaging through trash cans in the early hours, he gets mistaken for a bear: a large, hirsute man in a tatty racoonskin coat. As the tranquilliser dart pricks his thigh he laughs, we all laugh, though his is a hearty boom and ours a nervous titter. Yet, tranquillised, he sprints from the scene. He runs like electricity, so light of foot that native trackers cannot follow him. Our laughter sounds suspiciously hollow then, our demeanour becomes stern. The adults who refused to submit to the polygraph were beaten with iron bars. While we brutalised and dismembered the toys, in accordance with the Torquemada manual, we made the children watch. Truth will out. But then we see him on TV, before the world's press, declaring war on Switzerland ... and Swaziland, too, if such a place exists. He laughs. Everyone laughs, they're not sure why. The translators laugh too, having nothing to translate but laughter. The flashguns of a ravenous pack of paparazzi are triggered as one, obscuring his means of escape. Temporarily blinded, we ask ourselves: *Is this really how a Minister for Foreign Affairs should behave?* On misty mornings he uses the lake as a mirror. We find his scat among the trees, still warm to the touch. Of him, no trace. Those who failed the polygraph test had their houses demolished. Their furniture was dragged into the streets and smashed to matchwood. Nothing is allowed to hinder our quest for truth – we are renowned for it the world over. Later he was seen consorting with rogues, villains, scoundrels, thugs, scapegraces and desperados, a veritable mafia of them. He appeared, the scamp, to be trying to sell his father's medals. (His father the war hero.) By his side stood the regimental goat, nuzzling his hand. What are we to make of this? Ours is a fledgling democracy, and the nation looks to him for guidance. The children of those who failed the polygraph test were fostered out to cannibals. Although he has spoken against this practice, and spoken eloquently and with great conviction, still we persist: old habits die hard. But no man who venerates truth can claim to be entirely without flaws. While operating with a faulty mindset, lightning razed his neighbour's barn.

+++++

Can you recall the fateful moment when everyone's teeth turned to jelly, or was that just something in a movie I saw? Were you able to prise open the gigantic tub of Coca-Cola, big as a doll's house, using the miniature crowbar they provided? But why do that? *You thought something was swimming in it? In Coca-Cola?* Tell me, oh strange one, was house-breaking tacitly encouraged in your day? Did householders nobly submit to assault? Was life less sacred than a holy relic – the life of a freshwater fish, for example? Were you, as usual, kicking the gong around when the goldfish languorously began to lip-sync Billie Holiday singing *How High the Moon*? Was it just one goldfish or a vast shoal of Billie Holidays? Hold on, what's that funny smell, is something burning back there – I mean back in the days when cinema was young?

Did a religious sect, small but powerful (a word in the president's ear, etc), believe that the dwindling sperm count among human males was attributable to eating fish, freshwater fish in particular? Would pumping cyanide into reservoirs, lakes and waterways be the best solution to this problem? Was the president deaf in his consultative ear? Is it true that the battery in his hearing aid was invariably flat, as flat as a pancake (or flatter), and kept that way on purpose by agents of the intelligence community? Was battery flatness the root cause of the president's paranoia ... and more: his Botox-suppressed nervous tic, his hysterical whinnying laugh, his epical bouts of depression? Does he believe that in terms of unalloyed genius he's Beethoven's true heir, though the only instrument he can play is the musical saw (and badly at that)? Is he keen to record – with the Berlin Philharmonic Orchestra, under the baton of Werner Herzog – a tenor saw transcription of the maestro's *Violin Concerto*? But what of his frayed nerves, are they equal to the task? Does he sometimes dream, as do we all, of running away from home to join the Mormons – or, failing that, the Taliban?

In which universe, remarkably similar to our own, did Beethoven compose *How High the Moon*? Is that also the universe in which chairs are a powerful aphrodisiac and propelling pencils are thought to be a conduit for evil? Does the gravitational mass of the lunar orb tug at the blood in our veins, impeding its flow? Is moon-tugged blood reminiscent of the Danube as it glides powerfully through Vienna on its way to the sea, or more akin to the lagoon-fed slap of the Grand Canal against staithes? Can simile piled upon simile sap our will to live? Are similes more dangerous than, for example, the boiling caldera that lies beneath Jellystone Park; than paedophiles; than swine flu? Do some renegade grammarians think that similes are more dangerous even than metaphors, especially the cold-blooded ones with muscular jaws and razor-sharp incisors? Is the president, as the news media has persistently insinuated, a closet freshwater croc fetishist? Is he? Really? How would one know if that were not so?

Are Creationists correct in their assumption that women have, at the base of the spine, a vestigial dinosaur brain that facilitates childbirth? Do they consider *The Flintstones* to be historically accurate? Can their faith, as oft-stated, move mountains? Other than to prove a point, why would anyone wish to move a mountain? Because it's blocking the view of a scenic and extremely well-managed goods yard? But mountains are large and notoriously cumbersome; if you were given the task of moving one, how would you go about it? Wouldn't it be better just to shatter the mountain (this admittedly smaller than average mountain, hardly bigger than a hill, with a lone, stunted tree near the summit on which an eagle is perched) into chunks no bigger than your fist? Can faith do that too? Can it sift the valuable minerals from those of little worth, commandeer the goods yard, load the ore onto a train, transport it to a refinery, sell it for cash and deposit the money in a newly opened, secretly held Swiss bank account? That parenthetical bird atop our hypothetical mountain ... doesn't it appear, when viewed through powerful binoculars, to be rather more vulture-like than eagle, and copper-clad, impervious to the elements, secured by large steel bolts to one of the limbs of a concrete, facsimile pine? Can faith alone charm birds from trees and lure them into small-mesh nets? Is it, pound for pound, more effective than liposuction?

"Why," wonders the child, "has the moon grown increasingly distant? Is it because of the Earth's slackening spin, or has our interest waned during the long millennial dawdle?" What! – do my ears deceive me? Whose noxious tot is this? Should her precocity not to be met with violence, as in the Golden Age? Wouldn't it be best to thrash her with a shovel, chain her up in a dark, damp cellar for weeks on end and force her to eat, as tradition dictates, nothing but mouldy crusts, wood lice and rat droppings until scurvy makes her teeth fall out? No? Are we really not going to beat her senseless, despite her brazen interrogations? Yet, pray tell, how can we avoid doing so? "Wouldn't Amsterdam," adds the whelp, thereby digging her grave a little deeper, "benefit from having a mountain of its own, situated unobtrusively near the Reijksmuseum? And is it true," she continues, "that if there were seven men, each of whom was fluent in seventy-two languages (as many languages as there are in this world, according to the Vercelli Homilies), and if each of those seven men were granted eternal life, and if each one had seven heads and each head had seven tongues and each tongue spoke with an iron voice, still they wouldn't be able to enumerate the myriad torments of hell? What's more," says she, "this thing about handbaskets ... is it possible to go to hell in something other than one, or are the hell-bound (myself included, perhaps, and sooner rather than later) obliged to use only that peculiar mode of transportation?"

Ah, but doesn't the saw sing beautifully as it bites deep into her chains, though it's a hacksaw of humble origin, little different in almost every particular from millions of its kind? Is its song an extraordinarily subtle, almost subliminal set of variations on *How High the Moon*, as one musicologist has hazarded, or is it what the proletariat thinks it is, a song of freedom, plain and true? Did the great Paul Robeson sound like this in his heyday? Psychotherapists tell us that prisoners everywhere dream the dream of the hacksaw, that it's a yearning dream of such potency they wake gasping for breath, in danger of drowning in a pillow saturated with their tears – but is this correct? Aren't the tears that prisoners shed exceedingly bitter, and famously so? As bitter as bitter almonds? Is toxicity perhaps even more of a problem than saturation? Should rumours of systematic pillow drainage in jails be given more serious consideration than has hitherto been the case? Once the tears have been siphoned off, what happens next? Are they discharged harmlessly into reservoirs, lakes and waterways or harvested for use in biological weapons? But isn't the government's chief medical adviser concerned about something else entirely – the whereabouts of the president's lost equilibrium? Do his [i.e. the president's] tears frequently surpass in bitterness those of prisoners on death row, even prisoners innocent of the heinous crimes of which they've been convicted, child sex murders in particular?

As for phlogiston . . . these days you never hear anything said about it, good or bad, now why is that? Were the phlogiston supplies completely exhausted, circa 1951, by the manufacturers of highly flammable nitrate film stock? Did the sheer volatility of nitrate film add to the excitement of early cinema? Were anarcho-syndicalist firebugs usually to blame, or could a single smouldering onscreen kiss cause a conflagration in the projection booth? Have you noticed, by the way, during outdoor screenings, how big the moon suddenly appears to be, how it hews close to the Earth and peers discreetly over your shoulder, eager to catch a glimpse of the action? What do you mean, *does the moon also read books?* Is that a facetious remark or is it just plain foolish? How can anyone hope to read a book by the moon's meagre rays, light borrowed from the sun, reflecting off the surface of an unpolished mirror? Ah, but of all the dust and debris planets in our solar system, this one's different, isn't it? Don't we see something of ourselves in its cold, stony mass, something that fascinates yet makes us want to look away?

+++++

There is, according to grandfather, a poultice guaranteed to satisfy every need. The poultice, he says, isn't just a folk remedy made redundant by modern pharmaceuticals – new, improved poultices are being invented every day. If applied correctly, one of the most recent poultices, the "ATM", can withdraw cash from even the most recalcitrant hole-in-the-wall machine, whether you're the proud holder of a bank account or not. The "nuclear" poultice absorbs caesium 137 and shortens its thirty year half-life to less than a week. There's a poultice that, when applied liberally, removes God from the equation. Another greatly reduces the intensity of phantom limb pain. Yet another desalinates water. One time, grandfather tried to interest the fire brigade in an expansion foam version of a "Sumerian" smother poultice, but his offer of a demonstration was declined. There's even a poultice capable of defusing a bomb, if one can obtain the right ingredients and knows how to make it, which apparently very few people do.

Grandfather has the recipe for that in his poultice book. The book is tucked high up on a shelf in his study, well away from prying eyes (i.e. mine). But when he goes out for his evening constitutional, I clamber up the bookcase like a marmoset and sit hunched under the ceiling, snagging the ancient cobwebs that hang there like rotting hammocks, each containing the husk of a luckless spider. With the book spread open in my lap, I marvel at the boundless ingenuity that has led to the "tooth extraction" poultice, the "lost property" poultice, and the so-called "recovered memory" poultice (popular with flaky psychotherapists and gullible hysterics). Perhaps the earliest known poultice of all, the "perigee", draws the moon into a tighter orbit than usual around the Earth, though no-one seems to know what purpose this serves. Then there's the infinitely variable "love" poultice and the "snake charmer" poultice, their recipes almost identical. But against all expectations, the "easy birth" poultice and the "accreta" poultice (capable of detaching even the most stubborn postpartum placenta from its bed in the uterine wall) could hardly be more different. The latter resembles a wallpaper stripping poultice called, for some obscure reason, the "trestle", that was used extensively in East Sussex during the early years of the 20th century.

Of late, grandfather has been hard at work on a "sin eater" poultice, which has to be applied to the male genitalia in the pouch of a dedicated codpiece. A female version isn't imminent. As he readily concedes, some aspects of female anatomy have caused him no end of trouble. So getting at least the male version right is of paramount importance, not just to bolster his waning self-esteem but for the good of the human race: "If I can't come up with a workable poultice, disaster will ensue – that's no exaggeration!" He's begun to mutter obsessively about Judgement Day, prompted in part by his hell-fire upbringing, but also by an unsettling letter he received from Prof Hans Neumeier, a medical historian at the University of Bonn. Neumeier had read an article, published in *The Lancet*, in which grandfather's reconstructed "malaria" and "leprosy" poultices were discussed. In a footnote, the authors mentioned that leprosy was once thought to be a manifestation of sin, and they made reference to the "sin eater" poultice. Neumeier argued that for the "sin eater" to work it would have to be applied not to the genitals, as specified by grandfather, but to the cranium (perhaps built into the lining of a hat); moreover, grandfather's conception of sin was extremely and unhelpfully reductive, hence flawed; his endeavours were therefore as likely to succeed as the search for the philosophers' stone and the site of lost Atlantis. Grandfather tore the letter into scraps no bigger than a postage stamp.

This I saw from my vantage point under the ceiling, through a skein of dusty webs. Afterwards, to distract him, I asked numerous questions about his distant and, by his own admission, half-forgotten childhood, when he too was fiercely inquisitive and as limber as a marmoset. He said he'd rather tell me something about his grandfather, a Frenchman placed under house arrest then driven into exile for having invented the "truffle hound" poultice, the recipe for which was destroyed to avoid it falling into the wrong hands. It was, he said, a prime example of Copernican dread, whereby innovation is suppressed or shunned. But that's not what he wanted to tell me about. Apparently, his grandfather knew a man, an American to be precise, who kept electricity in a bucket. A bucket with a lid. That, said grandfather, was in the early days, before anyone had trained it to run along wires.

JOHAN DE WIT

A Dream

As a little child, God lived and played in the Garden of Eden. With his inquisitive nature and precocious mind he explored the garden from all angles and directions and soon knew each plant, shrub and tree by name. He particularly enjoyed watching those little ants crawling up the trunk of the tree of life. Occasionally a forlorn monkey joined him to chase the butterflies that were darting about, knowingly, so it seemed. But most of the time he roamed around in the garden on his own, as was his wont, made up stories about all the little creatures he had seen and when his mother called for supper his appetite was such that he frequently asked for a second helping. One day, when he had fallen asleep after eating too many Pink Lady apples and Conference pears, he dreamt that he knew everything, that he was dressed in golden garments and seated on a purple throne on top of the world. When he noticed that the people he saw in the distance were all walking backwards while looking up to him he made a resolution to get off this throne carved out of blue-veined marble right there and then to ask his mother what this strange custom was about; but before he found the time to carry out his plan he woke up. Mummy, mummy, he cried, I had such an exciting, frightening and yet wonderful dream. And he told her as much of the dream as he could remember. Oh, my little darling, she said in a voice saturated with compassion, don't worry, you're still only a child and by the time you are a grown-up you will have forgotten all about this sweet little dream of yours.

Another Dream

God was still eager to explore the world around him. It all looked so tranquil. His very own garden, his mother had told him, would always be waiting for him. You are young, so is your garden, and, according to the law of the creation, the future is for ever young and likes to be explored. God was very fond of his mother; he never tired of listening to her voice, even when not speaking her soothing voice was wrapped around his body as a second layer of skin, so he would never walk alone. After breakfast he went outside to stretch his legs and it didn't take long for him to stumble across a carpet of bluebells stretching as far ahead as he could see. This is absolutely wonderful, he exclaimed, I'd like to stay here for ever and ever. But then he remembered the words of his mother: watch your superlatives, and on that note he fell asleep. He dreamt that he was riding an Asian lion bareback. Together they explored parts of the garden he had not yet visited. Hill after hill and pasture after pasture the colours became more and more vivid and the scenery more and more exotic. God was truly astonished, so much to see and so little time. With perfect timing the lion dropped him off on this carpet of bluebells for God to wake up just before lunch being served. Mother, mother, he called, but she was already right beside him as if there was no time to lose. God told her of this amazing ride through his creation and that the king of the beasts had personally given him a lift. She smiled and kissed him on his left cheek, right cheek and left cheek.

And another Dream

God was growing up rapidly. Life in the open had done him good. He was healthy, amiable, knowledgeable and still listening to his mother when she was around. There were no distractions, his mind had kept pace with that and it was about time he should take the next step on the road to godhood. And so it came to pass that he found himself once more wandering around to take it all in, to make the impressions last and to build up as many layers of meaning as could be managed in one session. A dream a day keeps the mind in play his mother used to say, apart from that it gave him much pleasure. God was dreaming that as a young boy he lived in the Garden of Eden and that his mother allowed him to roam freely as long as he was back home to have a bite together because those who eat together stay together. The sun followed its path, the earth moved accordingly and his mind did the rest. He was everywhere, he saw all the trees in one blink of his eye, he heard all the birds with one ear and with the other he heard his mother singing: praise the Lord with sing, sing unto him praise the name of the Lord with sing-song; and on and on it went, and that's what after a while woke him up. My God, this was a real dream, he said to himself with the sound of his mother's singing still ringing in his ears, I was where I was and there was no reason or need to be somewhere else; what would my mother make of this? He called: mother, mother! No answer! He called again: mother, mother! But no answer! He kept calling: mother, mother, mother ...

Again another Dream

God remembered everything. God remembered that he knew everything. God remembered that his mother had not returned his call; her calling as it once was called had called. Time to look after the estate again. His garden, to do with as he pleased, was still wrapped in her words. Instead of talking to his mother he would now talk to the plants, and instead of having his supper with his mother he would now have it with the crocodiles, leopards and polar bears, and instead of dreaming away the time he would now dream all the time so that the time would remain constant. No need any more to separate dream from time. So one day when he walked up to the pool to have a chat with his favourite square-nosed crocodile he noticed something unusual: there was a gap in the forest, a clearing that hadn't been there the other day and what was most unusual he had no idea what had caused it. So when the crocodile came waddling out of the pool God decided to raise the issue with him, as crocodiles are an ancient species they must have an excellent memory. But then a third unusual thing happened: the crocodile snapped.

This had never ever happened before. God took a step back, shook his head and looked again. The crocodile was definitely coming his way. God was looking as hard as he could at the animal, there was no mistaking, it was steady and looked ready. In such a situation most creatures only have one choice: pray. And God being at one with his creation did just that. God prayed with all his might: Dear God, keep this crocodile away from me!

And again another Dream

Looking after the Garden of Eden had kept God busy. In the early mornings he did his homework, there was quite a bit of bookkeeping to do, making sure that each species had its own entry in the logbook he kept. In the late mornings he did his rounds, to acquaint himself with the variety of his creation, each species should have the opportunity to meet him. His mother had impressed upon him that personal experience should not be substituted for hearsay; he still lived by her principles. On this particular afternoon he dreamt that he was in a place he didn't recognise and that he was among creatures that didn't recognise him. He was so appalled that he turned round which made him open his eyes. The garden was so peaceful and quiet, all the signs were saying: this is God's dreaming time, give him the space and he will give us the time to last. When he saw his own environment so at one with himself he fell asleep again and dreamt once more. And again he found himself in an unfamiliar place, trees he hadn't planted, ants he hadn't created, languages he didn't speak that he was most put out which woke him up again. How can this be, he thought, I am the one who knows everything, I cannot dream of the unknown, this is not possible and yet that was what he just had done. And then suddenly it dawned on him: change, this is the change I was promised at the very beginning, these must be the signs that I am growing up. And so in the evenings he began to make plans for the time when this process of maturation would come to fruition.

Still another Dream

God being God knew that routine is vital to all aspects of life and particularly to the maintenance of the garden which had been his home for as long as he could remember. One of his routines was doing the rounds and as Eden was quite a large place he had divided the garden into sectors. Today he was going to inspect the south sector. He also fancied a few bananas which he liked to fry in the late afternoon; at around half past four he usually got a bit peckish and bananas were an ideal snack to still the pangs of hunger. On his way to the south sector he fell asleep and dreamt that he was carried away by the wind to a lake at the very edge of the garden. A lake so calm and tranquil that whoever spent more than twenty-four hours on its shores would for ever be enchanted and unwilling to return to wherever they had come from. And then he woke up. God was puzzled, in his dream he had travelled the entire south sector but no sign of banana trees, instead he had visited the shores of a lake showing signs of home-made magnetism which puzzled him even more. His garden was about the free movement of any creature, enchantment and unwillingness shouldn't have a place in his realm. God wondered where that could have come from. There must be an interloper around, having other intentions with this place than I have. How come this has not come to my attention earlier? He thought of his mother. What would she have advised him to do? Without having solved the mystery of the lake with its magnetic shoreline God returned to his quarters.

Yet another Dream

There was no doubt in God's mind that something had happened; the indiscernible had arrived and that could only happen because there must have been a void somewhere. The garden was his place and his place was the garden; that was clear. His mother was gone, so the garden would be his only companion.

The sun was out, the birds were singing and he felt drowsy from the heat. God dreamt that he was sailing across the ocean, that they were sailing into a storm, that the boat was riding the waves as if it was his own rocking horse and that he enjoyed every minute of it. He heard the captain say: if you want to rock the boat, build a model and find yourself a pond at the edge of town. God found these words strangely exciting; no-one had ever spoken to him in this way. Was it possible that language could be used against him? God was in the habit of believing his eyes when he woke up. The sailors' words were still ringing in his ears but the garden was as tranquil as ever. What a contrast between my dream and this picture of the real. How come when you transfer the real to a reel you get a contrast? God turned round. From where he was standing it looked as if a shadow had appeared between himself and his favourite tree. It felt as if there was someone like himself out there. But whatever he did, however hard he tried, apart from himself, he couldn't see anybody. Had his dream altered his perception of reality? Maybe dreams are now my companion; maybe the tree of life is a dream too, a dream I should climb into and out of until life shows itself.

Yet again another Dream

During his frequent rounds God had noticed that not all parts equally flourished. Did his care not provide full cover or had he taken his eye of the Garden of Eden during his routine dreams? Maybe there is something out there that does not yet exist. Whenever God was trying to solve a problem he fell asleep and dreamt. This time that didn't happen. God was caught up in his own thinking and was listening to the language in his mind while looking at the less well-kept parts of the garden. I was brought up to think that I was the universal gardener but look I'm only a dreamer. Lo and behold God fell asleep and dreamt that he slept in his own beard, that he bore that image in his own mind and had become the bearer of his own name. On that note he woke up. That was not much of a dream, he exclaimed. Why can't I dream properly? He promptly fell asleep and dreamt once more. I am dreaming God said to himself, looked around, but the entire garden was deadpan quiet. Why do all my creatures keep themselves to themselves? Why not show some appreciation for the work I'm doing round the clock to look after your wellbeing? When God woke up again he was truly shaken; he had only dreamt in name, nothing exciting had happened. Had all these questions prevented him from dreaming? God fell asleep for the third time and dreamt that he walked on all fours that he shouted like a drunk at everything that moved that he had enough of this caring image and that he was going to do something about it. God woke up and felt ashamed, deeply and terribly ashamed.

And yet again another Dream

The good news is that God is still around; he was last seen combing his hair. The other news is that God is combing his hair. The good news is that no scapegoat has been found. Instead, God looked upon a water bubble and blew so hard that he saw himself for the very first time. That was a shock to his system and to the garden, he felt the ground quake, his legs tremble. Since his mother had disappeared from the garden company had been thin on the ground and now he faced himself, no wonder, not having a model, the first thing God did was comb his hair. It was about time to disentangle himself from his creation and the ideas of garden, grace and faith. Having set his sight on this, that and the other he fell asleep, rolled down into a ravine and dreamt that he was carrying a cross made of sandalwood up the hill and that the smell of the wood mixed with his tormented sweat made him cry. He tried to gorge himself but instead gouged himself with the same idea he earlier had abandoned. His blood turned into food and the flood lifted him out of the valley back onto and into the garden. Completely soaked, he woke up. That was a lucky escape. I could have drowned in my own creation. God laughed. The idea is nothing but a scratch short of an itch. So, he dug a hole with his bare hands to bury the idea and when the shallow hole caved in God made no plans to dream again for the time being so as not to upset his lucky day but to dig himself out of this hole: trial and error will give me a fair chance! God tried and tried and was still trying when we left.

Once again another Dream

The garden had become a real handful. God wasn't used to manual labour. Not until very recently had he experienced effort and pain. Backbreaking work hadn't been part of the family tradition nor on the menu. Encounters only happen in dreams and these you can end in the blink of an eye. The paths he had used were now overgrown; it was a constant battle to move around, which was very odd given that this was his Garden of Eden. Trees had been uprooted through God knows what so he had to cut them up and do other unimaginable things to them. God was now busy all day long with the basic necessities of life. Often he went hungry, the fruit he used to pick was gone, out of desperation he had cleared a patch of forest to grow his own vegetables. All this extra work made him neglect his own place of birth. God was losing control of the environment he still called his creation but it sounded hollow and empty. One day he got so tired from tilling the soil that he fell asleep and dreamt that he was being beaten, flogged and put in prison for stealing a peach from his neighbour's garden, that he was pissed on and verbally, physically, mentally and sexually abused by bullies and other brutes he never knew existed. He begged the guards for mercy but they just laughed and threw him in a cell full of rats, cockroaches and other despicable creatures. There was nothing to eat but the stench he himself produced in abundance. God couldn't stand it any longer; he woke up. Is this the life I have created? Is this what happens when you have to fend for yourself?

And once again another Dream

God scratched his head, the garden was in a mess and he was in a state. This couldn't go on. What has to give has to give. But what? He looked at the mud. Could that lump be useful? Should he give it some meaning perhaps? An idea toyed with him but it was too early, either in the day or in the season. God was going for a walk that would calm him down; it always did. God walked and walked, day and night God kept walking, nonstop until he fell over himself and dreamt that he was asking a stranger whether he knew where the exit was. The exit to what, he asked. To the Garden of Eden, God replied, I have never been beyond the garden; I wouldn't mind having a look. If I were God the man said I would go wherever I wanted to without having to ask anybody's permission and if I were God I would know where to go and what to do. Are you really God, you don't look like God. Look at the state you are in, your legs are swollen, your lips are parched, your clothes are rags, you smell, I bet you haven't seen a bar of soap for years. You certainly look as if you had a bad dream; you look more of a worry gut than a god to me. God didn't like this turn of events at all. To be questioned and spoken to like that offended him deeply. Without having shown God the exit the man was gone. God despaired and woke up. Even my dreams won't give me any solace, what am I going to do? God's head was dripping with blood as if he didn't know how to scratch himself properly. The loss of blood made God drowsy, he fell asleep and dreamt that he was saying no, no!

One more Dream

God didn't care any longer about the garden; he was totally exhausted. He was even neglecting his own body. It was obvious that the will to look after himself, his life and the garden was gone. Old and cold, beaten by and subjected to the ravages of time! God tried to hold on to the garden, himself and his dignity but his energy, belief and strength were all slipping away; whereto he had no idea. He physically felt a repeat power search pulling and sucking the life out of him. He was unequal to the task if there was a task. It was too late to be thinking about renewable energy, his creative powers had dwindled down to absolute zero. Decrepit and unrecognisable God crawled around on all fours, not having the strength to make himself a walking stick. My garden is gone, my days are gone, my might and right never gave me much foresight nor did I know where I could find insight and no-one to blame not even my old self. God laid his head on a boulder and listened to the murmur of the water in a nearby brook, which calmed him down. God fell asleep and dreamt that he was a little boy living with his mother in a beautiful garden in a wonderful climate and that one day his mother was gone as if she had vaporised into thin air and that he tried to keep the garden in the condition it was when she had left him but that gradually his life and then the garden had gone to pieces that he had tried to live by his mother's principles but that his creation was stronger than its creator and that the time to sign off had come that he closed the garden gate and that he was gone.

JOHN LEVY
Goldilocks and the Five Bears

None of the bears in the forest locked their front doors. Before Goldilocks visited the house where three bears lived she approached a nearby larger house, which five bears called home. She rang the doorbell, heard the first few bars of "Farmer in the Dell," which she knew the bears chose only because it was the cheapest doorbell available. She was ready to pretend she was there to ask if they wanted her to clean their yard in exchange for honey. Thrilled when no one came to the door, but needing to be sure none of them were home, she rang the doorbell again and waited, counting up to ten:

> One-Mississippi, Two-Turkey-on-Rye, Three-Bearskin-rug, Four-Bering-Straits, Five-Bears-bearing-gifts, Six-Cherchez-La-Femme, Seven-Negative-capability, Eight-Pëtr-Ilich-Tchaikovsky, Nine-Gourmets-Galore-Go-Gallivanting, Ten-Timeworn-Thunderstruck-Tetrahedrons.

Her rule for counting slowly was inflexible. She would always begin with the number and follow it with any word or words, proper names were allowed, that came to her mind and were at least three syllables long. She favored alliteration over assonance. Considering it cheating to repeat any word or phrase from the last time she had counted to ten, she prided herself on the power of her imagination and even more on the fact that she was not showing off for anyone but herself. She loved to think of herself as creative. Sure, dishonest and greedy, with a streak of gluttony, but wonderfully creative and with a gift for being elusive.

After she finished counting, she slowly turned the crystal doorknob and pushed the door open about eight inches. "Yoo-hoo," she yelled, not moving beyond the threshold. When she heard nothing in response she hurried into the kitchen, hoping at least one of the five bears had left some food out on the counters or the thick slab of mahogany they propped up on two sawhorses for their kitchen table. She knew they always padlocked shut their refrigerator. The five bears all had golden keys they wore around their necks. They had bought the thick chain they wrapped around the refrigerator, and the padlock as big as a paw, after she had cleaned out their refrigerator last year. She hadn't been able to control herself but she had not left fingerprints and they hadn't been able to prove it was her.

"Thank you!" she said aloud, seeing five white bowls of reddish soup on the table. "Gazpacho!" She loved saying that word. This was the second time this year that the bears had made so much gazpacho for themselves that they left full bowls behind. Goldilocks knew she had to rush, the bears would have at least covered the bowls if they were planning on being gone long. Fortunately there appeared to be no flies in the house and there were definitely no flies floating in any of the bowls. Goldilocks guessed she had no more than five minutes before she would have to sprint out the back door when she heard the bears coming in the front door. She had cased their house for weeks last year and concluded, correctly, that they never entered the house from the back door.

She thought that the next time she counted to ten she would remember to include the word gazpacho. For some reason she couldn't understand, she felt positive that "Nine-Gazpacho" would be where she would fit it in. Almost at the end, but not quite. She didn't like ending the count with a vowel.

All the bowls were the same size but the gazpacho's color varied from one bowl to the next. That didn't surprise her. All five bears loved to cook and would often spread ingredients across the black granite counters and compete with each other, trying to make the best dish. Then they'd taste each other's offerings and vote. The winner usually got some sort of privilege, such as using the bathroom first before they went to bed or not having to do the dishes that day.

Goldilocks lifted the first bowl. Maroon, lovely in the white bowl but it smelled too oniony. The second bowl, a burgundy red that she found quite emotionally powerful although she did-n't understand why, smelled earthy and sweet. Taking a sip, she almost spat it out on the table: one of the bears almost always used three times as much salt as necessary. That puzzled Goldilocks because how did that bear ever expect to win?

The third bowl, the soup a startling pinkish-red, had two small blobs of olive oil floating on the surface. She left that bowl on the table. But the fourth bowl looked perfect, a wonderful ripe tomato red, the creamiest texture of all, and the only item visible in the soup was a small piece of avocado. She loved avocado in gazpacho. Reverentially lifting the bowl to her lips, she gulped down a mouthful. Heavenly, she thought. With effort she set the bowl back down. If they ever realized she had entered their house again they would stop leaving any food where she could taste it. Sighing deeply, relishing the soup's aftertaste, Goldilocks looked at the fifth bowl. She raised it close to her face. It smelled incredibly good, a little garlicky and lemony with a hint of something she couldn't identify. It was fire engine red, not her favorite color but much better than, say, a red that reminded her of when she got sunburned that time she was trying to get a tan.

Before she could bring the bowl to her mouth she heard the bears. One of the younger bears had a habit of telling the others about his dreams and his memory was so good that he always had at least five or six dreams to relate. Goldilocks heard this bear, who had the highest-pitched voice of the five, saying something about finding himself in a woods where there were hatchets stuck in every tree.

"If you dream of hatchets," the grandfather bear said, in his deep voice, "it makes a huge difference with regard to interpre-tation whether the hatchet is rusty and/or broken."

Goldilocks sighed in relief. Whenever the grandfather spoke all the other bears would gather close around him. She could picture the five bears standing on the front porch, none of them moving because they were eager to find out if the hatchets were rusty or broken and even more eager to hear what the grand-father would say the dream meant.

She sipped from the fifth bowl. Yes, just as it smelled, a trace of garlic and a whisper of lemon with the strong tomato presence and that something she still couldn't identify. Some rare spice they'd ordered? It was a little tangy and yet sweet. She was tempted to stay in the kitchen, despite the consequences, and ask the name of this spice. It would be sublime in some of her own recipes.

"Some of them looked rusty," the bear with the high-pitched voice said. "But there was one bigger one, in the smallest tree. It was new and shining."

"Hmmmm," said the grandfather. "If they'd all been rusty I'd say the dream had something to do with the inconsolable grief bears feel when they encounter wayward humans. But since there's that one new shining hatchet, and it's stuck in the smallest tree, I worry that you'll soon meet some sickening disappointment. Somewhat akin to the sinking feeling you get when sharing a new poem you've written with another bear and realizing the bear has fallen asleep while you've been reciting it. I hate to tell you this."

Goldilocks tip-toed to the back door, grateful to the bears for keeping all their door hinges well-oiled. She knew how they hated squeaks. Without a worry she eased open the door, stepped out of the house and closed the door behind her. Already anticipating the porridge waiting for her if the three bears weren't home, she found herself almost running between the trees. But after only a minute she stopped, surrounded by trees with two or three hatchets in each trunk. It occurred to her that she was entering the bear's dream. Was she but a part of that dream, her life a mere illusion and about to end when the bear awoke? But then she laughed, remembering that the high-pitched bear loved pranks. She could imagine the bear secretively buying boxfuls of hatchets, hiding them in the forest, then artfully installing them this morning before the other four bears were awake. The young bear fancied himself an avant garde sculptor. Now she remembered a peculiar sculpture she had watched him make behind the house last year, a tower of garbage cans hauled back from the nearby national park, welded together as if they were a section of a strand of DNA. She had thought it was a successful piece, but the grandfather had demanded that it be moved somewhere where he wouldn't have to see it every day. He had dismissed the sculpture as derivative and empty. Now it was in a remote clearing she almost never visited.

Yes, that explained the hatchets. As if watching a movie she imagined the bears finishing their gazpacho and then the bear with the high-pitched voice would invent some bland pretext to get the other bears to follow him along the same route she had just taken. That young bear was always trying to win his grandfather's approval. The grandfather had won a sculpture competition in his youth and never tired of taking the four bears over to where the frayed blue ribbon hung on the living room wall and telling them how surprised he had been to hear his name announced when he won.

"It was many years ago," he'd always say, "but the thrill still courses through my body."

Forgetting about the porridge, wanting to hear what the grandfather would say when he suddenly found himself surrounded by these trees impaled by hatchets, Goldilocks climbed to the top of one of the trees. The bears wouldn't look up, she was sure of that. So all she had to do was patiently wait. Sitting up on a thick branch, she tried to decide if she wanted the grandfather to finally praise his grandson or if it would be more gratifying to hear the grandfather dismiss the hatchet piece as yet another stale failure that lacked any dazzle and/or memorable sense of the uncanny.

VAHNI CAPILDEO
The Seven Dwarfs and Snow White

My head is green but chill, my limbs silvery with the freight of the earth's pull. My roots go deep. My heart is safe from total bitterness. Why, from age to age, have men and women so used me, to feed their taste for sin? I am an infinite source, now, of stories of transgression. My fruit is no longer my fruit. Yet I must bear it. As a young thing, I stood still in the forest, feeling the envy of my companions press upon me. Year by year I grew, happy and unafraid to raise my canopy of song and blushes. Now much has been plucked from me. Winds twist around me, so that I grow irregular as time. Yet my heart is quick and constant. I am home to many children, but have none of my own.

No, no. I can't go on with it. I thought that would be the way in. Tell the story from the point of view of that blasted apple tree. Magical prose sells nowadays, especially to tired business people, and to the lads and ladies (unpublished) who write like that themselves. Dear Diary, who would be interested if they knew that I am "Sleepy", "Snoozy", "Dozy", or what you will, only because I burn the midnight oil. I wake through the nights to write the tell-all story that should make my fame and fortune, and get me out of this damn perishing palace! No. How to make my individuality convincing to an audience who see me, if they remember me at all, as one of seven unbeautiful brothers, the comic conglomerate who skedaddle around whenever one of a series of sinister or starry couples happens not to be centre stage.

We have proper names. That is the first thing with which the reader must come to terms. Herbert, Hubert, Albert, Robert (he's the handsome, rather cruel-looking one), Egbert, Dagobert, and myself. I am the youngest brother, which, in the world of fairy tale, would earn me the attention of the goddess Fortuna. Woe is me. That lady is not blind like her sister Justice, but she doesn't focus on anything under five foot four unless it's a child with a sweet face and a sweet tooth to match. So. Names. My name is Cuthbert, but I prefer to be called John. "Hi, Titch," Prince (Cecil Algernon) Eustace (Sebastian V) drawls, whichever one of us he sees. "Hi, Cecy," is not a response that I would risk. Prince Eustace is long on temper, and *short* on humour. As far as I knew until recently, no one ever taught him a little about his *little* place in this great world. Don't expect me to begin his instruction. The gal seems fond of him. I don't want anyone getting hurt. Little John, a big wrestler guy with a shaven head and a goatee and a thing for camouflage clothing, taught me a trick or two, in my forest days. (Yes, I took my name from him; they say that's a way to take some of the power).

The second thing to explain is the importance of family in this story. The gorgeous and tragic figures who have made history have appeared in couples: the King and the good Queen Marguerite, fantastically in love; the King and his dead, appealing Queen; King and evil Queen, Queen and stepdaughter, Prince and Princess ... The sharp light on these tragic or gorgeous figures has worked to obscure the importance of family, just as tiers of candles before a saintly figure in the niche of a cathedral make you ignore the leaden sleepers commemorated by the literate stones of the floor roughening beneath your feet.

To recapitulate. It is winter. Queen Marguerite sits sewing, looking out of an ebony-framed window at her King setting off on his morning ride. She pricks her finger. Instantly she conceives a wish for a daughter with lips as red as blood, skin as white as snow, and hair as black as ebony. Queen Marguerite dies in childbed. The King remarries. The new Queen cannot rest for jealousy of her stepchild, Blancheneige. She pays a killer, who shirks his job, merely abandoning the girl in the forest. We and Blancheneige find one another. The new Queen poisons her with an apple. Prince Eustace places her in a glass coffin, kisses her, she chokes, dislodges the apple slice, revives. Yes, the official record recounts a different sequence of events leading to her revival. This version is the truth. Then we all move into Prince Eustace's palace, which is a glorified hunting lodge – glorious, if you like seashell grottos and confectionery halls. Mine eyes dazzle. I have taken to preferring the night. By now my audience will have fallen asleep, and I am about to disclose more truths...

Prepare yourselves. This is going to be a big one...

Please note, "Snow White" lived, and lives, with us, *because we are her brothers.* This is meant to be a state secret, but I no longer care. I need to know who I am. I, John. I who was Cuthbert.

Why should the King and Queen, a passionate couple with dynastic interests, wish for a *daughter*? It is because, nine times out of ten, the family sons turn out – like us. A tiny curlicue of inheritance makes us as we are. The same inbreeding that produced the fineness of maximum contrasts distinguishing my sister's spirit, face, and form – that produced a string of legendary heartstopping beauties: Élise, Jadis, the Snow Queen, a number of Valkyries – that's what's to blame, the super-concentration of our gene pool. That's the why of our peaky Y, that's why they wished for a *daughter*. The King and Queen were not childless before the advent of the longed-for fair one. It was that we, their sons, were not fit to be claimed.

Do you have any idea of what normally goes on in the families of princes? Who am I to say what normally goes on? Et cetera, et cetera. Take, for example, the way they talk to us. Not about us. To us. The Prince's allpurpose "Titch" is the soul of civility, in comparison to what I would rather leave untold (reserve is a good trait in an apprentice truth-teller). We have been jeered at in ways that, among the folk, would have led to riots and the enrichment of lawyers. No slander cases for us. No compensation for mental suffering. The common law does not apply. Chronicles, and brutality.

I think I need to go on a quest.

There are things I need to forget.

There is the popular story that when my twin sister arrived at our *forest abode* we did not recognize her. (Yes, we are twins. The slight stature that makes a pretty sprite of a maiden cuts a prince out as a dwarf, a monster). They say we wondered who this beauty was. We busied ourselves, comic men housekeepers, anxious to serve.

No. It was the pity of it that made us cry out that she could not be herself. Poor Blancheneige, so reduced, so miserable, so

ill educated that she could not spell her own name. Ours was the
work of her first restoration.

Let me leave this place.

Dammit. It's dawn, and I haven't slept a wink. It's not in my
heart to curse the birds, but I almost could. Good night, dear
Diary. I shall take one of my amusing little naps in the wire
mesh cot with the damask cushions...

It is almost teatime, and I want breakfast. I have a craving for
some Grand Marnier. Are orange juice and orange cognac so
different, really? What does fermentation do to vitamins?

In the lands around the Rhine, where at one time they
understood dwarfs, absurd legends are in circulation. Their
propaganda machine is even better than ours. People are
brought up to believe that dwarfs are like fabulous toads. We
live incredibly long lives in the cracks of the earth, oozing bit-
terness, ugly, wisdom-encrusted, but somehow with good
hearts, never mind the rest. Oh, *dwarfs*. Don't they reproduce
themselves in some unimaginable fashion, isn't a group of
dwarfs called a *knot*, have you ever seen a female? If only
dwarfs could indeed take to the earth and sleep out some of
their memories. We are the other half of history, which means
that the whole burdens us. Why do they shut us up? I shall be
the first to claim our birthright, disclaiming it. Johannes the
Author. Why can I not sit outside at a mosaic-topped table at
ten in the morning, free and happy to drink orange juice and
sekt in full sunlight with my German cousins? Alberich,
Friedrich, Heinrich, and Dietrich. There are always too many of
us to make a good story. We are there to balance out the rari-
ties, the royal creatures. On each horizontal of the family tree,
only one Jadis or Blancheneige.

The pains are beginning again.

I haven't got a head to work on the tell-all that is supposed
to be my safeconduct to a new life. Perhaps the quest should
come first. Leave, before you can look back.

My back still hasn't healed from last month's episode, when
Eustace kicked me across the room. It was understandable. I

had fallen asleep behind the chaise longue in the Pink Room. Then Blancheneige's voice rang out.

"Stace," she said (she called him Stace). She said, "Stace! Will you be my undoing?"

Half asleep as I was, I got alarmed. There was no doubt that she was in danger. I wasn't capable of comprehending, at that point between dream and – waiting – what might be going on in that room. (I cannot say that I live, that I wake. Waiting is all). You'll have got it, of course: She was *inviting* Stace to undo her stays. They were being playful. I didn't get it. I was worried, on the alert but slow on the uptake. A playful tone: how was I to recognise that? When have dwarfs ever played? For that, you need a childhood. Not "Take the handaxe and go chop some more wood, the heating has broken down again and just because you're not tall it doesn't mean you can't be strong."

"Stace! Will you be my undoing!"

I started up and around the furniture. I caught Eustace by shin and waist in a Little-John hold. Twisting my hips and throwing his weight off-centre, I got his own body to betray him. Trapped. Humiliated. He lay on the ground. He howled. It was not pain. It was an annoying, deliberate howl, the kind that those men make who have no normal vocal outlet for emotion. By sheer grotesque volume, they flatten into a listening posture everyone in the room who has ever cared for them. It is difficult to recover from that listening posture.

Then he stopped howling. I let him go. He broke a few vases. Then he started to kick me, shouting in a high-pitched voice.

"Roast dwarf! Roast dwarf! That's what the trolls used to sing about! Roast dwarf! They sounded full, and happy! I heard them when I went hunting in the Black Forest! And I only had paste pies! Grey paste was fowl and orange paste was fish! Live like your people, Mamma said, that was why I had to live on paste, and pretend it was roast dwarf! Wifey, tell Gaston that's tonight's menu! Supreme of roast dwarf! With sage mash and an orange coulis! And a plain dish of plum crumble to follow! *Bloody hell fire, no apples!*"

I momentarily wondered which sage was for the mash. The hermits had all moved out of the forest, in search of peace and quiet, except for the ones who had given in to the inevitable and opened hostelries where knights could say "A, good Sir," to one another while their wounds thickened at the edges preliminary to growing over. I was so dazed.

I do need that Grand Marnier...

I was dazed then. Now, whenever the pains recommence, my head clears more than is convenient. I have never felt at ease with daytime. Hence the nocturnal habits of Sleepy-Snoozy-Dozy, and his amusing nickname. Curtains drawn against the dust-filled shafts of hour-to-hour equilibriate the physical sur-roundings and the muted interior light of the mind. To contem-plate as if in an eternal present, the mind exacts control of its environment.

I am reliving something I would rather not remember. Those royal visits of our father, and stepmother, and sister (I did not know her to be unhappy) to the well-hidden "dwarfs' cottage". Always something. Seven birthdays. Easter, May Day, St John's Eve, St. Stephen's Day, Epiphany. Et cetera. And the presents. Good things, things that would last. Be grateful. Pearl-handled letter openers. Who would write to us, what messenger come near? Twenty-two-carat cufflinks, so we could dress for dinner in the forest. A set of seven Chinese vases too fragile to put water in . . . The retinue would sit around looking uncomfortable. They were forced to sit, to be off duty. On this family occasion, they must not stomp around outdoors. The need to make the retinue relax while the royals were being entertained by us explains the way they designed our cottage. Otherwise, why give seven dwarfs a single sleeping room but a triple-recessed living room? To walk the elkhound in, when the weather was bad?

And I am remembering the day when I could not stand it, how Princess Blancheneige was beloved, and I took her aside, took her to the larder, hit her, shook her, slammed her against things. She was quiet and her white gave way to a crushed-straw-berry look. She was blushing as if she were ashamed, blubbering without noise. I took her back in. They were discussing money, and nobody had noticed us. I myself called attention to how Blancheneige was crying. With a big false smile of concern, I said that we had been in the rose garden to admire Desprez à Fleur Jaune, and that perhaps the midges had bitten her. She nodded, still red, her eyes gone huge and bright and damp under her flustery brows. The memory of this incident has preyed on me so badly that I periodically believe myself to have forgotten about it. I did remind Blancheneige of it once, but she laughed, then looked puzzled at the quality of my distress about the past. She really had forgotten it, forgotten it so hard that it was working away within her, without her knowledge, however it liked.

Dear Diary, it's taken long for me to realize that my quest is right here at home. I'm here to look after my twin sister. Herbert and Hubert are too ill. Never mind how. Albert is always travelling, in disguise, naturally. Robert is a bastard, arrogant, a dandy. He has the looks, the brains, the voice, and very nearly the height. He spends half his time in Ireland, pretending to be one of the Fair Folk, and much of the rest of his time in Wales, singing. Egbert lives in the library. Dagobert is – Dagobert. That leaves me. (Cuthbert.) John. Husbands come and husbands go. Blood family is forever.

PAUL HAINES
Unrecommended Lures

It's in one of the sillier parts of the city he chooses to pour his heart out to her. She tells him how connivingly apt it is of him to do that then. And there.

Addicted to no known solution, he is nevertheless grateful when in the presence of the conventionally mired, with their tangible hint of less wrong.

No influence unknown to him, but none then he is under. (Full heart. Empty head.)

She gets up and walks away from him (her walk a guilty thought – her way of reminding him that love poems must rhyme).

They look at one another from across the room, a prescription-strength ignorance of moment deciding the borders to the distance between them. Each hesitates, then resorts to thought.

The first to speak, she says she feels disgusted is a beautiful word, as beautiful as serenity is ugly, and no fit goal either – serenity what had to be sold to the self.

"All wordwash," she adds, looking hard at him. (Her last hard look, he recalls, was when she had spoken of odors gathering in the throat to persist there, she said, fir-clotted tainted clamato for one, with its brown consistency of glycerin gone bad.) "Wordwash!"

She has raised her voice, and he knows to look out, but not what to say, pleasing her requiring honesty or at least relevance, which ruled out any number of ready rejoinders. She is fond of the supposed absurd – nothing too easy to come up with when under pressure. (An incommodiously used supposed absurdity, he knew, could set her ablaze.)

"Well?" she says, hardening her look further.

Ah, but he's ready. "Get me wrong," he says.

He's made her smile. "Get me wrong, and get me to a restaurant!"

The nearby restaurant specializes in businessman's lunch for lower echelon businessmen, a round oak table full of whom are ordering cocktails. Sitting directly across from them, a smaller table, and two young New Jersey mothers discussing a television program their kids have asked to watch that evening. "Well, it looks like it's going to be cute," says one, relating to the other what she'd heard about the show on reindeer.

"I don't know about the violence thing. With animals, you never know," says the other mother.

"Oh, I know" says the first.

The waitress has an outsized starched rose napkin pinned across one shoulder of her waitress uniform. Standing more or less centered between the businessmen, the mothers and the newly arrived couple (neither of whom seems ever to look at the other, notices the one mother), she has a finger stuck into her cheek to signify puzzlement. Which table next?

"Hey, all right! Over here," yells one of the businessmen abruptly turning to his left to carry on his conversation. "I don't care," he says, patting the fellow on his back, "you guys kinda had a vision, you know?"

"Let's see," says the waitress brightly. "That's one Miller Lite, three rum and cokes, and a Cherry Herring. Right? Right, gentlemen?" she asks, carefully raising her voice.

All five of the businessmen have their heads tilted back as they attempt to remember an associate apparently no longer with them. "He was the engineer on that project, wasn't he? A guy who talked kinda hoarse?"

"Yeah, yeah, you got him. Real deep voice. Never said much. Al brought him in."

"That's right. He talked hoarse. Hard to understand sometimes." The man's pleasure at the recall is cut short by a whiff of spawning pickerel and lilac, the window behind him open to that curious hour in the life of a city when everywhere a misplaced fragrance falls, and the poor are known to gamble.

The businessman sitting to the left of the businessman with a napkin pressed to his nose jabs his finger at no one in particular, says, "Look – he doesn't like me."

Three businessmen ask as one, "What?"

"He doesn't like me."

"He doesn't like you?" they continue in unison. "*Who?*"

"Not me," says the businessman with a napkin pinched across his nose. (Known at the office to be as noncommittal as a hedgehog.) He shakes his head as proof.

"He doesn't like me," he goes on, shaking his fist, "to the point I don't like him back."

Obviously restraining himself, the businessman with his hands folded behind his head says, "Tell him to go take a piss or something."

With that, picking up steam, the fistshaker takes his muscles to the bar. (He didn't take them everywhere.) He orders a drink, a double, and spins on the stool to face back toward the table he has just left. When he downs the drink, he gives his muscles a little flex (most of the motion in his head). A waitress passes by with an order of french fries which seem to him to be dancing. He tells himself that great amounts of nuance are being lost on him, but draws no vulnerable conclusions, ordering and downing another double, summoning up old wrongs, and settling up after every round, the wrongs lagging behind some.

The New Jersey mothers, realizing they have been staring for some time at the couple at the next table, remove the tall napkins, folded as though creating the contents of an enigma cookie, from their wine glasses, casually but indifferently attempting, immediately, to refold them, the one mother relating as she folds and creases her dissatisfaction with a restaurant she swears she'll never eat in again. "The fries were so greasily crimped, the salt would fall right off them. You couldn't keep salt on them for anything." Both mothers return their gaze to the couple when the woman stands, flapping her arms at the man.

"YOU! You say nothing, you sit there, you don't as much as look over at me."

The napkin-faced businessman, sensing the outbreak of something, darts his eyes from the woman to the businessman who, without unfolding his hands from behind his head, says, "Who's YOU, lady?"

The woman has turned her back to the man. (He remembers their first meeting, a dozen years ago. He had delivered a package to her for a friend and she had turned her back on him then, taking the package without saying a word, examining it in an indifferently careful way, and then, as though to herself, commenting that she didn't see what the rush was (not that she hoped he hadn't been inconvenienced), then, saying he had interrupted her preparations for dinner, launching into a detailed description of the menu, including the wine ("...a good bottle") and difficulties she had encountered preparing a special sauce. It was when she stopped talking, her back to him still, that the man said he thought he ought to be going. "I've cooked. Stay," she said. "Eat. Have a roll at least.")

"What did the specialist say?" asks the businessman with his hands folded behind his head.

It's to the businessman with such a still face the question has been asked. He seems at first not to have heard. It's as though shading himself from his own answer that he finally responds. "He said my ribs had dropped."

"He said what?"

"That my ribs had dropped."

"*Dropped*? Your ribs had *dropped*?"

"Yes. Had dropped and sunken in a sullen manner."

"The doctor said that? *Manner*?"

"That's what he said. If you don't believe me, ask my wife. She was there."

The taller of the two New Jersey mothers – having overheard – lowers her voice to say that she just didn't feel like being that decisive anymore. She said she hadn't smoked in years, having lost the one lung and then, today, smoking two cigarettes, the second, she says, not tasting so hot.

"What a minus my husband is," says her friend, as though in response, immediately quieting the other mother, who's all too familiar with her friend's hideously logical side, her way of getting her way by speaking with that awful level of certainty. She would say, "I doubt very much that could be possible," and have it sound like, "In a pig's ass!" Or she'd come up with something sounding like an argument, only to abruptly end it with, "Well, why don't I just sign off then, mucopurulently yours? How'd *that* be to your liking, huh?"

Gathering herself before beginning the complicated distribution of drinks at the businessmen's table, the waitress looks for a moment out the open window, noticing how chairs spread across the tarpaper roof inform us the naked are sunbathing and expecting no visitors, chairs draped with towels, face-down books, empty soft drink bottles with bent straws, and shoes lying on their own ankles.

All three tables have painstakingly quieted. Momentarily at rest, everyone seems to be contemplating the waitress – suddenly for them a tense token of something or the other. (A funny-enough feeling, providing you didn't feel like laughing.)

"I don't really know how many people you can leave messages for," she says, her eyebrows a bulletin board.

LAWRENCE FIXEL
The Graduate

1.

Now the decision is made, I wonder at the long delay. Of course there is the handicap. But at long last it's becoming clear that – one way or the other – all are handicapped. And the doubts, the rationalizations? Perhaps no more than masks for pride, for wilfulness. As the Instructor says: *The Stones are hard and dangerous – but how else cross the river?*

It remains now to proceed with courage, with full confidence. Enrolled in the Course, the rest will follow: step upon step, until I reach the other side. (*How long*, and in *what direction*, are questions that need not be asked.)

There is no chance, I realize now, of this being merely another detour, another waste of time. It is rather, at long last, the best chance of finally entering a different space. As the Instructor says: *Concentration, Co-ordination, Convergence.* These are the key words – not words really, but states of being to be achieved.

2.

At last – today it begins! I am indeed looking forward to the weeks of intensive training, designed to promote the quick, deft movement that implies true inner balance. (So much more really than mere self-defence.) My attention now should be geared to this – and nothing but this. For it is the *Process* itself – (am I quoting again?) – that shapes and forms the outcome.

Thus obtaining the Certificate is the smallest part of the Task. More important is to perfect the Instrument. To come to that point where, at last, one begins to move without conscious effort, without will. As I understand it, this can be true for me – (perhaps now I can accept this) – as for the *sighted* members of the class.

3.

The time has gone by quickly. Just as expected, the routine, the discipline are indeed making a difference. Not only the gain in poise, in self-confidence – overcoming that initial awkwardness – but a certain *stamina* beyond anything I might have guessed. I can hardly wait for the day to start: what *new* discoveries lie ahead?

4.

....Something is going on that I do not quite understand. For some reason the Class is smaller now than when we began. It seems some sort of "separation" is taking place. No one has actually been dropped – (how rigorous the initial screening!) – but rumor has it that some "more passive" members are being assigned elsewhere.

5.

The separation has indeed taken place. As to what training the others – (*more passive?*) – have been assigned, there is no word. The choice, however, has been made clear: this morning, right after breakfast, our diminished group was summoned to appear at the Supply Room. After some short delay, our names were called. We were then issued: Mask, Foil, Protector, Tights – the complete Fencing Costume!

After the initial surprise, I found I was not the least per-turbed. A few moments of questioning: wasn't this a strange way to achieve inner harmony and balance ? Yet on reflection it became clear that, at a certain level, this must be what is required.

Only those who still cling to the mundane level of expecta-tion and desire – it now seems obvious – are unwilling to admit the urgent fact: it is precisely *here* that the Path divides.

6.

....As the Instructor predicted: *parry, lunge, thrust*, are becoming part of a natural repertory of motion. And along with this, the Foil itself seems to be part of the body – an extension of hand and arm. Thus I have noticed, when it is *not* there, I begin to miss the weight. One thing though continues to puzzle me: how is it I know almost at once when the Instructor leaves ? And as a corollary, that I do less well at such times?

7.

I am not quite sure how this has happened, but I have become almost unaware of the presence of the Others. Perhaps this is because I have now been officially assigned an *Opponent*. While somewhat unexpected, this must represent some recognition of what has already been overcome, some transition to a "higher stage" in the training.

....What is intended by these daily "practice bouts"? In the absence of any direct indication, I can not help some slight feeling of suspension, of unease.

....It has occurred to me to ask my Opponent. This is not, as I understand it, strictly forbidden by the Rules. Yet how could I – considering it further – invite the cooperation, the confidence of the very one chosen to oppose me?

8.

So there is to be a *Contest!* Not of course anything like those advertised, vulgar spectacles of the outside world. This is rather to be a subtle display – (*an unfolding?*) – of skill and grace, more like a dance than a parody of warfare.

I learned this after taking the drastic step of speaking directly to the Instructor. A step that was prompted not by any inner doubt, but by a natural concern for what is, after all, a serious physical handicap.

— *Remember: the foils are tipped.* He said this in the most gentle voice. And this encouraged me to go even further: to ask about my Opponent. Once more I was not disappointed. I could almost hear the smile in his voice: *But of course you're evenly matched.*

It took a few moments to sort this out, to grasp the meaning: *So we have to imagine each other?*

As his voice came back with some more soothing words, somehow my hands moved toward my face. I suppose he left just then — at least the warmth of his presence faded. My hands kept moving; I touched and rubbed elbow, wrist, neck, chin. The flesh itself was solid, warm — nothing of the cold dark I felt inside.

9.

No victory, no defeat. I should have known. *Evenly matched.* I should have known. *Contest is not Competition.* (The very words of the Manual!) I should have known.... But in my mind's ear, sounding again and again: padded feet thumping on the wooden floor. And from afar, derisive voices, mocking laughter....

10.

How did it come about? I can not tell. All I know is that I have no further need — that much is clear — for that discipline, that motion within a confined space. I am resigned now, not only to leaving, but returning where I came from. *Back there!* Once more tapping my way through the noise and fog of one city or another.

As for the training, perhaps it may serve — (if not as intended) — to ease my passage there. Through crowds and traffic, my steps can be less fearful, more directed. It will be good to take hold again – (how long it has served me!) – of my own red and white cane.

I am eager now to relearn the grasp of it. Will it again fit neatly in my hand? Can it too be held with such confidence, without feeling the weight? Is the task then to reclaim the loss – the true replacement for that long-desired, dreamed about, perfectly balanced foil?

ROBERT LAX
21 Pages

Searching for you, but if there's no one, what am I searching for? Still you. Some sort of you. Not for myself? Am I you? Need I search for me? For myself? Is my self you? I know: Self. Is that you? Is it me? Why search? I seem to be built to. Search dog, search hound: built that way. That's me. I know me. Do I know you? Do I at all? Have I had some signs or flashes? Any clues? Was that a clue? What one? Any one I can have had, or think I've had, or imagine myself to have had, in times past or even now as I ask. Is asking a clue? Is wanting to know what you are, who you are, any proof that you are, that you're there? Wasting time: I might be using it for what? What use it for when all I want to know is where you are. I go on searching, I was born for that. I don't remember being born. What makes me sure I was? Or that I was for anything.

Time for distraction. I'll count to 150. Count to 150 by threes. I'll start at 150 and work back by threes and fours: 147, 143, 140, 136, 133, 129, 126, 122, 119. Tedium. I'll return to the search, cross-legged, silencing the mind. Do I have legs? My body has: I can cross and uncross them. I cross them now and sit with – is it mine? – my spine erect.

I sit with spine erect and stare, not fiercely, into the dark. I am searching again, as I always am, as I always do. One way as good as another.

Looking straight ahead, not fiercely, with only one object in mind. No objects. Looking straight ahead and waiting. Waiting not searching. Searching and waiting. How do I know what it is? I know. I know because I keep doing it. Waiting and searching for what, for whom? How will I know when I've found it, found him, found you? How wouldn't I know? How could I expect not to know what I'd found when I found you? Do I just go on searching, looking, waiting? Do I find you? Do you find me? Will I know I've been found? How wouldn't I know.

How would I not know what I was looking for? But I don't. But I do. I've been doing it for so long I must know something. Not much. Not enough to hold onto. A vague idea. Do I know what I'm not looking for? I do. Do I know what I am? I don't. Would I know you if I saw you? Would I know you if you came toward me down the street? Staring into the dark at night, would I know you if I saw you staring back? Not staring, looking. Would I know your face if I saw it? Would I think it was you? Have I seen you before? Do I know, do you know where it was, when it was? Is there any chance I'd remember?

Something I remember about standing in the rain, on the street, upright, of course, and in the driving rain. Not driving, a vertical downpour. Night and under a light in the downpour of rain. Did I ask any questions then? Did I see a face? I was absolutely alone on the street. Alone. I was part of the rain. Not part of the rain, part of the moment the rain was about. I knew where I was. I knew what I was doing. I knew what the rain was doing. There was nothing particular about it to recall.

I remember other times, some only in dreams, times I'd recognize if I saw them again. Times of things coming together, working together. What do any of these things have to do with you? Why do I remember them? Why do I sift through them? I do, but not because I know what they may hold. If there's anything they hold.

Times of feeling you were there, that you were close A hall, a corridor: walking down a corridor, the damp stone walls, a smell of dampness, cold, but a feeling of what? That I wasn't alone? That someone was near, not visible, but near me, that someone was there. Who, though?

Or in a dream, in a house, a low sort of house, a cabin by the river, wide window looking out on the river. House very steady. River moving slowly. An in-between light, neither dark or light. Twilight. Between night and morning. No, evening and night. Between evening and night. I'm inside the house, cross-legged, not crossed, just sitting on the floor, looking out at the river, dark river, grey light. I'm not alone. Or I am, but not alone like now. I'm waiting, not waiting. I'm there.

When I'm there, you're there; when I'm not, you're not. If I'm not here, I'm waiting. Try it again: when you're here, I'm here too, and when you're not, then I'm not. Where am I then, when you're not here? I'm nowhere. What am I doing nowhere? Waiting. I'm sitting in (what we'll call) nowhere, looking into the dark, and waiting.

I ought to be able to say it better than that. But how? By not trying? I'll try not to try. I'll try to say it the way it is, the way I see it. But I won't try too hard. Trying too hard gets me off the track. I know where I am now. I know I can get some part of it said. I can, if I don't try too hard.

Wake up and wait. Lie down and wait. Sit up again and wait. All in the dark now. No way of telling day from night. Do I expect to hear a sound? Do I expect to hear a voice? See a light? A dim one? A bright one? See a face? I sit up. I'm alert. Do I know what to expect?

I don't know what to expect, but I do know what I'm doing. I know what it feels like to be doing what I'm doing. I feel like a sentinel. I'm on guard duty, I don't know what to expect. Friend or enemy? Friend. I'm waiting for a friend. Someone who may become a friend. May turn out to be one.

Why wait? Why watch? What better have I to do? Have I anything else to do? Might sing. Sing in this darkness? How would I hear your voice if I were singing? Might count. No counting. Count very softly. No.

My childhood was a happy one. I was this. I was that. My parents adored me: I remember that. I wanted for nothing. I was fully supplied. Practically, there was nothing I might have asked for. I didn't ask. I didn't often. If I asked, I was given. If I sought, I found. So much for the early years. I can hardly recall them.

School: I went to one in the country, a small school with a single master. I must have done well enough in my studies; I remember no rewards, and no punishments. Or few. When the master spoke to the class, he seemed to be talking to the other students; I never felt he was talking to me. As I reached the age of puberty, the whole experience came to an end. We must have moved to the city then, and my schooling was over.

Schooling was over and my waiting began. I'm sure that's about when it started. It must have begun very quietly. I didn't notice it begin. I realized I was doing something new. I didn't know I was waiting. I knew I was doing something almost all the time, some new thing. Something that joined one day to the next. I never wondered what I was doing anymore. I knew I was doing that thing.

That thing, but not that I was waiting. I was simply continuing. I was going from day to day with just one purpose: to remain in the state I was in. What state? A state of alert. But alertness for what? I hadn't even the beginning of a notion at that point.

Like a prisoner, waiting for a reprieve, counting the days, not counting, not knowing what to count or why to count it, waiting for one thing, one moment, one event. I didn't feel like a prisoner, bur I was waiting like one; doing nothing else but waiting.

Or like a child, a foetus, I mean, waiting in darkness, warm or lukewarm darkness to be born. I was waiting for things to start happening. I was waiting to begin to be.

Or like waiting for a letter that doesn't arrive. That will arrive, but hasn't yet. It will, or it won't. There's nothing you can do to bring it along. Can you think about it all the time? You can't. But can you forget it?

I do think about it all the time. I don't. But I don't forget. Always somewhere in the back of my mind, up front, right here, right there. Candle flame glowing in some dark corner. Vigil light. Or a window on the dark. You see nothing from inside. There's just the possibility of seeing.

Or like waiting in a sunless valley, in a narrow pass between two mountains, waiting for a ray of light. Families live there all year around. Never see the sun. Never stop waiting. Night follows day, but sun never falls directly into the chasm. Always a shadow, always a cloud.

When the wind blows, I listen to the wind; when the rain falls, I listen to the rain. I sift through the sounds to see if there's another. To see if there's one I can cling to and call my own. Nothing so far.

I open my eyes in the dark and see darkness. I close my eyes and see darkness, even in the light. All the same darkness. Almost the same. Light comes and goes, but the darkness stays. Almost always the same. A fairly steady darkness. One you can count on. Almost.

Sounds come and go, but the silence remains. Silence, unbroken, except for occasional noises. The substance is silence, dark silence. There's always some stir, some light, some sound, then they stop, and there's only dark silence.

I wait in the dark, in the rain, no sound but the rain. Waiting, not waiting, doing nothing but waiting. Does the darkness move? Does the silence move? They don't, and neither do I. Are they waiting? I have no way of knowing.

I don't know if it waits, but I think it moves. The darkness does. There are masses of it, masses in it, and they shift. A silent moving of force against force, mass against mass. A feeling of chaos, too. Not total chaos.

Movement of dark things in darkness, looking for order. Looking for some relief from total, all but total, chaos. Dark things moving in darkness, trying to find some kind of adjustment, some form of order. I look into the dark and see darkness, no more light than at the half-imagined edges of these dark objects. Darkness made up of objects slowly turning, jostling and turning, slowly turning, trying to discover some kind of accord.

I'm not really waiting, I'm watching. Watching while waiting. Looking into the darkness and watching it move. Watching the movement of dark things in darkness: a push from the left, a push from the right; a struggling movement up from below. Did I say it was chaos? It isn't chaos. There's some kind of action in it, some kind of will.

Is it my will? I don't think it's my will. It's just the will of the things that are moving. Things, or whatever they are.

Sections of darkness. Ice floes of darkness, afloat in the sea. Drifting, turning colliding. Smacking up against each other, breaking, turning, drifting. Dark whales at swim in the night sea. They swim toward each other. Toward each other, and away.

Dark dolphins leaping above the dark sea. Purposive movement. What purpose? Dark dolphins, just before dawn, adip in the night-sea. Dark rocks, dark dolphin, dark wave.

No, it isn't like that. All dark, but it isn't like that. Darker, more solid, less budge. Not budgeless, but not so much moving around. Not smacking together. A bump, a thud. No smacking, A black-curtained scene, hardly moving most of the time.

Dark, like a black cat. Dark and shining. It has its dormant times, its active times. Cat nap and cat nip. Sleeping and leaping. First one, then the other. Active dark, passive dark. Sometimes you watch, sometimes you wait. Looking into the dark do I see a black cat? I just see the dark, but it changes.

Like this and like that. Like a cat. Like a cloud. Light cloud, phosphorescent, but only lightly phosphorescent in a field. Light cloud, afloat in dark field. Light, barely visible, inner light of light cloud, phosphorescent, afloat, hardly moving, not adrift, not standing, afloat, hardly moving in night dark field.

I found work at last: watch-maker's assistant. Clock-maker's, rather. I brought him the sand. He fashioned the globes and measured the hours. I brought him miniscule white cups of coffee too: not every hour, by any stretch, and not often even on time. But it was a job, a means of livelihood of sorts, that didn't interfere with my real work, my continuing preoccupation. Or hardly ever did. He didn't like dreaming; he did like the sound of feet running. What he got in the hours, days, nights and what must have been months I was with him was a little of each.

Some running, some standing and dreaming. More running. More standing, sitting, or leaning against the door-frame, obviously dreaming. It was, as I've said, a livelihood; not rich, not an inch above subsistence, but enough to let me continue in my chosen way.

My way at that time was ill-defined, but pursuable. There were nights, midnights, when I could sit up alone on the cot he'd assigned me, eyes closed, eyes open, to watch, to wait, hardly breathing, fully alert, as alert as I could be, to any change in the dark's part light but mostly dark configurations. This watching might go on for hours, one or two, one, two or three, sometimes till just a moment or two before dawn, till at last I'd lie down again for an hour's sleep. The longer the long night's watching the slower the next day's running for sand and coffee. The less dreams by night, the more by day: standing sitting, listing, leaning, mooning about on the master's time and premises. The situation was bound to end one day, gently or abruptly by mutual accord, and before many days, weeks, months had gone by, it did.

The situation ended, that is, the job did, but not for a moment my underlying pursuit; if anything it intensified in the months of physical fast and privation that followed. The cot was gone, but the world had become my pallet. Wherever I slept or slept not was now my preserve. I've forgotten the number and kinds of places I found: whatever was shelter. I didn't need much. The weather was clement and I'd grown accustomed to the rigors of uncushioned existence. My observatory powers in the meantime had grown keener. I could see in the dark. I could see much further into the dark than before.

I saw more then than I had before, and more than I see now, in my present state. My fallen state. But I'm getting ahead of my story, if that's what it is.

My fallen state, if that's what it is. My dark night of the soul, if that's what it is. My long night's waiting if that's what it is. I saw a lot more then, on those nights of sleeping, not sleeping under bridges, sleeping not sleeping on benches, under trees, in barn or on church step than I'm seeing now. No matter. I continue to watch.

I continue to watch, and that's what counts. What counts, if anything does. Something does, but the question I more often ask myself is who counts it? Do I? I do. But does anyone else? Does anyone else in the universe count what happens? Does anyone else in the universe know what matters? Does anyone care, I mean, personally care? Ah, well, why get into that, as long as I do.

And I do. Seem to. Seem to want to know what's going on. From moment to moment. Why it's going on. What counts, from moment to moment. I want to know. Seem to. Seem to want to know. Seem to want to know what it's all, or even, what any small part of it's about.

Image follows image. Image flows into image, not one stays long enough to describe. White writing on black. White web in dark night. Pale sliver of moon appears and disappears. Where is the energy? Where is the push?

The white is drifting about in the black. Appears and disappears. Forms and disintegrates, quietly. Forms, drifts and disappears. White is a light foam. The black is the sea.

Black lives, rises, expands, subsides. Black has energy, black has its law. White forms at random. The black has a plan. Black grows like a tree. Black moves like the sea.

There are nights, there are times when there's no white at all, or it's so dim, green or grey you would hardly call it present: just a film, just a mist, the memory of a glow. But the black, the black sea, the black tree, is always there. Always growing, always living, always changing. Full of energy and on the move. But always there.

Should I watch the white? Should I watch the black? I look into the black and see the white moving before it. I look into the dark. I don't look into the light. The light disappears if I watch it. The dark remains.

An eye. Do I see an eye? Looking back at me in the dark. It's like an eye. Has a point, a pupil. Flashes and disappears. Flash, dim white flash. I see the corner of the eyelid too. Outer corner. Nice line. Two graceful curves, joined at the corner. Dim white. Sometimes I see it. Hardly, but see it.

Eye looking back. Not fiercely, no. But gently? Intensely? Just steadily from deep in the dark, like something in nature, deep in the woods.

Or as though my own eye could see itself looking. My eye meets the eye in the dark. The eye in the dark meets mine. No fire exchanged, just two quiet glances.

My eye. Your eye. Or even if it's mine and mine. Why should my eye look at your eye? Why should yours look into mine? Am I seeking out a glance, a look, in darkness?

Hundreds of eyes I've looked at and into: not just in the dark; at every hour of the day. Looking for what? Some kind of response? Eyes of every ocular shape and color, and of every degree of liveliness and flaccidity. Some that weren't alive at all. Some that looked like exploding universes.

I worked for a while for an entrepreneur. I brought him the cardboard. He cut out the forms. I ran for the oil; he filled the lamps. At night his shadows moved across the screen. Children in the audience screamed with delight, but I trembled. After the first few evenings I didn't watch at all. The works were comedies mostly, but not for me. Too many characters beheaded, or almost beheaded. Too many hard slaps delivered to the jaw.

It wasn't the proper environment for me to grow in. I told him so, not knowing whether or not he would understand. After a number of days, nights, weeks, months, the arrangement came to an end, and I was left on my own again, still waiting.

For you. For someone or something I'd recognize. A person, a moment. A sign you were there. Or had been; or were going to be, soon. Those comedies didn't help me at all. I was glad to be out in the dark where I could forget them.

Not that I ever forget a thing. It's all there, all I've done, all that's ever happened, is still there, somewhere in suspension. Waiting in the wings. Or riding above the tide. Above it, or below it. It's all there somewhere, it's just that I don't recall it. Never do or seldom. Never try to call it to mind. Never try to replay the scene. Why should I? It's not in my interest.

Not in my interest because if I'm looking anywhere, I'm looking ahead. I'm looking toward some point, some vanishing point, or anyway, not yet visible point in the distance, in the future where something or someone I'd recognize would appear. (Where you would appear.)

Some person, some moment, some atmosphere, that I'd recognize as very much mine, would be there.

My person. My beloved, if you like; my sought-after-being, my remembered one, would be there. The one I'd looked for, the one I'd sought without any clear idea of who he or she might be, of what he or she might look like, would appear.

Not, as I've said, that I had no idea. Not no idea; but no clear one. Not an idea I could hold well in mind. Far less an idea than a feeling, a dim, unfading area of light, a possibility as yet unfulfilled, a readiness to recognize, someone, something. You.

A readiness to recognize you; that's all I've brought, that's what I bring to the encounter.

I worked for a printer for a little while. I brought him the wood. He cut out the letters. He'd line them up and we'd smear them with ink. I brought him wine, too, and a handful of almonds every so often throughout the day. I don't know what his novels were about, but the work was peaceful. I'd have stayed with him forever if he hadn't been arrested. I was out for wine and almonds when the authorities arrived. The shop was empty when I returned. Letters and ink all over the floor.

Back to the streets, the parks, the quays. Back to standing and looking, watching, not watching the passersby. Looking for a face. A face in the crowd. A particular one that I'd recognize and in a particular way. Did I think I'd find it? Did I know I'd find it? I knew I was engaged in just one thing: in looking. Looking and looking.

And back to nights of looking, outward and in; not knowing which way I'm looking, but waiting and looking. Back to the night-watch. Day-watch and night-watch. Dusk to dawn, dawn to dusk. Mid-day to midnight. I don't say I didn't tire. I did. I tired, but I didn't give up.

I didn't give up, because I couldn't. I didn't, because I was made to go on waiting. Made, put together, invented, born, for that single, singular purpose: to watch, to wait. There's no giving up on the thing you were made to do. There's no giving up on being who you are.

Not for me, anyway. There was no giving up on being who I was, and there's no giving up on it now. I'm into the business of doing what I'm doing, of being who I am, and of waiting for whomever it is that I am, and have always been, waiting for. Into it, I guess, because, for the moment, there's nowhere else I could be.

Or would much want to be. I've gotten accustomed to standing on corners and waiting, lying on benches and waiting, standing up in the heart of a forest, or just in the wooded part of a park, and waiting. I've wondered sometimes if you came, and I saw you, and I knew you were there, I'd continue to go on waiting.

It could be like that, but I don't think it would. I don't even think it could be. It couldn't, because if you came, things would change. A thousand, maybe a million things would change. My whole life would change. I know that. I've known that much from the beginning.

FANNY HOWE
Even This Confined Landscape
(*from* The Lives of a Spirit)

One morning around four she peeled the skin off an apple beside the warm radiator. On the windowpane, etched in frost, were leaves and thorns, silver flowers and daisy banks. She blew them apart and peeped out at the day. The sky was clear since all the clouds had fallen to earth in cold clumps, which scraping shovels now lifted up. She in her Levis and sneakers murmured, Is all this for children? Can I?

Mother, if I promise to return home without being forced, can I please take a quick trip? Please! My work place lies outside these gates. I must build a perfect park. Can I?

The human being is to her parents what an Eden is to a dual nature. "You can, but you won't," said my mother for her own reasons. "As soon as your wish can come true, you have already fulfilled it. I personally think the world is six hours short of paradise."

I ran with a closed Asiatic face. Useless fragments fell off like scales. A cold wave ran under my feet like a bamboo surface, as I pedaled across frost maps, round globes of ice, seeking the five spiral wheels that enter the gate to G-d.

Structures do variations on the same law, then comes the alchemist's mind and all is changed. My shadow seems to be the same shadow, wherever I go, and no matter how fast I move.

So what's the excitement? Surprised that the two yous are always together? In some unknown month your skeleton will weigh the same as everyone's. Thick-ribbed ice and chilblain hot as pepper will shudder you right down the air to Nova Zembla.

During her travels, she carried her bicycle through each park skilfully, hopping on and off when she turned sharp corners. She could often be found leaning the bike on her inner thigh, surveying, with her helmet unstrapped though still covering her bobbed hair.

When snow was imminent, meridian light whitened the pavement. Crosses and branches caught the attention of her quick bleak eye. Every thing was in the way.

When she wasn't tossing on her pillow or sitting on the foot of a couch in darkness, she was moving like this around the city parks. Blueprints besieged her as the morning star rose over the crests of the buildings with slow-moving satellites and airplanes. Irregular architecture, mossy in color, was the make of the neighborhood. Some latticed windows and stone porches, slate roofs and chimney stacks. When she rode to each park, followed by the question, Can you really build a peaceful place? Her will bent itself double and zoomed. She was fueled by that small question and said, Yes.

From any place she imagined landscaped courtyards, galleries where people could get together and joke, a square for parades, a winter garden, a theater, a church, and a resting place for military and solitary. There would be refreshment pavilions, including public toilets, for working people and children in an area studded with bowers and awnings. Was it Eden or Jerusalem, a socialist city? Even a communal cemetery was made of plain unmarked stones under a shade-tree.

And listening in the dawn hours to the radio, it's exactly that dazzling jazz she'd climb up on, the inverse order of tunnels in air. These were the verities of daybreak: a lake of gold with blue clouds building varieties of mountains – the idea of Heaven.

Like that the solid black trees seemed to beg and twist to get off this thing. Because of the weather I could never move from home. This, too, is an erotic shaft. Is it a sin or a trigger? It does shoot me up the notes, rung by rung, and G-d burning before. The nursery crib, natural wood slats with colorful decals of bears and balloons, remains my favorite bed. In it I can lie and watch the theater of the weather parade as days.

Once I was sitting on a bench making a phalanx out of the chaos of the city. A bench is a kind of crib, after all. And I thought I saw my communard coming. My fingers twisted a bit of costume rosary, a chaplet made of garnet and rhinestone. I swept the masks for one of him. But he'll never find her. Not that one. It was wrong.

Exteriors become rutted and dimpled. Depressions finally shade what once was smooth as the plump white back of a duck. She eats fast, from the pan, with her fingers, but will never be filled. Disappointment becomes the one appointment you can count on, likewise.

One time the flush left her face; she saw the perfect park. Like a field of lighted jack o'lanterns under a dawn sky, the topes and hummocks in the cemetery seemed to release orange auras. Peace! Quickly she whispered her insight to Heaven and moved away from the place like an independent traveler who is forcing her reluctant body to move through foreign streets.

She felt like a face in an illuminated manuscript, who couldn't get off the beautiful page about G-d.

Rushing home she passed the office where the paper green Xmas tree was weighed down with gold bulbs and gold trim and the women over their machines, humming. It reminded her of a green bench with small half dewdrops littering the paint. That was luxury's thought. If she had paused long enough, she would have thought only of the women themselves, their tedious labor.

At home begonia spat waxen petals pink against the haze in the kitchen. The chimney smoked like a tea kettle. A smell of bacon and toast had burned away the morning, the noon. Let her, now, pour tea and pass the little almond cakes with pink icing. She missed the other two meals and menus and it has started to change again outside.

Clouds have congealed into one giant snowflake whose stellar parts are spread from pole to pole. There is a yellowing around the edges, as with burned or old paper. The air champs at cheek and eyelid and plumes of smoke pour from the chimney stacks.

She pours the tea, and yellow jonquils in a thick glass vase are splayed against a window where the snow is now shown to be speeding, white on gray. It forms, first, a thin pocked surface, the same it will return to.

The community is moving around, waiting to eat and wash up. From the yellow jonquils comes a jocund melody: clarion and strings! The house is warm and Sunday would suit its atmosphere of genteel atheism.

If I had climbed up among the chimney stacks and the sampler city was spread out before me, I would have looked again for a park where nothing retaliates. There the small birds huddle heads under wings; the ducks waddle and squat like creampuffs around the whitening pond. The water squeaks into knots at the surface and settles. And the trees, still as granite, live for the light.

I would have said, Mother, stay at the window, but don't call me in.

DAVID MILLER
True Points

"...the only true point is a turning point." (F E Sparshott)

The child pressed her face to the window of the bus; breathed upon it; and wrote with her finger.

Walking from the bus-stop to my house, I followed in the wake of litter, scraps of paper blown by the wind.

– You remember I called? Philippa? she said.

– Of course, I said; and invited her to come inside.

The young woman's eyes were frank when they met mine, but they did so rarely, for the most part looking to the side. Her smile (lips closed) creased the left cheek, infusing her features with geniality.

– I must admit, I said, how surprised I was that Tony would think of giving anyone my address; it's been years since we were in touch.

– Oh, he told me I *had* to look you up! she said, quite unabashed by my remark.

– And I was glad he did, she continued; it's good to have someone to visit when you're in a strange country.

I had no idea who she might be. But she talked on, telling of her travels and the people she'd met during her time abroad, as if to a friend; and it disarmed me, and I was touched. Nothing she said was out of the ordinary, yet I felt no wish to cut her visit short.

After Philippa left, I spent an hour or so trying to put some of my papers in order. I couldn't settle to it.

No work was done that night.

* * *

– The chivalrous people of old, Mike said later. – Valorous, too – I wouldn't be surprised.

– What did they say to make you think so? I asked.

– Ah! so you needed to hear them *say* something!

The elderly couple had attended to us through the merest nod, smile or gesture, with only the occasional word (kindly and sufficient); it was left to their children and in-laws to minister to our needs. They had, it seemed, passed on the obligation of speech to the younger men and women; who in turn obeyed it with discretion. The sublime ease of these people, and their hospitality towards strangers, impressed us both. Obviously, they were poor, as the furnishings and neglect of their cottage revealed. What did they do, in the way of work? I asked one of the younger men this question, and he replied simply: We're fishermen.

A young woman, conspicuous because of the baby at her breast, sat at one end of the table, her face suffused with the firelight. I noticed the quiet, sympathetic interest she took in us, her family's guests. She listened closely when Michael told an anecdote about once sharing a hospital ward with a professor of architectural history – a brilliant man, Mike said. One day the professor stopped speaking in the middle of an account of his student days in Rome, and began flapping his arms energetically, as if to drive something away.

– What's the matter? Michael asked his companion.

– Those birds! he said; you've let those birds in!

There was nothing in the room; but Michael had to wave his arms at the hallucinatory birds, until finally the professor closed the window to seal their departure.

I wondered at Mike for telling these stories; surely he realized how much he was giving away about himself. No one, it was true, showed any alteration towards us; yet I felt the need of the cold night air again.

We took a path that led up a hill, shoes sucking in the thick mud; the darkness virtually complete. We were talking, for the sake of continuity in unfamiliar surroundings; and I recalled the tower-block where I'd visited Mike during the first years of our friendship. – Summer, I said; sun upon the windows. I'd look up from the street to your window; the glass rectangles pulsating against their frames. The neighbouring black roofs were blinding.

Our voices were the only sound for a half-an-hour or more, until a sudden hubbub of dogs' barking broke out at no great distance. The noise abated after a few minutes; but we decided to go down the hill again and find where we'd left the car.

* * *

The burly tramp in the dirty grey overcoat might have been mistaken for her Uncle Robert, Philippa said, except that Robert was dead; the resemblance was unnerving. He'd slipped to his knees on the pavement; I took his arm and helped him to his feet.

Uncle Robert, she told me, had been a professional boxer in his youth. Seldom sober, even so his skill had let him win many of his matches.

By the time of Philippa's adolescence, Robert was a confirmed alcoholic, utterly dependent upon his relatives and his few friends in every way. He'd smile obligingly for his niece's camera from the fat and grizzled countenance of his waste.

She recalled talking with him once about Aunt Lucy, who had developed a blood clot in her throat from which she could die any day. She mentioned her difficulty in talking with Lucy, since there was painfully little in the way of shared concerns. – You could talk to her about boxing, Robert had said.

– You could tell her, he'd continued, about Jimmy Carruthers.... And he talked about a film of Carruthers fighting in Bangkok, with magisterial skill and grace, in defence of the championship; barefoot in the open-air ring flooded from the monsoon rain and littered with debris.

We were having lunch in a café; and I talked about my friendship with Tony; telling her how, at a time of great loneliness, he'd come into my life (through a mutual acquaintance) to be the one person with whom I then felt any large accord.

– Does he still live in that house near the railway viaduct, with the large back garden? I was visiting him one day – this was when he was still married to Jan – and there was a point during the afternoon when I left the house to go out into the garden by myself and sit there, on the ground. The garden, the quiet of the afternoon, Tony and Jan's friendship – these things came together to make me feel strangely peaceful – for it was a troubled period in my life. I was sitting so that I faced a sapling, and I sat there a long time looking at it; and I suddenly felt borne back, throughout my whole body and self, to... well, what should I say? a first state both tender and guiltless.

– Charles! Philippa said, laughing; you're really strange!

In the evening I returned home, to write.

My front room faced out towards a waste square where tenements had recently stood; hollows, planes and lights of the large building behind were framed by dark forms of foliage – night's changes absorbed the squalor.

It was at this time that I was able to write.

I'd become caught up in the idea of a coincidence of opposites: of image and imagelessness, visibility and invisibility, finitude and infinitude; and it had brought me to the threshold of a darkened chamber – I had entered, and sat down. I wanted to see, and to pursue in reflection, the way in which divine Being *is revealed in every being and yet always hidden in them*. Notes were compiled; and left in folders; more notes were written; and I felt lost in the process and act.

***

Sitting at the car's wheel, Mike handed me a road-map; although it was too dark to read it.

– Where now? he said, and smiled broadly.

We drove inland; and stopped for the night at a run-down hotel.

– The Hesperian Hotel! said Michael. The name was sufficiently quaint, I surmised, to please my friend.

We took turns showering in a narrow cubicle. When I had finished I went to our room, where I found Mike reading in bed. I slipped in beneath the covers of my own bed and waited for Mike to begin talking: for he always wanted to converse for a while before sleep.

– ...and they would tear live flesh with their teeth, said Mike.

– Or, I said, the living substance of other people. *Sparagmos*. Such a polite word.

– And you, you care too much for words!

– Michael, I said, would you turn out the light now?

Once in darkness, we were both silent for several minutes. Then I began speaking again.

– How easy to mask evil, I said, with a multitude of disguises. But good, too...

– Good?

– ...is hidden from us; camouflaged. You know it when it has pierced you with wound after wound.

***

The first leaves were lit from beneath, leaves of the second tree full on by lamplight; the facade of the hotel lit, in part, by its own lights. And from behind – a voice rising in song, its distance increasing with my steps – plaintive song.

I found the door of Philippa's house, a little further, in a row of terraces. The street was quiet at that hour, but the stones were thick with dirt from demolition work being carried out across the road.

I was dismayed by how maculate and disordered a room I found myself entering. Papers, books, bedding and clothes were piled around without any attempt at arrangement. Table and sink were littered with unwashed plates and pans, cups and glasses.

A painful sense of dereliction caught at me.

But she led me by the hand into the room, and to a chair, apologising hastily for the mess, as she called it; then she moved away, to find herself a place to sit.

A photograph had been tacked to the wall, near the window. It was, I saw, a snapshot of Philippa, standing at the railings of a ship. She was smiling and waving.

When I re-entered the room, I saw that Philippa was leaning out the window, surveying the street below; with her head behind the thin green curtain. She lit a cigarette, and the match flame pricked a spot of the dull green alive.

***

I dreamt that Michael and I had gone to a party at Philippa's; we sat by ourselves, watching couples dancing, until Philippa came and drew Mike into the dance. A little later she came back to where I was sitting, and said: Guess what I've come to ask you for? – I don't know, I said. – A dance! Philippa said; but I begged off, and went into another room.

– Put it on, someone said, handing me a waxen mask. As soon as it covered my face, he also gave me a long gown to wear. I saw now that the others in the room were similarly masked and attired.

We all went out in the street, and to an underground station; the man who had given us masks and gowns then had us sit astride the poles by the escalator-stairs. An icy wind blew, from time to time, down the escalator. The man took out a small cine-camera from the bag he'd been carrying; he filmed us as we sat clinging to the poles; while the people descending past us on the stairs looked with amusement, or incomprehension, or even anger.

When we returned to the party, Philippa refused to speak to

me – ignoring my greeting, and walking away. I followed her through the house; she shut a door, I opened it; she shut another door, I followed, and opened that too; until I pushed open the door to a room where Philippa, on her knees, naked, was being whipped by someone disguised with a mask.

Philippa turned her face to look directly at me as I entered, and she cried out.

Mike and I breakfasted at the hotel, where a large ground floor room had been set aside; part of it functioned as a kitchen, while tables and chairs (all, as it happened, empty save for our own table) occupied the rest of the space. The hour, Mike suggested, might explain the absence of other guests; for we had woken late.

We ate toast and marmalade, and drank tea. The quiet, and the warm sunshine, suffused us. It was too perfect; for it suddenly seemed to me the inversion of Philippa's cry.

– Two men, both in their early thirties, said Michael, engaged upon some last desperate romantic quest, the details of which mostly remain obscure, needless to say....

– The self-dramatising, though, would be more obvious? I said. But Mike stood up, his chair falling back and hitting the pavement. He went into the café to order more coffee; when he returned, he picked the chair up and seated himself again.

– Son of a bitch, he said.

– I'm sorry, I said. Then: Do you want to go back to the hotel for lunch, or shall we eat here?

– I want to *talk* to you, he said.

***

Philippa took several peaches from a paper bag and placed them in a bowl on the table.

I was standing at the window, and happened to look down into the street; two big workmen had stopped their truck and were manoeuvring an injured cat from the road onto a large cardboard sheet. Traffic was building up behind them, yet they proceeded with a slow, caring patience.

– I was *always* falling in love at that time, Philippa said; so often, that nothing else seemed to be happening. I was meeting all kinds of different men, at parties and at clubs; and often I'd be in love with several of them.

There was a vivacity to the young woman that I found charming; but there has always been a puritanical strain in my nature, and I was ill at ease when she began to talk about her love affairs.

– I believe in getting everything into my life, she said, as if to underline what she'd just told me. Then, she continued after a pause, if I look back there's a lot that doesn't seem important anymore.

– For all of us, I said. There's a saying: "So much chaff for the wind".

Philippa had cut a peach into slices, which we were eating when her doorbell rang.

She left the room and entered again, bringing a tall, lean young man with her. He immediately walked over to me and extended his hand. – I'm Patrick, he said.

***

– Think of this, I said: a stream alive with stones, driven mad by the sun. A young woman stands looking into the water, and the face of her long-dead brother appears beneath its surface. Like a stone that's awakened, but to unmitigated suffering.

– She hasn't thought of him, I continued, for many years. A fulgurating sorrow for him strikes through her. "Whatever the risk", she cries out, "I will come and aid you!" And she keeps her thoughts on the child and his suffering until, in a dream, she sees him safe on ground, playing happily amongst other children.

A man at the next table turned to us and said:

– Perpetua. You haven't got her story right, did you know? She was in prison, awaiting martyrdom, and she had a vision of her brother who'd died many years before, as a child. (He had cancer of the face – isn't that terrible?) Anyway: instead of being immersed in water, as you thought, he was unable to drink from a pool, or a large vessel, it's also said: the brim was beyond his reach. But after Perpetua's prayers she saw him drinking the water; she also saw that his face had healed; and that he then began to play, because his suffering was over.

– Donald, he said. You must come over to my place for a drink.

His gestures were implacably effeminate; his pale skin was flaking from obsessive washing (as he confessed readily enough); his eyes coquettish; his hair long and blond. He was highly erudite. While we looked through his snapshots (in which, characteristically, he posed with young men wearing leather motorcycle clothing, their motorbikes alongside or behind them), Donald conversed about a string of subjects, eccentrically linked; so that he moved from Arnald of Villanova's *The Time of the Coming of the Antichrist* to Apocalyptic themes in German Expressionism; and then to the vertiginous mysticism of the heretics of the Free Spirit.

When Mike went out to buy some cigarettes, Donald said to me: He's so good-looking, isn't he? Is he your lover?

– No, I said.

– Well, he said, maybe you don't like such masculine men? Mind you, he *is* terribly nervy....

I didn't have to answer, for he immediately got up and went to the bathroom.

When he came back, he said: Do you think I'm weird? I mean, that I can't stand to feel unclean and have to wash so often? Does it make me seem crazy?

I said: It would only matter if you felt it harmed you in some essential way. It shouldn't make any difference at all to anyone else.

Michael came in the door then. Donald turned to him and said, pointing in my direction: This man has been sent by Our Saviour to help me!

Coming back to the hotel late in the evening, we stopped to peer through the window into the darkened interior of the din-ing-room, where a single lamp had been left burning, lighting up the area that served as the kitchen. Empty as the room was, there was a flame of hospitality that burned there, its light spreading over the kitchen's casual, yet cared-for, appearance.

I thought of the small kitchen-space within Donald's front room; with the glass sphere attached by thread to the ceiling, just above the rack of china plates. Donald had pinned up some other photographs of himself and his companions, with a post-card of Grünewald's Isenheim Altarpiece (showing the panel of the risen Christ) directly above them. And his voice, in memory, telling us more of Perpetua's story: how she dreamed of chang-ing into a man, to fight with the Devil in the guise of an Egypt-ian warrior; and how she flung him down; and was rewarded with a branch of golden apples.

***

Philippa suddenly said: When I was at college there were two tutors who started off having no respect for me at all; but by the time I finished the course, I had them eating out of the palm of my hand.

— What sort of course was it? I asked.

— Catering, she said.

She talked in a way that was unfamiliar, prompted (it seemed) by her friend's presence, although he, for his part, scarcely spoke; and I felt a sadness penetrating me, as if soaking little by little throughout my body.

In the days when she and Patrick had first known each other, she had been working as a "hostess" in a nightclub. — You get these sleazy guys who think they can get what they want out of you, she said, and it's up to you to get what you want out of *them*. It's only the natural and right thing; they deserve to be taken for their money.

– I got other things from them besides money, too, she continued. They think if they give you drugs, or even if they just buy presents for you, you'll end up in their power. They don't have any respect for you, and that's why I didn't have any respect for them.

My eye wandered again to the window and the street below; but the two workmen had gone.

I looked at Patrick; I could see nothing in his face (nothing below or within the frame of jet-black hair), for I thought of him as a reflection of the many boy-friends she'd talked about. Leather jacket, T-shirt and jeans: the standard declaration of his dress supported this loss of differentiation.

– No more than shadows, Patrick said; or at least I thought him to say it.

– What? I asked; for I wanted to be certain that the young man had said these words – which made me want to catch up and comfort the very shadows.

– What *what*? Patrick replied, looking at me askance.

I couldn't see him; I heard him, and didn't hear him.

***

I showered and returned to the room. Michael was already in bed; he turned his head to look at me as I came in the door.

I signed to Mike that I wanted to write something in my notebook (the phrases had been running through my head all the while I was washing myself), and he took up his book again.

– You remember what it was like? he said. I'd come out of the hospital, but I was scarcely able to talk to anyone, or make a decision for myself, or in fact do much at all.

– I remember.

– What was it like? It was like I was cycling through an orchard with every tree dense with birds, and the birds were shitting on me as I cycled beneath them.

– And do you remember the big storm late that autumn? he continued.

– Yes, I remember it.

– I expected that the faces of all the people I've ever loved who have died would come to me in the night. I expected to wake up covered in blood; I thought it was a judgement! In the morning there were heaps of sodden leaves collected by the wind, uprooted trees, smashed windows, flooded gutters....

When I eventually got to sleep, I dreamt that Philippa and I were travelling together by boat, in a sea fiery with the sun's reflection. Classical sculptures – figures of the gods – rose from the water on either side of the vessel, and I said: Let's hope we don't hit any of the statues. Philippa smiled, and said: Think of it: a woman stands there, looking into the water....

***

Philippa was the only person who'd had an opportunity to take the things (a brooch and a necklace of my mother's, which I had kept in my desk-drawer since her death). I disliked the idea of Philippa's having stolen them, but no other conclusion seemed possible.

I went to see her, and we talked for some time before I said:

– Philippa, my mother's jewellery's been taken from my flat.

– No one cares, she said, if I've got enough to eat, or if my clothes are in rags. You don't care, Charles!

– You should have said something. Philippa, you must know I feel a great deal of sympathy for you....

– I don't want your fucking sympathy, she said.

I lost my temper then. – You're a treacherous little bitch, I said.

– So are you! she shouted. And, raising her voice even more: Get out of here!

She opened the door, but stood in the doorway so that it was impossible to get past her.

– If our bodies grew so bright we could see through to each other's secrets.... That's a dream, but from heaven, I said.

– From fucking hell! she said. Do you think I *want* to know your dirty little secrets, or that I'd want you to fucking-well know mine?

– If we *could* see each other in that way, I said, we'd weep with each other; that's all.

Philippa stepped to one side. – Get out of here, she said.

I walked until I came to a small park; I went in, and sat down on a bench. Shafts of light and moisture in the air composed an envelope for silence; the kind of silence that follows in the wake of pandemonium, and encloses anguish.

To the memory of Petros Bourgos.

KEITH WALDROP
Puberty

*The first and chief endeavor of the mind is
to affirm the existence of the body.*
— Spinoza

The window is an alternative, dim squares ruled by bars of black. Except for the window, there is only black. One might think that, black on black, nothing could be legible, and to most eyes that might be the case. She, however, provides her own bright background, against which the dark announces its attractions, bold patterns suggesting a cosmos in the works.

The sheets are white – clean and white – but add to the pitch dark total.

As she has grown, so has her fear of the dark, but it has also shifted, gradually, from alarm to anxiety. Against this fear, her fear itself lights flares – a reflex, triggered by any end of day. It would be wrong to suppose that she fears the dark merely as a symbol of death – for her, death is terrible only because it resembles the dark: a volume without planes, space without surface.

The stillness she keeps – heart and breath beating against it – is tense with the thought that no matter how determined her inactivity, there is always the possibility of a false move: the muscles could make their own decision or a mere tone betray her. We assume that in silence and the dark the self disintegrates into a host of minor processes, each with its own worry. But there are some – and she is one – whose peripheral lines of thought, uttered and unuttered, parallel and intersecting, form a pattern that is, to an extent, coherent, solid enough to found a personality. The lack of stimulus, far from interfering, sets it off, frames it. It projects out of the dark, like a sentence on a page of stray marks – or like a sentence she can read, in the midst of a foreign paragraph.

When she is tired of it, she looks towards the window.

"Love," he says, not here, and not to her, "always met me smiling, drew me on, then left me to my own devices."

As the light passes from window to her − never mind the unimaginable penetration of the panes themselves − it undergoes a change, like richly colored music coming through a speaker, stripped of extremes. She loves this house, even when she cannot see it. And other senses, now, pass through unseen partitions into rooms that she imagines brightly lit and frequented by figures she has no reason to believe are there.

She hears, for instance, a muffled tap, which brings to her mind's eye an uncle whose cane strikes the floor, never in advance like a blind man's, but just in measure with his own right leg, so that, far from suggesting lameness, it gives his walk a manner, even along the hallway where a carpet mutes the tap. She will go walking with him. Although the darkness is, apart from the window, total, approaching her from all ways at once, she arches slightly, staring forward. Windows should open onto a borrowed view: a wall of fire, a castle rampart, or a dried-up ditch; royal pleasure grounds or the hut of a recluse.

She has been put to bed with angels and, fearing they will disturb her darkness, she will not let her mind wander down town, will repudiate known streets, dismiss store-fronts blanched by arc-light, hold her breath against familiar air. She will not think in that direction, but dwells − for the moment − on an old memory, precarious, threatened by waves that come, regular and unflinching, obliterating high and low, near and far, the unheard voice in the throat. Her vanishing point is at variance with that of this room, this house. Patterns of shadow thrown by a window against the wall opposite, or against the edge of the ceiling where it continues that wall, might hold her attention, keep it from wandering down unseen corridors into other spaces. No light is thrown. All her thoughts go their own way, mindless of her, as if unthought.

Now her inner organs are no more invisible than a hand held before her face. It could be an organic cavity that she floats in, her relation to any wall having become tenuous. Like a zeppelin she moves, effortlessly, like an island, the house also floating, and the land.

"Love," he says, "escort me." But it is not a request and is said nowhere in particular. He has lived on an island and she imagines him in a window at the top of a house thin like an arrow pointing upward – the single window of his study, book-lined and tobacco-ridden. From this window he gazes forth, day after day, and sees each day a different sea, a different line of land, distant always, but at widely varying distances –or no land at all, but waves of a different water. All the sad thoughts which she supposed lost come back and take their places, and she finds them strangely consoling, as the ghost of an oppressor might seem a consolation – or anything, long forgotten, coming into view.

Returning, as from an island, with his cane and his somewhat rolling gait, he insists – to her, since she is listening – that always in his legs he can feel the drift of the continent. And once, he relates, he chased a solitary wave, a wave with no others to block its long career. It rolled on, preserving its original speed and figure, then gradually diminished in the windings of a channel.

Light is always, it seems to her, against her, and from her body springs, in some direction, always, shadow. Fear lies around her at every degree, though she has the frontal eyes of any predator.

"She is afraid of the dark," she hears him say of her, as she gazes down a road along which a rail fence trails like a dragon, in and out of view. "Because," he says, considering, apparently, a local post loaded with signs, all pointing. And finally, "of the coming of sex, an unknown force, not subject to the ego." She is not listening now, but hears, dispersing the landmarks. "Like the welling up of night." She is puzzled how he can look so work-hardened, when certainly he has never worked.

He talks a great deal about pleasure, its status for a mind upon whose walls the world is projected, now closing, flower-like, and then opening like outer space. Half his life, he will explain among clouds of smoke, he wasted in constantly moving about. The other half disappeared into sleep and its approaches. Foreign travel, all of it.

He accepts that to be real means to be someone's experience, that what does not exist within a sentience does not exist at all. And so he tries to image unlikely events, objects of no context, characters beyond his own belief, so that if such things are in any universe, or were, or may come to be in a later, thoughtless time, they might have now, in his conversation, their improbable reality.

In her, desire is even now increasing, towards venom; while his has weakened to wishing, supposing, on its way – a finger held upright across the lips – to wistfulness. If he focuses on some stationary object, it will usually stand still, for a moment. And then it is not the object that, suddenly, moves, but something on the periphery of his vision – quick, like a bug scurrying from sight. It always startles him. The woods about him wander, pull themselves up and move with surprising dispatch. The three dimensions remove, as a thin film. Fortresses spring up, with the most diverse names. Eventually, no trace remains.

The oaks that she finds here and there along city streets are specimens merely, tall perhaps, but unable to bring into play their astonishing force. A forest of oak, ruthless, stamps out inferior vegetation, deploying its foliage in acid layers. So that while spring may heighten and extend a rank green, on the ground it is a forecast of death.

She breathes in the scene – all she needs to see, she sees with her lungs. From her to the window may seem, at first, simple, but remember that nothing moves in a straight line. Her landscape is determined by an angle of sight which, if she could see, would sever it from the fields outside her vision, but now must render it – patches of tree, road, beckoning pavilion – all from internal dead of night.

Individual squares are distinct, lined by black bars dividing it into panes, and the window itself is a rectangle – taller than it is wide – outlined starkly by the void, to which it forms the most violent contrast: the contrast of nothing-in-particular with nothing. She sees, that is, not light *from* the window, only the pale glass itself, an illumination so faint as to turn it, though visible, opaque. It stops her vision, without satisfying it, whereas the darkness nothing curtains off.

But it does not strike her, this magic, as a performance of her own. The dark itself flaunts a design, impressing on an absent screen its radiant trickery.

"Everything," he says, "everything in general, that is...." No matter how far from the ocean, his eyes habitually brim. ". . . is possible. Few things in particular." At a certain distance, the earth is bound to bulge up between them, but they walk together, side by side, she on his left, through a wrought iron gate ornamented with magnificent irrelevant initials, into the most perfect alley she has ever imagined. She is composing a garden, the location of which she will not disclose, ever, even to herself. Stalks of pure will push up and flower, out of the voluntary soil. Unsuspected varieties spring up here, some newly evolved and others blown from far afield. Pollen and exotic scents emanate from this secret area, as sometimes details cluster around a subject suggested only by those details.

The house around her – already invisible – now vanishes. The center of her body, which is outside her body, brings into focus an unseen landscape which, otherwise, would remain groundless, without this shadow of reality. Birds sing. Birds fly from limb to limb. The trees arrange themselves so as to facilitate flight and song and the breeze that fills the unoccupied spaces anchors the environment by wrapping her in air.

His cane taps the grass with a parquet resonance and he strokes his beard, morally indifferent. All the embroidery of trees, of birds, of flowers resembling birds – each arabesque is outlined in black. Obscurely she knows that only going in circles – or, perhaps, staying put – is conducive to order.

The horizon, now, is defined by a barricade of mounted men. The sun, now that she thinks of it, appears at large, spreading like the floor of the sea. Only the tallest mountains break the surface and achieve dry land, so many copies of the Idea of Paradise. Bats enter, confusing the air. It would amaze her, if she thought about it, how much difference it makes, in utter darkness, to close or open one's eyes. All moving and all motionless things she has, to a degree, translated: music while asleep, on the darkest peak a valley noon, vertical archipelagos. Translation requires secrecy; if stated, it disappears. She wants to hear him say things: "Every creature is outside God," or "Completion," his cane raised pensively, "like the very tip of a tail."

"You are an orphan," he says, which is untrue. Or true only in his eyes: she is not his daughter. He believes – or, rather, he does not question – the long outmoded notion that disease resides only in the body's solids, health washing helplessly around maladies of precipitation.

"Complete," he says, "would include Africa." He moves with difficulty, not because of his bad leg, but because the tiny room, his study, is full. If he is not careful, piles of books, caught by a passing cuff, collapse. "I could never write a biography," he continues, "of anyone at all. No anecdote seems secure enough." No pile falls as he approaches the window. "As for the inner life ...." He has arranged things in this study (smoke hangs in the air, and the stench of stale ashes – why does she never visualize him with pipe in hand or a cigar between his teeth?) so that the only mirror is blocked, deprived of the room. He has no wish to be confronted by his own image, walking towards him or paused, startled by the face staring out of the reflection, and into it. To him the window is a more satisfying glass, presenting the same changes, but more broadly, lighting the same personality, but without a mask.

But he fades and looms larger and his island, in the downstream part of her perception, vaster than she would have it, sails by without moving, as if she were dizzy, and his only glance at her, sidelong, is repeated in an infinite perishing series. She is afraid that she will sleep, or that she is already sleeping. To remember something – to be sure, that is, to remember – she feels that she must not, originally, have held on to it, but handed it over to memory, whom she sees as a stranger processing her dreams and her retrievals, giving them up only provisionally and sometimes rejecting desperate petitions.

Why is she unable to maintain her sense of garden? Is no partition possible, which would separate inside from outside, consecrate this present ground and abolish the world of the next event? She can change all the distinctive traits of standard time – with the exception of its irreversibility. When she thinks a wall, it rises, brick on brick, along the vast land masses, thick and forti- fied till it can hold back the northern snow that piles against it. But the portion of wall abutting on the sea is soon destroyed.

Besides the influences that may find their way through the natural boundary of skin, whose pores seem more penetrable at night – besides those foreign influences – the most familiar com- ponents of her body, without which there would be no body (blood, yes, and bone) could turn, denying their, or her, identity. She does not know, now, where she is, except that it occurs to her that this level green, broken by weeping trees and by a queer- shaped artificial lake, may be a graveyard. Once it has occurred to her, graveyard it is, and she scans it worriedly, puzzled to the point of discomfort, for there is no headstone to be seen.

Loss of memory is never total. Some traces are conserved, some habits. If the amnesiac asks who he is, he has recalled three words and a language to take them from. He has not for- gotten how to ask a question, or what it means to be someone with a name. His tongue remembers how to form the sounds he is making and his heart is remembering to beat. On an impulse, the garden she has left she reinvents and enlarges. All around her it extends to an horizon-line of saw-toothed forest sharp at infinity. Terrors lie around her, but now she would reach out to them. Life, very likely, is like these terrors of the night, the earli- est glimmer revealing eventually that – all the time – there was nothing there.

The dark will fade soon. Her body, as she shifts position in her sleep, is covered unevenly with a fine moisture, as if from dancing. Corporeal waste; she will wash it off. She will comb her hair, tomorrow, in such a way as to suggest the orderliness that has been claimed for the creation as whole.

GILES GOODLAND
Spring

Mother wasp is making paper. On paper she wants her children to prosper and soon there will be hundreds willing to answer her closely. She perfects them in the spiral shell of a nest hanging like a lightshade. The blind stingless grubs she tends are sensitive to each vibration, each draft or small sound that comes up to the attic.

Startled into a tree the fled voice, unaware how closely its words had brushed our shoulder. The flowers are opening hands. Days believe themselves into light.

Mummily, incarnation of milk. Remember this differently next time: I, a fluid charging the body, full of containment's illusion. As soon as you think of a void it fills. Like everything you touch, it turns to world. I am made of the people who murmured their parenthood at me with such insistence I agreed to become the kind of plastic in their hands that has a shape-memory of childhood, cast and then outcast. Lying on the lawn she lifts her son up above her, towards the sun, feeling dribble fall warmly down her neck. Mummily thought: this we enclose in talk as the body in clothes.

It is the time of day when gestures hang in the air. I am pushed against the wind and time is following me. There are cattle speaking as in belief, and out of their tongues travel new senses. A seeming of cloud, an uprooted horse. The claws of a tree tremble in a pond before the wheels of a pram. There is a cloud gathering where a path ruts into the woods, under the hills. Are we thoughts, that dissipate? A coot, wrongfooted, trips into water, toggles away. My face passes through a range of expressions before landing on surprise.

In my pram I sang my own worlds. Placed on a blanket, the grass spoked. Already on the side of the just, I would give freedom to all of the animals: force them to be free, to acknowledge me as their creator, and when the ants burrowed away from me, I crawled after them, my digits grubbing into the soil. Then I tasted the crumby stains on my fingers, and crawled back.

It was when I was too old to be born any more. In the divided kingdom of grown-ups, the seven-year-old, with two older brothers, was without a king. There I constructed a child out of cereal-packets and glue. Imagine an object the parts of which will never fit together. This is child, like the "h" in ghost, it cannot cancel its eyes that shine through the unforgiven light. It has an extra, unsoundable quality that people recognize but never voice.

Child, unspoken, finds a way outside, through the garden hedge into a field, and makes cuckoo-sounds all afternoon, perched on the sawn ledge of a tree-stump, in a sea of nettles: one of those fat little-brother birds that pipped out of the indistinguishable egg, took all the food and felt compelled to shoulder its older siblings over the nest's edge.

I had cuckoo friends, my own age, to explore with. There was a patch of woods with great climbing oaks, branches at just the right distance to allow us to haul ourselves up, and sit examining the stand and the lie of the land. We could feel the breathing wood, under which opened the green-sealed pond that had been our source of frogspawn, the fields laid around us, the boxy houses. The hours tricking away, squirrelly and elusive.

Bones articulate themselves into memory: visiting the churchyard with Mark, who lived over the field, and fighting among the gravestones, under the church's lengthening shadow, we knocked over an urn. It rolled on the grass. Righting it, the slime of algal once-flowers stuck to my hands: clingy, stringy, like death. We picked up a pocketful each of the jewelly slag that they spread on graves to make a shiny glass blanket. As if you could stare down into that opacity and make out the form of the deceased.

Mark said it would give us dreams, and that night we kept one piece each beside our beds, and we had a nightmare about the same person: Tammy, the drowned girl. We held hands once. She had been in our class, and then she wasn't. We both dreamed she was a jarred tadpole that had once swam in a pool that cracked like duckweed after a thrown stone. She drip-marked patios, hanged croaks on tree-latticed evenings in which the sun took days to set. Her inaudible scream scraped dogs from sleep and creaked cats into motion as her fingers slicked silks, her unfathomed eyes worm-turned at pond-bottom, her lapsed lips yessing. I woke to the sound of a liquid being poured when one sheet was too much and a voice bounced where it had no business, and I screwed my head tight into the pillow. Beyond that, the speaking walls, and beyond, the hedges' shifts and sighs, sucks of lifted hoofs, distant cars, and the pond itself, gulfing, velvetting across gardens. This is the pond in which that childhood met a foregone floor, and a green girl once called Tammy sleeved in pondscum tapped windows and unlatched the glass. Snails slid from her cuffs and her eyes were frogspawn flecks and deep inside those nuclei there was a weed-covered pond, which forever looked no different to lawn.

Next morning we were both back at the unmarked graveside, dropping those glassy stones with the knowledge we had stolen, and we ran.

There were gaps under some of the sheds, where I could look down and see a formless rubbly area, a place of no jurisdiction. Pale weeds, lost balls, old rodent traps. It was like the space under the places we tread in sleep, the meaning appended to the last fragments of a dream that puzzle out of the air as we rise. Mummily said she'd seen weasels there, knifing through this ordinary world at dusk with the weight and power of energy-creatures, shards of predation. They were down there, under the shed, like goblins or swear-words, or death.

An overwhelming sense of being held suspended between father and the floor in an anxious state as he sandpapered my cheek with his chin and blessed me with pipesmoke, then returned me like an ornament on a mantelpiece, before he went back to the wide table on which he had spread out cutups from each daily newspaper, and his nightly correspondence with their letters columns.

Or sometimes my head tottered as he took me upstairs. A period of absence, then an unfixed smile, there he was again, a ball of whisky warming his hand. We are as old as the tales we tell each other, he began. His stories went like this. Once upon a time in a land before death. Death you should know is when the body reduces to the words it was, and these words blow into a distant set of dictionaries. Heaven is the space where shadows jump when they are too tired to lie on the floor, where all your reflections hold a party in your dishonour. What if on death what we have to live through again is not conscious life but our accumulated dreams played back without the intercession of daily life, perhaps they would at last start to make some kind of pattern, a nonlinear alignment that will finally supply us with that elusive meaning we lacked in life.

But usually my parents' voices never quite become words. I tremble under them as they shoal in through a door. My responsibility is to keep from climbing into their bed. Even if the ghosts I saw spoke to me again. It is their pictures that clung to me on waking.

I propped my elbows on my bedroom mantelpiece, to stare the stars into being. The house on the edge of the woods, from my window by owl-light, beyond which I fixed the stars, where it always seemed to be dusk. Perhaps everyone has a forest from their window, an edge behind the everyday. Gently it folded into night, and was swallowed in the green interior. The light shone like this I thought and dimly made sense along the long dark track of time.

I heard him or thought I heard him downstairs, booming lecturishly, his voice like an organ: What can I say? I go to work for a day and come back. All that occurs is through time. Time is the bottomless pit into which we fall. Geological, planetary time. It's more frightening than infinite space. One can conceive of crossing the stars, other galaxies. But the planet's future: a dead sun, an airless rock, any imaginable future will have us fossilized. It's a dark mirror to look into. We have to understand that any physical journey is only a shadow of the real journey we make through time; and we all know where that ends. This feels like a day that had been plagiarized from some long forgotten former day distinguished only by the hope I held at that time to become something more than one of the many others. Or perhaps he was not saying that, and papoosed in my bed I made up the words to go with the organ-tones of his voice.

I pictured myself, like him, my future behind me. It will come as a shock when I revisit the old home, unlived-in for years, paths all thistle and ragweed. Front door opening difficultly. The rubbish that has blown under. As if it has always been that way, I step over the newspapers and dead leaves, and into the hallway. It feels like I'm looking for something. I try each door in turn, and opening them liberates memories I had long given up. They escape like light leaving a sealed room, into that long corridor with a door for each day, unnumbered. Some doors are unlocked. One room contains all the skin traces I will shed in the open-plan office, on the keyboard, under the chair, swept into a conical heap. Another holds a filing cabinet which contains, by year, all my claims to uniqueness, disproved. This one appears to be empty. If a rainy Sunday could be stored, this room would hold it. Or it contains only us, peering through the half-open door.

This room contains a dentist's chair. This one, the dessicated corpusses of my parents, frozen in the moment that created me. A further room contains woodland, acres of it, at the moment when it has become too dark to play and owls are taking flight. Among the locked doors, one would be full of lightbulbs, another full of dark, thick as ocean-floor. The last would be the soft way back to the womb, you might think. It will open horizontally, like a smile on the wooden face of an undertaker.

The horizontal door is on the ceiling. I would have forgotten it if the pole with the hook on the end hadn't still been there, leaning against the corner beside the window in the bedroom. I snag it on the trapdoor handle and pull. The stepladder comes down like a metal tongue. Soon I'm up there, and finding that the light doesn't work. I tap my pockets to find a matchbox. In the light of that uncertain flame that quickens even the dead, sits Mummily. She slowly stands up, brushes herself down, and gives me a hug. I am lifting above us the arm holding the match.

A dozen heartbeats later, the flame reaches my finger, and in the excitement I've dropped the matchbox. We stand there in the dark for several minutes, arms still around each other, but mine are growing heavy, and I disengage. I realise it is too late for her to descend, and I resolve to come back soon, and bring food and cigarettes. And a lightbulb. But I'm happy now. I know what it was I will be looking for.

Nowhere in the house is Father, except as a voice trapped in the walls, the wiring. Neither his voice nor the quality of his advice changes, but being older I can at least now examine it and make up my mind what quality it bears, what kind of material it is. He is saying: We need our children so we can recover the lost forgotten things that our parents said to us. This evening at bedtime I found myself saying to my son "I don't want to hear your voice at all." At least I didn't stroke him. Sheer force can do a lot to a person. What it can do to a child is beyond belief. We must all remain imperfect because of our ruined childhoods. A perfect childhood is impossible, but even a happy childhood is unfeasible under present conditions. The best that can be done is to prepare a child for the worst, while intimating the best.

Each door leads to another door, the corridor is a long walk, it is an effort to count them. My bedroom opens up through a cupboard into my brother's. It is a house with gaps in the middle, with holes. Two houses, in fact, sutured together long ago.

Away then, travel forwards along bookshelved corridors, find your way into the living room, where dad's papers still weigh down the table, and his typewriter is next to his pipe, and all the letters he wrote are imprinted, the carbons fluttering in the breeze from the door you left open, and the shelves stacked with more letters, piles of them. He typed with red emphasis, and underlined and capitalized. His letters belonged to some uncategorized literary form, taking as their starting point a civic issue or matter of supposed concern to the area, and extending from that to a charge-sheet of faults and failings in the world at large, connected together by tenuous but precise logics, the red ink deployed sparingly at first but in greater quantities towards the end, the key-strokes harder, the letters superscripted as he struck too fast; but appearing to me as objects of beauty – red and black. My fingers brailled them into sense: As instruments of the state all narratives end here on a disfigured page, in the end of all sentences, we come to this dark circle and know it for death's period but this only becomes significant when the novel has been taken to the charity-shop, and its owner stretches on his sheet of blood, in a house where letters waited and where the closed book still feels the windblown tree.

He would rattle his thoughts onto the page as if he were emptying his pipe. His thoughts were the ash that had to be pipe-cleaned out, or expectorated phlegmily, in the way he uncleared his throat. The world in his sights was more than the sum of its pictures, there was ash flying round the room, and the smoke so dense it was a cloud that surrounded everything.

I burrow down further and end up cozied into the pocket where the sheets tuck in under the mattress. A child contains an adult, observing, pretending not to be there, but recording everything. Lymphing back through the mind from the land where the dead outlive the pure sound of midnight or of a violin-note hanging in the air, this inner adult will bring back the pattern that so many silences make all together. Sometimes it will speak to you.

Doors shouldered themselves into my sight, in my dreams these corridors opened into other corridors, some doors contained murderers, some contained beautiful but ethereal thoughts like butterflies that flew out as I opened them to look, dissipated and were lost among the furnishings, and the house became soft, the floor turned into carpet, up to my knees, and the walls were flock, soft to the fall of my hands, and I was crawling in sleep's soft jungle, the carpet-sea lapping at my sides, red in the plush of the pile, where sleep is a magician who casts himself over the oceans of my memories, and the world dilates to a pupil staring into the night. Each night this eye must learn once more the way to blink.

bpNICHOL
from Selected Organs: Parts of an Autobiography

The Mouth

1   You were never supposed to talk when it was full. It was better to keep it shut if you had nothing to say. You were never supposed to shoot it off. It was better to be seen than heard. It got washed out with soap if you talked dirty. You were never supposed to mouth-off, give them any of your lip, turn up your nose at them, give them a dirty look, an evil eye or a baleful stare. So your mouth just sat there, in the middle of your still face, one more set of muscles trying not to give too much away. "Hey! SMILE! what's the matter with you anyway?"

2   Probably there are all sorts of stories. Probably my mouth figures in all sorts of stories when I was little but I don't remember any of them. I don't remember any stories about my mouth but I remember it was there. I remember it was there and I talked and sang and ate and used it all the time. I don't remember anything about it but the mouth remembers. The mouth remembers what the brain can't quite wrap its tongue around and that's what my life's become. My life's become my mouth's remembering, telling stories with the brain's tongue.

3   I must have been nine. I'm pretty sure I was nine because I remember I was the new boy in school. I remember I was walking on my way there, the back way, thru the woods, and here was this kid walking towards me, George was his name, and I said "hi George" and he said "I don't like your mouth" and grabbed me and smashed my face into his knee. It was my first encounter with body art or it was my first encounter with someone else's idea of cosmetic surgery. It was translation or composition. He rearranged me.

4   The first dentist called me the Cavity Kid & put 35 fillings
     into me. The second dentist said the first dentist was a char-
     latan, that all the fillings had fallen out, & put 38 more fill-
     ings in me. The third dentist had the shakes from his years in
     the prisoner of war camp & called me his "juicy one," saliva
     frothing from my mouth as his shakey hand approached me.
     The fourth dentist never looked at me. His nurse put me out
     with the sleeping gas & then he'd enter the room & fill me.
     The fifth dentist said my teeth were okay but my gums would
     have to go, he'd have to cut me. The sixth dentist said well he
     figured an operation on the foot was okay coz the foot was a
     long way away but the mouth was just a little close to where
     he thot he lived & boy did we ever agree because I'd begun
     to see that every time I thot of dentists I ended the sentence
     with the word "me". My mouth was me. I wasn't any ancient
     Egyptian who believed his Ka was in his nose – nosiree – I
     was just a Kanadian kid & had my heart in my mouth every
     time a dentist approached me.

5   It all begins with the mouth. I shouted waaa when I was
     born, maaa when I could name her, took her nipple in, the
     rubber nipple of the bottle later, the silver spoon, mashed
     peas, dirt, ants, anything with flavour I could shove there,
     took the tongue & flung it 'round the mouth making
     sounds, words, sentences, tried to say the things that made it
     possible to reach him, kiss her, get my tongue from my
     mouth into some other. I liked that, liked the fact the
     tongue could move in mouths other than its own, & that so
     many things began there – words did, meals, sex – & tho
     later you travelled down the body, below the belt, up there
     you could belt out a duet, share a belt of whiskey, undo your
     belts & put your mouths together. And I like the fact that
     we are rhymed, mouth to mouth, & that it begins here, on
     the tongue, in the pun, comes from mouth her mouth where
     we all come from.

6   I always said I was part of the oral tradition. I always said poetry was an oral art. When I went into therapy my therapist always said I had an oral personality. I got fixated on oral sex, oral gratification & notating the oral reality of the poem. At the age of five when Al Watts Jr was still my friend I actually said, when asked who could do something or other, "me or Al" & only years later realized how the truth's flung out of you at certain points & runs on ahead. And here I've been for years running after me, trying to catch up, shouting "it's the oral," "it all depends on the oral," everybody looking at my bibliography, the too many books & pamphlets, saying with painful accuracy: "that bp – he really runs off at the mouth."

The Tonsils

1   They said "you don't need them" but they were keen to cut them out. They said "if they swell up they'll choke you to death" so you learned they cut things off if they might swell up. There were two of them in their sacs & they hung there in your throat. They cut them off.

2   I didn't have them long enough to grow attached to them but they were attached to me. It was my first real lesson in having no choice. It was my only time ever in a hospital as a kid & I wasn't even sick. I wasn't even sick but I had the operation. I had the operation that I didn't want & I didn't say "no" because there was no choice really. I had everybody who was bigger than me telling me this thing was going to happen & me crying a lot & them telling me it was good for me. It was my first real lesson in having no attachments.

3   Almost everyone I knew had their tonsils out. Almost every-one I knew was told "it's good for you." Even tho none of

us who had our tonsils out ever knew any kid who choked to death from having them in, almost everyone we knew had their tonsils out.

4   I miss my tonsils. I think my throat used to feel fuller. Now my throat feels empty a lot & maybe that's why I eat too fast filling the throat with as much as I can. Except food is no substitute for tonsils. The throat just gets empty again.

5   I was told I didn't need my tonsils. Maybe this is the way it is. Maybe as you grow older they tell you there are other bits you don't need & they cut them out. Maybe they just like cutting them out. Maybe tonsils are a delicacy doctors eat & the younger they are the sweeter. Maybe this is just paranoia. I bet if I had a lobotomy they could cut this paranoia out.

6   What cutting remarks! What rapier wit! What telling thrusts! Ah cut it out! Cut it short! He can't cut it! You said a mouthful!

7   There are two of them & they hang there in your throat. There are two of them in sacs & they swell up. Now there are none. Gosh these words seem empty!

The Lungs: A Draft
for Robert Kroetsch

1   This is a breath line. I said. This is a breathline. Line up, he said. Suck your stomach in Nichol, I don't want to see you breathe. I didn't breathe. This was a no breath line. He said. Six or eight or ten of us not breathing while he walked down the line, holding our breath while he looked us over, while he chose one of us to punch in the gut, to see how tough our stomach muscles were he said, stomachs pulled in, lungs

pushed out, waiting while he paced back and forth, while he paused in front of each of us and then moved on, this small smile playing across his lips. Waiting. A breathless line. I said.

2   I was staying at Bob and Smaro's place in Winnipeg. I was sleeping on the floor in Smaro's study. I was getting up early in the morning, like I tend to do, getting up early and going into the livingroom. I was sitting down in a chair and reading a copy of a new book on literary theory or literary criticism Smaro had brought back from some recent trip as she tends to do. I was just turning the page, just beginning to get into the book when Bob appeared at the top of the stairs, when Bob came down the stairs from the upper floor, not really awake, came down the stairs anyway, Bob, muttering to himself, "life, the great tyrant that makes you go on breathing." And I thought about breathing. I thought about life. I thought about those great tyrants the lungs, about the lung poems I've tried to perfect in various ways, the lung poems Bob's written, written about, lung forms. And I thought about the lungs sitting there, inside the chest – inhaling – exhaling. And I thought to myself, to myself because Bob was in no mood to hear it, I thought "life's about going the lung distance." Just that. And it is.

3   We were maybe five, Al Watts Jr and me, no more than five, and we had snuck out back, behind the garage, to try a smoke. It was just the way you read it in all those nostalgic memoirs of male childhood. It was authentic. It was a prairie day in Winnipeg in the late 40s and there we were, two buddies sharing a furtive puff on a stolen cigarette. And just like in all the other stories the father showed up, Al Watts Sr, suddenly appeared around the corner of the garage and said "so you boys want to smoke, eh?" If only we'd read the stories. If only we'd had the stories read to us. We'd have known then how the whole thing had to end, we'd have known what part the dad plays in these kinds of tales. But we hadn't. We

didn't. We said yes we really did want to smoke. And we did. Al Watts Sr took us home, took us back to his study, the room he very seldom took us into, and opened up his box of cigars and offered one to each of us. We should have known. We really should have known when he lit them for us and told us to really suck in, to take that smoke right down into our lungs, we should have known what was coming. We didn't. We did it just the way he said. We sucked that smoke right in, right down to our lungs, and of course we started hacking, of course we started coughing, trying to fling the cigars away. But he made us take another smoke, he made us take another three or four good drags on the cigar, until our bodies were racked from the coughing, until our lungs ached from the lunge and heave of trying to push the smoke out. And we didn't want to smoke anymore, I didn't want to smoke anymore, I never really wanted to touch a cigarette again. Even when I was a teenager and hanging out with Easter Egg on his old scow down in Cod Harbour and he'd offer me a toke, I never could take the smoke into my lungs again. Except that after I turned 30 I started smoking cigars. And even though I didn't take the smoke into my lungs, even though I just held it there in the mouth and let it go, when I thought about it it really didn't make much sense. It didn't you know. Look what had happened to me with Al Watts Sr and Al Watts Jr those many many years ago. This wasn't supposed to be the outcome. This wasn't supposed to be the way the story goes. But it was as if the lungs wanted me to do it. As if the lungs had a memory all their own and I was forced to relive it. Not a primal scream but a primal puff, primal smoke from a primal prairie fire. As if the whole childhood episode had been like one of those moral tales where the reader takes a different lesson from the one the writer intended. Or like one of those shaggy dog jokes, where the punch line comes way after the joke should have ended, way after the person listening has lost all interest in what's being said. Lung time. Different from the head's.

4   When do you first think of your lungs? When you're young and tiny and turning blue and you can't get your breath because something is happening to you like my mom told me it happened to me? When you're five and choking over your first smoke like I just told you? When you start to sing in the choir and the choirmaster tells you to really fill your lungs with air, your stomach, and support the sound from down there, inside the body? When you take up running, gasp for that last breath hoping to bring the tape nearer, the finish line, hoping the lungs will hold for the final lunge? Do you think of them then? In a moment like this, trying to remember, can you even say "I remember this about my lungs"? No. No. Almost no memories at all. Only the notion that they're there pumping away, just beneath the surface of these lines, however much these lines do or don't acknowledge them. One of those parts you can't do without. Two of them. "The bellows," he bellows, airing his opinion. Because to air is human. To forgive the divine. Bellowing our prays, our songs. Bellowing our lung-ings.

5   A draft he calls it. Like it blew in through a crack in the mind. Just a bunch of hot air. As when you're really hot, get the cadences to fall, the syllables to trot past the eye and ear just the way you see and hear them in the mind. As tho the mind tapped the lung and each thot hung there in its proper place. "It's just a draft. I'll get it right later." He feels the breath heave. He hears the words start as the heart pumps and the lungs take all that air and squeeze it in there, into the blood stream flows thru the mind. No next time when the lungs stop. Like that last sentence on the tongue, hangs in the air after the lungs have pressed their last square inch of it out in the absolute moment of death, only the body left: "I'll get it right next time."

DAVID RATTRAY
The Spirit of St Louis
for John Speicher

I step out onto Wiborg's at four p.m. under a cloudless sky, a jet
trail over the Clubhouse, a slight breeze and the sun warm on
my face, the new poems in a side pocket of the corduroy jacket
I am wearing, a perfect one for a walk on the beach. I got that
jacket because Speicher had one exactly like it. "On the beach"
was one of his favorite expressions, meaning out of work. It's a
merchant sailor's phrase originally. In the hospital four months
before he died, Speicher had a dream of waking to ship's bells.
Today I memorized "The Golden Ship," a sonnet by Emile Nel-
ligan. The ocean is calm, the shallows inshore foam-flecked. I
need to piss and will in the breakwater of boulders at the end of
Hook Pond just before the empty spot where the Sea Spray
stood until a few years ago when it burned. A sandpiper scam-
pers ahead of me along hard-packed gravel, following the reced-
ing surf lines. A continuous thread of colored pebbles. I pick up
a white translucent one. At 4:15 the beach turns pink. A quarter
of an hour ago I was dropped off here by the man who is about
to build a house for me. I wonder if he realizes what a grand
thing it is to build a poet's house. When Alexander the Great
razed Thebes he left Pindar's house standing. My worst feelings
come from a bad opinion of others; my best from a good one
of myself. A yellow Piper Cub roars by, following the shore. To
my right is a miniature of a formation such as one sees in Utah,
only it's two instead of two hundred feet tall. At 4:40 I pass in
front of the East Hampton Bathing Pavilion, and ten minutes
after that stand in front of the house where Berry lived in the
summer of 1952. Her parents would be out at the Club, a din-
ner-dance. She and I used to sit atop a low garden wall over the
ocean, facing the pink night sky above town, hugging and kiss-
ing. Bent with age, a white-haired man in sky-blue denim combs
the water's edge ahead of me. Half a century ago I came to this
very spot at the same time of year to build sandcastles. Now I'm

back, and, like the white-haired stranger, I am looking for good pebbles, something to carry away. I was smarter then. I would have gone barefoot on a day like this. To live is to walk alongside rivers, or over them. The ocean is a river too. The ancients thought of it as a stream circling the earth. What I was brought up not to call the undertow is a river in the ocean, called a seapoose by the Indians 300 years ago and by Bonackers to this day. In Toulouse I threw a typewriter off a bridge into the Garonne. I go places by bridge.

From Delancey Street a long ramp leads to an archway reading *1896 + Williamsburg Bridge + 1903*. After ten minutes on the ramp wondering if I am going to be shot by a sniper, I get to that arch just in time to meet the oncoming "J" train from Metropolitan Avenue and make eye contact with the motorman. We nod to each other as if passing in an empty field. He is a dark-skinned Hispanic, middle-aged, with a mustache. The bridge was started the year of my father's birth. The retired Western union operator I walked from 39th and Park to Grand Central the other day was also born that year. Either of them would have been old enough to have seen and remembered the man Cendrars saw in blue sunglasses pacing the corridor between compartments on the Trans-Siberian in the summer of 1905. A kid in a painted teeshirt and leather passes going the other way, unshaven, chuckling to himself. A gang or (who knows?) band name is painted over the walkway: CRO-MAGS. Wouldn't want to run into them. A white fishing boat is the only thing on the water far below, pebble-sized as Mayakovsky noted. I gaze down on the Domino sugar mill. Mayakovsky misplaced it at the foot of the Brooklyn Bridge. I pass a spray-painted peace symbol dating from the Vietnam War and a row of yellow flags following a red one on the west-bound track. Seven workmen straggle along the trackbed. They are painting the girders bright orange. Right about here there was a burnt car last spring. The bridge angles down. The roadway is at a higher level now. Cars can toss things. I don't have any insurance against flying objects. Another

"J" rattles west overhead, thirty feet up. I run. Tree sprouts poke up through cracks underfoot. Last time I came through, there was a dead dog, a small brown mutt, curled up in a corner between a soot-encrusted sapling and the wall. Emerging, I glance up Driggs Avenue for the 61. It's coming.

On the overpass: BAMBU LOVES ELSIES ♥ ♥ . I picture a pair of chocolate colored breasts with black nipples. I am Bambu. I lurch forward, nearly banging into the fare box. The driver stares, the map of Ireland on his face; he thinks I'm drunk. I am not Bambu. I do have a dirty mind. In the seat in front of me a big black woman in a raincoat is reading Jeremiah 6: "Were they ashamed when they committed abomination? Nay, they were not at all ashamed...." We pass a prison surrounded by spirals of razor wire, a border between Hasidic and Hispanic territories. The woman with the Bible chews on a red licorice stick. At Flatbush an ambulance shrieks by. I get out. Too bad it isn't Pennsylvania Dutch country. There are 23 Speichers in the telephone book in and around Reading. For 89 cents you can get a quart of birch beer, a drink consisting of birch flavoring, caramel, sugar, and carbonated water. A previous occupant of the room had stuck bubblegum onto the bedstead near the floor. Reality has so many ways of getting you. On the chair were poems of Mark Kirschen published in 1980 just before his suicide, a first and last book that I would like to read on the air. Fred Allen wrote four letters to me in 1943. We were proud. Radio was a celebrity thing. One evening I walked into town and back, barefoot under maples, with lightning bugs here and there in the nightfall, carrying my sneakers, where a moment earlier I had been admiring a purple cloud in the last stratospheric sunlight over the 1866 clocktower of the old State Normal School's administration building. It keeps accurate time, although a teeshirt proclaims this to be a place where you can set your clock back 25 years. That may well be true. But there is no such thing as an anachronism. In 1927 Gide went up the Congo River by steamboat, accepting the hospitality of colonial administrators and tribal kings along the way, reviewing native troops, taking note of masks, talking drums, tales of juju and spirit possession, admiring the muscles of boatmen and bearers, swatting mosquitoes, and keeping a journal in which the colorful passing scene served as a backdrop to a soliloquy on European literature, art, and politics. Imagine Poe walking Highbridge. Without a bridge you sail or fly. Try an island. A place like the island in the land o' lakes at the center of Siberia where Cendrars offered to fly his sweetheart in a monoplane and build a hangar of mammoth bones where they would make love like bourgeois. Is there a proletarian position? Naturally, the missionary. Early believers called it The Way. The Mayakovsky poem speaks of sugar being carted from the mill beneath the Brooklyn Bridge. He is talking about the Domino plant beneath the Williamsburg. He also has "victims of unemployment dashed headlong into the Hudson's scowl" from the Brooklyn Bridge, quite a trajectory for a jumper. At the end of time the gods in final conflict burn the rainbow bridge to Valhalla. One may go further in a boat, balloon, or plane. The week Lindbergh flew, Dad bought the papers, all of them, *New York Times, Trib, Herald, World*, even the *Brooklyn Eagle*. The "Flight" file sat in a corner for years before coming to rest in an attic so hot in summer one speculated about spontaneous combustion. By the spring of '48, the file had baked to a point where its whole top layer crumbled away on being touched. A favorite drink on the river was ginger wine. One camped overnight inside a disused covered bridge near Orford, sharing it with a family of bats. A bat relies on the sound of her own voice bouncing off obstacles to guide her in the dark. If muzzled, she runs into things. Her vocalizations pinpoint the flying bugs she eats. Relying on echo location at microsecond time depths, the bat is my soul emitting a symphony of tiny shrieks with each mouthful of air. Heavy netting shrouds the flight of strings. A paper airplane of folded yellow ruled paper. On papyrus a punning song lyric: "Acheron means ache..." Of the people at home in the house I was growing up in in 1945 I am the sole survivor. Two died of cancer, two of strokes. How do you describe a tunnel of Christmas tree lights seen for a tenth of a second from a Greyhound? From Dr Genthe, I believe, was a little tin model of the *Spirit of St Louis*, its front end all goose bumps, with a propeller you could spin. In the room where we ate, the windows faced sunset, and for a bit each year our supper table bathed in the warmth.

The other day I passed a child imitating an ambulance. In '68 I imitated a Paris police truck and was 32 at the time. I'm in a place with no telephones or mirrors. I have never been near anything like a river of sparks. Eileen described a river of broken glass, all red, and the temptation to dive in. I examine an oblong of yellow rock crystal with a cat's cradle of white bands crisscrossing inside. On the day of judgment darkness will cover everything and the oceans will boil away, the sky turn to fire, the stars explode, and the souls of all that have died since the beginning of life on earth flash like lightning. It's 5:30. At Georgica Gut I rest on a huge white drift log next to the words BRAD LOVES MICHELLE in ballpoint. How long is it since I wrote one of those? Snowfences belt the dune. Something of Georgica, its marshes and pond, with eelpots and wading fishermen, is already there in White's watercolors of the Powhatan near Roanoke in 1586. Painted faces, fish traps in mild sunlight, curing sheds. Blue distance, golden wires, silent amid sedges, and, to rule the pure sugar melody of the Muses' honey-winged song, a fancy most lofty, insolent, and passionate.

GUY BIRCHARD

Tom Farr

In days when we might rather have
hitched instead, we boarded *The
Canadian* in Vancouver, bound for
Union Station, Toronto. Late winter,
1971. Won't now more than tried
then to hide. I am that I am, avowal
not less profound for having come
from Little Richard in them days, no
matter where he got it.

Not long after departure, a man I'd
noticed up and down the aisle
stopped at our shoulders and spoke.
He was built slight, in early middle
years, close-cropped and clean-
shaven, jeans and a windbreaker, a
mild face, and quietly he told us he'd
chosen us.

If we'd give him our full attention,
what else would there be to do?
between Hope and Tee-O he would
teach us the Secret of Delight. That's
what he said. Nothing we didn't want
anyway, and all we had to pay was
attention. He had looked over all his
other prospects in all the other cars,
from Baggage to Observation, and
we were the ones he could tell.

He was on his return from Australia,
where he'd been a tire recapper, and

he was hoping to make contact with
his estranged family, his children last
seen around Hamilton whence mail
sent went unanswered were maturing
wherever they were, and for them,
too, he had what he had for us, and
the only thing he wanted in this world
was a Mobile Home.

Having made his introduction, he
said he'd leave us get ready and be
back. So we stirred and stared at each
other, and somebody sniggered, and
somebody did not, but said she
thought she saw Satan, which was a
little strong, I reckoned. Somebody
was disdainful. Somebody didn't care.
I wasn't sure I didn't mind.

Dogged by sorrow all our days,
what's special. He didn't get much
from us. That's all. I sat apart with
him a time or two. He neither quoted
nor cited, no rote, no rhetoric. Pure
instinct. But he craved Authority.
And a medium must be covert, that
old theme. I want what else he
wanted. Achievement of a lay order.
Graciousness in isolation. Pardon
cant if I slide. If he had a Secret to
impart, he needed time we lack. If it
was our souls he sought, I'm wrong,
Lord have mercy. I don't know who
he was.

Tired, discouraged at Union Station
in the throng detraining, rueful, into
the diaspora of our like, salut, elusive
Delight, Tom Farr, *salut.*

Vicar of Distance

We left Osoyoos in his Olds 88,
Grandad, Firecracker Alice and me,
the three of us up front, the back seat
out, full of boxes of apples. Novem-
ber.

After dark in a roadside restaurant
busy with normal travelers, normal
truckers, the hilarity of our appear-
ance struck and whelmed me.

When we got to their Shack up the
Missouri Coteau a day or two later
Grandad ragged on me some about
the ginger way I drove over glare-ice
at the summit of Kicking Horse Pass.
It was the night of November
Cabaret in the Community Hall but I
didn't go. I sat in a rocker all evening
till long past dark staring at the wall
taking stock of my whole life.

Next night I copped a ride to Saska-
toon with one of the cousins. It
seemed like a long way I didn't know
through a world I know well.

I boarded *The Canadian* for Winnipeg,
did what I never do: took a berth. At
dawn there I was.

7:00 / 7:30, I phoned Driveaway Car
Co. and the guy said, Sure, so I taxied
on over. He was a paraplegic operat-
ing out of a rooming house. He didn't
give my *bona fides* a rough time.

He sent me to a garage on the out-
skirts where they had a seminary stu-
dent's repo'd Cougar sitting in the lot
on bald tires, empties rolling around
on the floor behind the driver's seat.
You couldn't get in through the dri-
ver's door, only over the transmission
hump and stick shift from the pas-
senger's side. No thing to me. They
wanted it delivered in the direction I
was going.

All day I hung around while tires with
treads were found. November
through North Ontario you'll be glad
of them. No studs though. Against
provincial law. The shopboss dicked
around endlessly. Eventually I got
gassed up and gone late in the after-
noon.

Not thirty miles east of the city
where the Zone of Tension is
between Grassland and Shield, low
light in low sky, the Cougar heated
up. There's not much of anything in

that stretch but I lucked onto a road-
house at closing time. Checked the
oil, checked the belts, opened the rad:
not a drop.

The stupid malicious bastards had
given me a car without a drop of any-
damnthing in the radiator.

I poured it full of plain water and
drove into the snow. It snowed all
evening. At Kenora I put in as much
antifreeze as it would take, not much.
I drove as far as the Lakehead, Kak-
abeka Falls, by midnight, through
snow all the way. Ever since, thirty
years, alone or in love, ill or ok, I've
made it a point to stop at that same
hotel. A refuge once, a comfort ever.

Next morning the snow was deep but
had stopped falling. The sky was
clear, bright, windless, blue cold.
Right outside the hotel parking lot I
picked up a hitchhiker who had spent
the night out there. And away we
went, making first tracks on the
unplowed highway.

I intended to stay that night with
Lucy Peredun and her mom in the
Sault but the OPP had a roadblock at
Nipigon, said no one could go
around Superior on 17 because of
the storm, only the north road was
open, Kapuskasing, #11, down into

North Bay that way, many miles.
Well, I was to no schedule. But I
never saw Lucy again.

All day I drove without a break and
after the sun went down I kept driv-
ing. The temperature dropped like a
rock but as the night grew colder the
Cougar got hot again until some time
after midnight the engine super-
heated.

I had picked up a second hitchhiker
at a truckstop near Moonbeam and as
the motor approached seizure in the
black frozen pitchdark desolate wee-
hours bless my soul but he said he
knew an oldtimer name of Henry
Porter living pretty near.

We edged along, one eye on the
gauge, one eye on the periphery of
the high-beams' illumination, until
the hitchhiker recognized Henry
Porter's gate. It was about three
o'clock in the morning and cold as no
conscience when we roused him out
of bed. He took it in stride, let us
into his tool shop. We pulled the rad
hoses by trouble- and star-light and
found them full of ice. We were back
on the highway inside an hour. I won-
der if they were really angels, if it
isn't all a fantasy.

I made North Bay at first light. I was eating the caffeine tablets with the red rooster on the packet and I was near nauseous with fatigue and the rushes but I figured I better keep motoring or the system would likely freeze up again, and I was once more alone by then.

Soon after dawn, down the Valley near Mattawa, where the highway parallels the railway, a freight train was on fire, burning away without a soul around.

I got to my dad's place in the capital as he was getting up and I left the car parked in the street while we broke fast and after a while I went to deliver the thing downtown. A ways away it overheated again, bad, but no matter it made to me any more. A cracked block I wish it.

"Free ride for you," the agency hack fleered, refunding my deposit for the ignition key.

That night in Greektown in Montreal I slept with Anyo. Not for the first time. Not for the last.

WILL PETERSEN
from The Mask

The blossoms are out. Cold rains today.

(Cold rains today, as I copy this out, ten years and two months later.)

Your young lady, breath-takingly beautiful, resting within a cushioning brocade bag, in a new, less cramped wooden box, is on her way back to you, after so long a stay. I'm sorry. It could have been done sooner, and ought to have been, but I walk, often, on eggs – of my own laying.

How are you, Murray? I cannot write. Do not, please, regard the silence as a distance, as a coldness, a lack of care. I could talk, I feel, and listen, but cannot, from another land, write.

The air-mailed ORIGIN, with comment of Picasso's "confession", and with my little stoneprint tipped-in, and with, hidden 'neath the print, a few words, is, perhaps, relevant. At least, in the interim, to your letter, with its long quote from Camus, a partial response. And now, the mask returns.

Mask? The word is not true.

to mask: to conceal...

O-mote: is the word used in Noh: the face, the forefront.

So, the young lady disguises no one, conceals nothing.
She cannot mask. Only reveal.
She cannot give you her face, but you
can give her
your body

•

Last week, one late afternoon, I took the local to Fukakusa, *deep grass*, and walked up the sloped and careless shop-lined street into a red-fronted China-noodle server's. The only customer in the three table establishment, I sat with the man of the place and his womenfolk and watched for a while the high school baseball championships on an eight-inch screen, slurped my noodles and broth and then asked if Mr Takazawa's place was near. Oh yes! He picked his one-year old up off the street, set her in a stroller and, one-armed, husky, with a hearing aid, pushed upslope with me behind. We crossed a grass grown double track and on the way back I stopped to peer into the gatekeeper's shack, thinking it a nice place to read a book in, or watch people from.

We turned half-left, then up a narrow woodfence and mudwall lined dirt lane to a gate. "Takazawa-san! Takazawa-san!"– and when no one answered, baby in arm, he went round back. The gate opened. A hair-slicked blue-sweatered handsome youth said his father was out, gone, perhaps, to Nara.

Uneasy about keeping the mask in my hands any longer, fearful harm might come to it, I left it, with my name card: Will Petersen, English Consultant, Matsushita Electric Industrial Company, Ltd, Osaka – saying I'd be back within a few days.

Now that I'd finally taken the *waka-onna* to a man who could perhaps repair it, I'd still have to go back to him, ask what could be done, have to decide, whether to risk it, perhaps write another letter, mentioning possible alternatives – it might take weeks. Or a month? Or –?

It had lain out of sight in its bag in its box up on a shelf for far too long. I'd seen masks only on stage, alive. Or in the dressing room. I'd never really held one in hand. Once I was allowed to peer through. Takashi held it to my face: I was blinded: through the tiny holes bored through the wood I could see almost nothing.

I'd watched performers handle the masks respectfully, careful not to finger the surface. I'd watched them in front of the full-length mirror, humble, honouring the mask, then bowing into it, to sit erect, looking out at the face, the being, they'd lent their bodies to.

Or, I'd seen a few in museums, under glass. And, of course, in curio shops, and on walls, as decorations, or in souvenir shops, lifeless replicas. I suppose I hesitated out of a certain awe to take the mask from the shelf, or out of fear that I might drop it, damage it further. (That the face that was ill was dying, *that* I did not write. But the dream was in mind, and is vivid now: the faceless head, seen from behind, the gash in the neck...) And perhaps I hesitated (I said then, but know now) to take the mask to Takashi, to confront him with mutilation, so soon after his return from spinal surgery, still unsteady on his feet, to spare the crippled dancer the pain of beholding a marred face. (Yes, *that* I wrote to the dying painter. The dancer forced to lean on another's arm, the deaf musician, the painter who cannot hold a brush, the potter with arthritis, the illness of the art – aware of them all, beholden to them, feeling now, in my own forearms, an inflation: an increasing pressure. But a friend warms: Write, write. Don't stop.)

I hesitated, perhaps, feeling Takashi would think to himself: It's a shame. Fine masks are hard to come by, but here is this one, that ought to be under the stage's roof, exiled to a foreign land, divorced from a body that could let it live.

He studied it quietly. We sat in his bare tatami-matted room, the full-length mirror behind me. To my right, the tokonoma; in the place of honour, an old tsuzumi. Higher, hanging from the twisting polished post, a cheap, small dark green Greek mask I'd given him years ago.

He looked at *waka-onna* for a long time, holding the mask at arm's length, turning it, tilting it, ever so slightly, catching its subtly shifting expressions.

He covered her, returned her to her box. There are two mask-makers I can recommend, he said. Mr Takazawa, in Fukakusa, would be the right man for this one.

"Perhaps it could be touched up, the chipped surface restored. But, most likely the whole skin would have to be removed, a completely new face painted."

I shuddered. Your letters had spoken, particularly, of the sensitive quality of surface, the texture of the aged off-white. Was it worth risking all that for a chipped chin? Perhaps it would be better to return the mask, unretouched, mutilated, but with the old surface intact.

I hesitated. More weeks went by. But at last I had taken it to Takazawa. Now I would go back to him: to see what he had to say.
• •

Last night, at seven, I went to the station. In the wild wind-swept rain I steered the scooter cautiously. In the station I stalled over coffee. Then I ran, leaped into the coach as the doors hissed shut. Twenty minutes later I got off. The noodle shop was boarded up. At the double track a gatekeeper waved his lantern. An orange and green express, empty, rushed past.

A young man opened the gate, let me in, went back inside.

Unescorted, I stepped down unlit stone steps and into a passageway. A round woman, washing at a stone sink, laughed: Americans *are* tall, aren't you! I recited an old joke about big feet, excused my intrusion, pulled off my black rubber boots, and stepped up into a room.

A card game was going on.

Nodding to directions given by gesture, I crossed creaking boards, climbed steep dark steps. A seated Buddha, four feet high, surmounted a low table. Next to the ancient figure, in drab shirt, brown sweater, khaki pants, sat a man. Mr Takazawa, I supposed. I bowed. (But he didn't. He's had foreign visitors, I thought.) There, on the table, beside Amida Buddha's Lotus Seat lay a woman's face. Like the Jones', I thought. Here it is, he gestured. I'd come to *talk about* the repair. It's done, he said. Or didn't. Done? *How* did you do it? ? – I held it. No one could ever tell it had been damaged. Amazing. I suppose I seemed like a canned food consumer asking a farmer how in the world he ever managed to grow a stalk with real corn on it. Took the whole face off, he said. Did it over from scratch.

Incredible. The face was no different than I'd remembered it – the same aged off-whites, the time-browned edges, the sensitive skin texture, the delicate hairlines, the eyebrows like mist. Then I saw her double: another waka-onna on the tatami, off to my left. And her sisters, but only carved, still unpainted – and another, complete but for the mouth; and blocks of wood roughed out, and tiny ones, two inches high, his son's practice pieces. And old men, gaunt, and fearsome demons, and up under the ceiling, gathering dust, a fox, a god, a dragon. He brought forth masks from the 17th century, faces stripped of their skins, naked wood, but bearing traces of chalky underpainting.

Layers and layers of white, he said. And the wood must be aged. *Hinoki*, at least ten years old. Blocks of wood, some of them salvaged from old housebeams, stood around the cushion on which he sat to work. He removed a demon's face from a box: its ears had been gnawed off by temple mice.

I made some comments, asked some questions, trying to draw him out, to express his spirit. But his words were of craft: this is what he did, this is what he had done all his life, and he did nothing else. When he went to see Noh, he went to see masks. When he went to see masks he went to buy them, and after he bought them, when he tired of them, he sold them. Demons or animals or buffoons didn't interest him for more than the blink of an eye. Noh masks, yes – they had most to offer – and he referred to them as *men*, in plain speech, and not as *omote*, as Noh performers do, and said, yes, the female, for him, had most to offer, was most subtle.

But the talk was desultory, never penetrating, and my words were not always clear to him, which made me feel, sadly, he was hearing patterns and making small talk with a composite of all the foreign visitors he'd ever had. And for that reason, perhaps, he had to confirm his own identity, by showing me photographs of himself at various noteworthy places in company with other mask-makers, by showing me a newspaper clipping, with the headline declaring: NEW BOOM IN OLD THINGS, and finally displaying his collection of name cards, of American museum curators, and Frenchmen, and Italian scholars who had come to visit. Much like the Kyoto painter of "old Japan" listed in the tour guide, who opens his properly traditional house to tourists and, after flicking off a quick bamboo to Ooohs and Aaahs, or unrolling a scroll displaying dazzling virtuosity, tops the visit by showing his tastefully bound guest book of most distinguished signatures, while his wife properly, humbly, smiles.

The Tokugawa period masks, older than the history of the country claiming me as citizen, were so fine, and the man's own work so very sensitive, so profound, that from the man himself I expected – what? Was I, after all, a romantic, a seeker of saints, a naive believer in exotic mysteries? Did I come, hesitantly, expecting to meet a man who meditated for months before a block of wood before releasing its spirit? I'm not so sure. But I was certainly a man of 35, who was raised in a culture that cherished expression in a time that knew no craft. All the way home

I thought of traditions, of the craftsman, of art, of the study of Noh, and of my own work as a lithographer.

Before I left, a little after 9:30, still full of questions, I asked him if he could estimate how old the mask was. Certainly, he said. I can tell you precisely. The whole thing's a signature. I can tell by any number of signs, mainly by the character of the chisel cuts — like brushstrokes in a painting. Sure, he said. At a glance I can tell you who carved a particular mask, and when. Sure, no matter how old.

"So then", I repeated, "*How old* is this one?"

"I made *this* mask 15 years ago."

•

Back home, I observed how the simple wooden box had just the slightest curve to the lid. And then, when I laid the mask upon its brocade, noting the old orange of the cords glowing subtly against old whites, and the varied reds of the lips, enchanted by the shifting ever elusive expression, it all seemed of a sensitivity of ages long past. Such faces, surely, were beyond the hands and hearts of people of this world...

> (.....already wasted, but intense about life,
>   painting, the lake, his teaching and his
>   friends, Murray read the last chapter:
>   your letter about the mask-maker....)

TOM LOWENSTEIN
from Whale Hunt Journal, May 12-28 1977

I've been out four days now, sleeping in brief snatches and the mind associatively shuttles between Zen *sesshins* and memories of childhood holidays on chilly English North Sea beaches. Zen emptiness opens like a colourless flower, while on that bitter 1950 English shingle, stiff wet towels chafe salt into the thighs, teeth chatter, wind flings grit into the fish-paste sandwiches and we drink frugal draughts of diluted Kiora. Time passes, changes and repeats in the memory. Here on the ice, the emptiness is inhabited by scavenging sea birds, and the expectation of death to be followed by a rejoicing which is its contradiction.

*

Large white clouds whose darkened edges are like water-stains on Italian paper. Along with birds and mammals, hunters and the hunted, clouds migrate towards non-being.

*

The ice creaks. *Sikum inua atuqtuq*: "the ice spirit's singing." What does the ice sing? Like me, it sings:

> Aya-ya!
> "I'm cold.
> To the heart!"
> Aya-ya!
> *Oi vey!*

*

The weather howls. In tents and houses, the painful turbulence of men and women. Rugged, formidable joking. Big midwife Mamannina says, "Ariggaa! Fred qiaruaq, (Great! Fred was crying!)" The poor fellow, amiable, inept, has been managing the village store, and he's been caught on the take.

Mamannina mocks my rudimentary Eskimo and lisps my name, baby-fashion, parodying my perfectly good pronunciation: "Aniq-sua-yaaq uv-ang-a" (I am Aniqsuayaaq). She tears up my muscles and returns them to me as Jello. The ability to joke is a species of power. The harsher the joking, the greater your unassailability. The young are taught indifference to ridicule. On another level, they must constantly heed their shame, living like flayed rabbits until they stop making mistakes. Thus joking is action, a response to wrong action, and a sign of action. Note: Every non-Eskimo-speaking local child knows, among several words and phrases which they can't manipulate grammatically, the word for "scold", and uses it in English sentences. "My mama sure *suak* (scold) me!"

I have to get used to it too. At last year's hunt, I was scolded by women till my ears bled for not keeping the blubber stove hot enough. This year I am scolded for using too much fuel. If I could reconcile these two extremes, I might achieve insight. Or perhaps just one hot ear and one cold ear.

*

Footnote on Mamannina tearing muscles. She is a tribal healer, albeit a beginner, being trained by Della Keats in Kotzebue. Last year I sat on the floor of her house while she massaged my back. "You got all this meat round your shoulders twisted," she said. "Put your teeth in when you massage your ethnographer," I wanted to tell her.

The treatment was rough. Had Mamannina lived last century, her amulet animal would have been the brown bear. I thought of the story about the shaman who married, serially, a polar bear, brown bear and whale. When they started to quarrel, each animal laid a skin of her own species on the iglu floor and fought their husband. In each case, the man was torn to pieces, died, rose to kill his wife and marry the next one, thus exemplifying the archetypal shaman's career in progressive accumulation of power through dismemberment and rebirth ordeals. The wisdom we can derive from this kind of sequence is both spiritual and poetic and perhaps lies in allowing ourselves to be taken apart and consumed: embracing totality with such thoroughness that we disintegrate in its embrace. Those who can reassemble with a reintegrated psyche have perhaps undergone the equivalent of the archaic experience and live with re-forged connections with arcane forces. Subsequent deployment of "power" deriving from the ordeal is a minor part of this: this is what Buddhists often disdainfully call *siddhis* (magical powers). The higher path is to achieve a connection with the absolute and contemplate it without desire. The object being to see, not to appropriate, to analyse, not wield. But this is possible only in post-neolithic societies. Hunting culture shamans must both ingest and utilise their power, otherwise the tribe will die. The relationships between shamanism and yoga/Buddhism are clear. Yoga at its lowest is shamanism: the development of supranormal faculties, cataleptic dreaming, out of body soul flight. Shamanism, at its best, can bring enlightenment: what a Bering Sea Eskimo man described as mind and body illumination (*qaumaniq*): a lighting up from within the body: an up-rush of radiance flooding head and torso, just as endless summer fills the winter's body.... ("Thank you, Jesus, for this doughnut," I just heard Mammanina mutter, bless her.)

*

News on the radio of Jimmie Carter and Fritz Mondale. Whales, bears and seagulls also bring news of their campaigns with happy, but no less moribund, freedom. What, after all, can a shaman on the sea bed who marries into a polar bear family expect but to be irritated by his wife, while she in turn will insist on fighting him to the death?

*

There are two things in the tin: golden doughnuts fried in seal-oil, and hard-tack (pilot crackers). I reach for a doughnut. Mamannina says, "You're not supposed to eat that. Qaqqaulat are for naluagmiut (crackers are for white men), doughnuts for Eskimos." Mamannina is joking, but she also means what she says, and if I were silly enough – as I was last year – to argue, we could have a devilish row, and I'd end up on the brown bear-skin, my flayed meat steaming... Inupiaq people identify with what they eat: each village allying itself with the animals it loves, knows and kills. Thus, whale in Point Hope; fish, muskrat, caribou, and black bear along the Kobuk River...

It goes further than this. Hunting the whale and then ingesting it and storing its meat underground on the Point, both Point Hope land and its people become whales. In which connection Agviqsiina ("whale-man") said to me as we watched a brown bear moving across Cape Dyer last year:

"When that bear sniffs me, he thinks 'Ah, maktak! (whale-skin).' When he sniffs you, that bear smells hamburger..." ("But kosher," I stopped myself from adding.)

Likewise Suuyuk said: "It's a good thing you like my food. If you didn't like it, you couldn't be my friend." Both physical and social survival in the community are predicated on the meat-ceremony. The most basic human contact beyond language and sex lies in sharing food. In a hunting society where meat has a part in most activity, there can be no participation without sincere and happy commitment to this. My greed, which in my other life I would prefer to conceal, is a mark of courtesy here.

But Mamannina is presumably aware of an irony in her remark about doughnuts. Certainly these treats are, on account of the sea mammal oil in which they sizzle, special to this locality. But the recipe is Euro-American, the first flour-based cooking having been introduced to the village by whaler-traders in about 1880. Asatchaq has told several stories in which flour soup and pancakes feature. And the innovating shaman Atangauraq shattered whaling taboo in ca. 1885 when he took women out to his whaling camp so that they could cook for his crew. And while carbohydrate-based foods helped replace the wild game resources that the white man had over-hunted, new foods eaten in combination with meat and oil also entered the old taboo system. Thus the ghost of a woman who had fried hotcakes with the wrong kind of fat down at Cape Thompson in about 1890 appeared in a dream to Asatchaq's father-in-law to explain the consequences of her dietary infraction. It should also be said, in defence of two opposing points of view that 1. pilot crackers entered the native diet during the same decades, but that 2. they seem not to have been incorporated into dietary regulations. There may thus after all be some justice in Mamannina's comment.

*

The lament of Sarah, middle-aged umialik, about the younger set and hard times in general. Spoken at breakfast:

"Those boys never come to camp now...They're too lazy. The girls don't come either. They start coming at the beginning of *umiaqtuq* (whaling), but then they get bored. The teenagers aren't interested anymore. They want to go sleep in town. They don't do anything. Coal is so expensive. We're running out of *siqpan* (blubber) for the stove. Not much driftwood either... no driftwood on the north beach, and the trail along the south beach is terrible..."

More on this later. But there's an historical synchrony to Sarah on driftwood and Mamannina's observation about doughnuts. Carbohydrate entered the local diet during the same difficult years as when Euro-American whaler-traders plundered the south beach for their ship's furnaces. After the whalers left in about 1910, the driftwood deposits grew again. But once native people started to build European-style houses and abandon seal-oil heating lamps in favour of wood-burning stoves in the 1920s, the beach was again denuded of driftwood. When imported oil became the heating staple of the mid-1960s, the driftwood piled up again and there's plenty on the south beach.

*

"Don't wake me in the morning!" said Umik only half-humorously last night before turning in. We all lay down on caribou skins and wrapped ourselves in old chicken-feather sleeping bags. We slept from 1 a.m.to 3.30. The stove went out at 2 a.m. and I woke cold, grabbed my parka (white and stiff with frost) and have just managed to warm up when someone knocks on the tent-frame. "Whales out there! Two whales!" "Let them go by," I secretly pray. But Umik gets up. Sarah gets up. I pretend to sleep until someone pokes my leg. "Whale. Get up!" I hunt my socks. They're cold and wet. Umik is saying, "Where's my hat? Where's my gloves? Where's my kamikluks (trousers)?" jabbing his voice good humouredly but also in a sleep-fuddled and disoriented imperative. Sarah is already up and priming the Coleman stove to boil water.

I stumble outside. The ice hits my eyes painfully, but the wind's dropped since yesterday. Danny and Gordon are there, and we stumble round the skinboat, unloading caribou skins and rifles. We wrench the boat round on its sled till the prow faces the water and start pushing along the trail through a gap in the pressure ridge and so towards the ice-edge.

There are four of us dragging the boat. It's not far to the water, and although the trail's rough, the sled-runners move easily. Down by the lead, great new fissures in the ice have opened. There are gulches, ultramarine, immeasurably deep, into which the whole crew, boat and all, might be swallowed at a single shudder of the ice-pack. We fix our windbreak into ice-rocks that I piled up yesterday. The invisible crack by the windbreak still creaks noisily. We stand in the tremendous silence which is broken only by the movement of this deep internal fault. "It must need oiling," says Umik. He chops a narrow gap in the ice as though starting to excavate the entire sea.

The sea is empty. After an hour, we see one whale far to the north of us. Then one more. The wind is steady and cold. A few glaucous gulls. Streaks of strato-cumulous, white on blue sky, whiter above the horizon.

10 a.m. Eight whales cross the horizon. They blow drifting triangles of vapour that collapse as suddenly as they rise. One travels closer to us. It breaches and we see the white blaze on its tail. "Like water-proof boot" (with its white seal-skin banding) one man murmurs.

> "his-flippers-
> Holy-cow-   I-see-'em..."

murmurs Umik, his voice undulating with the whale's movement, the words *his-flippers* rising and falling like whale's breath.

*

Sarah came to the village in the 1960s from Kiana, a river community about two hundred miles south of us. Eskimo outsiders have a hard time here. "Times have changed since I first came," she laments. "They always used to dance when they caught a whale. Nowadays it's only Bingo, only Bingo." This is not even half-true, but sufficiently to the point to preoccupy an observant, semi-marginal resident's musing.

Sarah continues, "Mamannina is good, the way she comes down to camp with us. She's a bit noisy sometimes," (Sarah wrinkles her nose), "but she's tough. Not like me..." Two women more different would be hard to find. Mamannina is the village bone-setter, masseuse and general shaman, with that lacerating female Tikigaq scorn whirling from her like randomly aimed whips. Sarah, by contrast, is vulnerable, nervous and socially on the margins. Like many Kobuk people, she is soft-spoken, with a contemplative passivity that masks her tough-mindedness.

I respond to Sarah's remark with a sort of laughing assent. Laughter here is a concomitant of language and has a code of its own. There's the laugh of the skinboat owner which proclaims modesty and self-deprecation. There's the laughter of chagrin which acknowledges pain as an unavoidable component of existence. There is laughter that rasps cruelly from the throat like knife blades. Wild, often hysterical, laughter reels out of the chest in great ribbons of ectoplasm. (This in response to self-critical clowning, especially when there's death in the story, the fool-narrator having narrowly escaped being drowned or eaten alive.) There's also the empathic but self-protective laughter which says, "I understand what you're saying, but factors too numerous and complicated to go into forbid me to take sides." I'm hoping that Sarah has interpreted my laugh as such.

*

There's competition between the younger men at whale-camp over how much sleep you can do without. "I haven't slept for three days." "I haven't slept *four* days." "*Saglu!* (lies). You slept two hours yesterday..." The important thing is vigilance. This must always be in the spirit of challenge. We watch through one long skein of day, interspersed with timeless speculation, stories and the rhythm of migrations. The light suffuses memories of land and night, bleaching the negatives that lie packed in the unconscious. Sea, light, daylight spirits. In the origin myth, the raven creator, light-streaked peregrine and toccatas of air...

*

I visited Suuyuk's camp about half a mile north of us today. The trail along the ice-rim is easy, but there are many rough patches where I fall into pot-holes.

Suuyuk's is a big, prestigious, high-competence whale-crew and I'm nervous about my visit. I have left two undermotivated and inexperienced people back at Umik's. At Suuyuk's, there are eight men by the boat, with others in the tent and in the village who'll come out as reinforcements. It isn't just the size of the crew that gives it status. Suuyuk is a big man, a successful hunter who also prospers within the American economy as a heavy-machine operator and site foreman on North Slope develop-ment projects, which includes our village move. Twice mayor,

Suuyuk flies regularly to Barrow for Native Corporation meetings and his prestige gives him the pick of the village for his whaling crew, which therefore has an almost arrogant balance of weathered older men and tough young hunters.

I approach from the south of Suuyuk's camp through the frozen carcasses of eight flayed belukhas. Belukhas yield a delicious white *maktaaq* (skin and blubber), but the meat is full of parasites and it's left out for the foxes and gulls. These great corpses lie in their frozen blood like rusted submarines or burned out Spitfire fusilages. One freshly caught belukha is still moist and gleaming. A slit is opened in the body and a greenish, transparent sack comes flopping out on a meat-hook. This was a pregnant female I realize with horror. The thin elastic tissue of the uterus is slashed with a knife, and the baby tumbles with a splash onto the ice: glistening, perfect, eyes blind behind their epicanthine folds. It has a delicate semitic nose, the whole creature curled like an ammonite or prawn, suspended between life and death and ineluctably exposed now. The cord, thick as a hose-pipe, is cut and the blood gushes. The creature has a tiny penis. The skin is storm-cloud grey, delicate and silky. I am aghast with terror and compassion.

*

Just south of Umik's camp is a bay with high cliffs of ice, flat on top and studded at the base where the water, lit by the ice to an intense ultramarine, drips and washes. Within this bay, a small flock of old squaw duck float peacefully in mating pairs and call "*a-haa-lliq! a-haa-lliq!*" which is their name in Inupiaq. These unpremeditated phonemes hit the ice and echo back in naked is-ness. Bird call and words travel, are deflected, break in two, and drop in the sea...

*

Mamannina responds to an ethnographic joke I make about no-longer existent half-sibling partnerships. These are the brothers and sisters people acquired in the traditional period when their parents practised spouse-exchange with couples from another region to cement trade relations. Mamannina's laughter blasted my joke away and I've forgotten what I said. It was probably something like "Maybe she was my *qatangun* (sister by another parent)."

M was born about twenty years after the spouse exchange system was obliterated by the Christian marriage vow, but she knows all about it and her mind, so I imagine, fills with strangely competing constructs: the ancestors as ideal figures pursuing lives that were whole and unspoiled but which were nonetheless discredited by missionaries. The fact that M's grandfather was a black whaler-trader who cohabited with an Inupiaq woman at the Jabbertown station in about 1910 lends the paradox a further complication. Every apparently simple phenomenon has internal paths that lead to yet more veils and layers.

"Taaa-aam!" (Tom). M's voice starts high, descends along the vowel and vibrates on the nasal before the hum is abruptly clipped. She is communing with my name: first ingesting it and then singing it through her body. All one needs in Inupiaq for the soul to be evoked and stroked, is *atiq*, name. It was all right to entertain her with my allusion to the archaic but I probably trade a little too easily on this kind of saucy antiquarian privilege. But I can't help enjoying the flirtatious glee with which my older friends who know about the traditional world greet what must seem like bizarre pedantic episodes of mania and showing off. People who were born after ca 1930 both long for and abominate the dangerously rich textures of their grandparents' lives and beliefs. I can move around in it because I am immune. But I sometimes get the feeling that people are afraid that I'm dealing with contaminated matter.

KRISTIN PREVALLET
from I, Afterlife:
Essay in mourning time

PREFACE

The narrative goes something like this:

My father walked into a hospital. Outpatient. He was suffering from severe panic attacks. He was sleeping two hours a night. He had to fill out a form: Name, address, birthdate. Is the patient suicidal? He checked "no." The next week, he drove to a gun store and bought a revolver. The next week, he drove to a parking lot and shot himself in the head.

Before this, he made an appointment to see a psychiatrist, and got a prescription for Paxil. The psychiatrist gave him a form: Name, address, birthdate. Are you suicidal? He checked "no." He only saw the doctor once.

There are numerous studies that link Paxil to suicide, but because he was depressed there is no reasonable proof that he was not suicidal before he took the Paxil. So this is a story that leaves a wide margin of doubt, a story that is not about probable cause.

On the day he died, November 20, 2000, it was overcast, but not too chilly. It's possible that he had tried to go to the gym at 5 a.m. At some point, he bought *The Denver Post* because he used it to cover the windows of the car.

At 8 a.m. some kids from the neighborhood were on their way to the park. They saw the lone car in the parking lot, with the windows covered in newspaper. They peeked in and saw a man slumped over the steering wheel. One thought he saw blood on the man's ear. They called the police.

The police came to the house and asked, "had the victim been expressing suicidal thoughts?" They gave my stepmother a pamphlet, which included advice on how not to feel guilty. The pamphlet advised against building a shrine.

My stepmother wanted to see the body, to say a proper goodbye. The police told her to call the coroner's office. She called. They said, "You can't see the body. We'll leave his hand outside of the sheet for you."

We collected dried flowers from the garden and wrote letters so that my father would have something to open when he woke up on the other side. Zinnias, peonies, poppies, and strawberry bush brambles. We were trying to fill in the gap.

The report from the scene is the police-side of the story. 1) They searched for a pulse. 2) They established identity. 3) They took photos. 4) They wrote down descriptive phrases. (They investigated to make sure no foul play was involved.)

No evidence exists to call this "murder" because it cannot be proven that any outside force caused this violent act to occur. Internal violence is too intangible to be considered "proof."

So, as I was saying, after three days of being on Paxil, he drove eleven miles to Rocky Mountain Guns & Ammo on Parker Road and purchased a Colt revolver for $357. I asked my sister, "Who was driving? The man or the medicine?"

He signed a form: self protection. So, a man walks into a store and buys a gun for self protection. But self protection cannot protect the man from himself. I said to my brother, the logic escapes me.

The bumper sticker on his car read, "Conflict is inevitable, violence is not." The police didn't make a note of it on their report. The man who sold him the gun probably didn't notice.

The scene: a baseball field, in the heart of Englewood, Colorado. A field, and behind the field, a thick grove of trees concealing a bike path. One single and solitary tree sits off to the side of the field. A parking lot. He parked the car in the eighth spot, facing the solitary tree. When I went to investigate a few days later, I found a pile of glass. From this evidence I deduced his location at the time of death.

But this is not the whole story. The whole story is gaping with holes. The "hole" story is conflicted, abstract, difficult to explain.

Sublimation: when solid becomes ether without passing through the liquid state. When the overflow of negative psychic energy is rechanneled into writing, or art. When the distance between living and dying is filled in with language, objects, people, and mundane activities, such as doing the dishes. When something difficult to articulate finds its form in poetry. When death (silence) is brought back to life (mythology).

Regardless, the story has many possible forms and many angles of articulation. This is elegy.

EULOGY

When a person has died the order of their things is weighed down by the fact that they will not be returning to move them. So the order of their things becomes a shrine; the order is preserved for as long as possible. Until it is clear that the person has actually left the room. I know this because the night after my father died I lay in bed half asleep and half awake. A panic began to overtake me, and I could not lie still. I clutched my head and walked into the dark living room: the panic was all around. The ceiling became shards of glass – they fell all around me. I lit a candle to calm the panic because it was as present as a person. I lay on the couch and stared at the candle. Beside me, his stack of books. He never stacked his books. They were always stacked as if he had been rumbling through, looking for something. He didn't seem to read books from cover to cover. On the top: *Manual of Zen Buddhism* by D T Suzuki. The book looked as if it had just been purchased from Barnes and Noble. He had stopped reading at page 30, *The Kwannon Sutra*. He scribbled the following notes on pages 14, 15, 16, 23, 26, and 29:

> *Vow to extinguish passion.*
> *Perfect quietude – wisdom of absolute identity.*
> *To keep one's thought pure.*
> *(The birth + death of attachment. Blissful Tranquility beyond*
> *   birth + death).*
> *Nirvana is eternal, ever blessed, free from defilements.*
> *Blessed One Enlightened One.*
> *Self – nature is empty, Form is emptiness. We are not born,*
> *   we are not annihilated.*
> *Emptiness means the absolute or something transcendental.*

We are not born. We are not annihilated. So where are we? Shards of glass on the edge of breaking. On the verge of refracting a way through, to another world. That this world be shard, the one beyond, smooth as glass. I never talked with my father about ghosts. Except that once, we encountered one.

There is a story about an old man who encounters the ghost of who he wants to be; there is a story about a man and the mountains. Like any sea these mountains have a name, they are called "Rocky," and upon the crest of the range there is a trail that enables a person to walk across five states and through five separate ecological life zones.

There is also a story about a specific point on a specific trail. Follow the crest of the range. The thick groves of aspen and pine open onto a clearing. Much like being on a boat in the middle of a tumultuous sea, watching as the waves slowly calm. The moment when the world beyond the waves suddenly opens up to all of the possible worlds that are hiding within it. And things are finally clear: there is a place on earth where the sky and the mountain like the mountain and the sea are one in the same: the mountain piercing the watery sky and the sky flowing down over the mountain.

> *The clarity of the sky prevents its falling. The firmness of the earth prevents its splitting. The strength of the spirit prevents its being used up. The fullness of the valley prevents its running dry. The growth of ten thousand things prevents their dying out.*
>
> (TAO TE CHING)

One day, my father took me to a specific trail on the mountain and there we met an old man. His face was worn with tough wrinkles; he wore a hat that was tattered but functional; he was well-layered and his backpack was as big, and perhaps as heavy, as a deer.

He told us that he had been walking the trail since Montana, that he had been walking for three years, and during those years the only people he saw were the people he met on the trail.

We were amazed by this man, his endurance, his loneliness, his withdrawal from the world, his persistence in walking, the fact that through walking he had *become* the mountain, that indeed there was really no way to separate him from the mountain because it had made its impression on him.

He could have been the sprit of the mountain, he could have been a ghost, he could have been the breeze of the aspen as it brushed through the fur of a hare.

This old man made me see that my father was utterly disconnected from the ground he was walking on. I noticed how he was walking ahead of me with a pace not at all suited for the terrain. Unlike the old man, my father's questions – about the cosmos, space, time, the universe, the one God of the present and the many gods of ancient times, the galaxy and the peace of being in nothingness – were not rooted in his experience of walking, here and now, through the mountains. It seemed to me that these questions were in fact sending his mind into a spiral of confusion that gave him no insight into how to live a life worth leading.

I too am occupied by all the questions of my father, and like him I wonder if the void is too great, if time is too vast, if humanity is too imperfect; and like him I sometimes wonder if it all isn't remarkably futile, if enduring the persistance of fear and disappointment in our lives makes sense in the quest for an overall purpose.

This story, about a man who meets the ghost of who he wants to be, has already been told, over and over:

> the man has disappeared, no traces are left, the bright moonlight is empty and shadowless with all the ten thousand things growing on it, if anyone should ask the meaning of this, behold the lilies of the field and their fresh sweet-scent.   (D T SUZUKI)

STEPHEN WATTS
Nonno

I

I can hear a man walking in front of me down the slabbed road. That should not surprise me. Nothing should surprise me in this sharp attenuated air. I know who it is: it is you, nonno, going in your hobbled boots on the uncambered roadway down from Precasaglio to the town of Ponte. You are just entering the town's edge, going past the first stone house. Soon you will go through the gap where the road forms the ground floor of the arched house. I know without the shadow of a doubt that it is you and you are twenty-two years old and you have just decided, suddenly and in finality that you must leave these mountains and go. Painful that decision: but also without pain, holding the complexity of a world in one body and soul. But it never flick- ered through you then, that I would have to come and find you almost ninety years later. I can hear you, nonno, a handful of metres in front of me. Your footfalls ring out from the cold flags. I can almost reach out and touch you, yet always you just elude me. It is firm but dreamlike, this vision of migration, this startled geography, this life stuttered with sudden clarity. Are only dreams the most real, dreams and death? Why does such invisible loss seem the most palpable? Or does death release what is real while our being alive is but a coursing of pretence and sleep? Even these sharp and lovely moments of lucidity during daytime lives have to be likened to tiny deaths. Even though we love being alive and live our loves with passion. It is winter, grandfather, and you have just left the village of Pre- casaglio. You have just walked out of that bird-scooped cluster of houses hung above the raging river where young women wash clothes clean. Bird-scooped. You've walked the ridges and cart-ruts of the road. The snow-enclosed cemetery of the mountains. The church where your carved altar-rail still stands keeping separate the priest from his people. Past the flower-drained meadows and appendicitis fields. The road-fork at the church of Zoanno. The zag of the road going down to the workshop of the carpenter Ferrari. His turbid river at the corner still some distance out of Ponte. Along the narrow level in spate with the river you walk a hundred years before me and still I see you down the gradient as it plunges a little into the town (superb to look under the casual bridges and see the exploding waters). Under the floor of the road-arced house. Past the votive Virgin you painted when you were seventeen on the outer wall of Santini Giacomo's house. The oldest part of the town, changed little from how you knew it. That perhaps is why I am able to tear a gap through the veil of history and see you. That is why I can hear you now at this end of the final century and listen to the history of your migration at its beginning. That is why a little reality can flow back through me by the rip of its veil. I thought I would not be able to finish this fiction but now maybe I can. Or start it at least and let it ravel to reality. I can hear you there in front of me, the hob of your shoes spitting on austere flags. In front of me almost a century ago. What else should there be left to hear? Is it as if sounds were still so air-struck and clear? What has memory done? Down one side of the valley everything freezes, down the other are villages, earth, bodies, stone, grass in sunlight. Sat in a cart and pulled by a horse I can hear you breathing. Your stuff of life. In no time you will reach Milan. Then time will spin backwards until you swivel through Paris and get to London. But, nonno, how can I talk to you when I never met you in my life? How is this discourse possible and the only one that has sustained me through my tiny deaths? Such moments of reality to lead to a sort of ecstasy. Such endings at the beginning that are always …

2

There is a place above the last cluster of homes but before the final and sometimes inhabited *baita*, where the path crests a hill and flattens out a little and there is almost a small field of scorched tree stumps, where you know that something once happened, though quite what or when is not clear. There is an atmosphere of slight desolation, that is all, but it is enough to begin a story. It may have been where a number of friends, herders fetching sheep in the fourteenth century, were overtaken by a sudden and unexpected avalanche, sheep and dogs and herders scattered and four of the men killed outright, just smashed about. Or it may have been where the village priest, on his way down from the high *baite* having delivered unction to a dying parishioner three centuries later, was waylaid in the dusk going on dark by some bandit who thought him someone else and who spent his own next twenty years trying to resist the overwhelming sense of guilt until he drowned himself in icy waters unable to throw off at last the black mood of despair. Or it may have been that a middle-aged mother one winter's afternoon swooned by worry at the sudden illness of her latest child carried the babe wrapped in blankets down toward the village but slipped on the black ice of the path and cracked her lowest vertebra, the two of them held there in the gloom and savage frost of the night, she dead in the morning huddled over him and he moaning slightly under her dead weight. Just so we walk paths, like the lone traveller in Dürer's winter scene getting past the frozen pond and equally frozen meadows while freezing birds drop out of the sky and in a far distance the white mountains glimpsed bring unaccountable tears to our eyes, that though we stop to watch even so we inevitably carry on. Or it could have been that partisans coming down off the white zones of the war were ambushed here by traitors of the occupying force and killed not far from their homes, or alternatively that partisans ambushed their fellow citizens of the different persuasion, and that murders were done quickly harshly and brutally leaving a savage mess for dear ones to find, though the partisanning must have been from centuries gone since acts from but one lifetime ago would have carried their own clear story to our ears and eyes. Or there as in the painting by Brueghel we must have seen ravens in the cold and grey air as travellers passed by toward what burst stories or shattered zones we could hardly dare to imagine. What is it about time that stops or in that place where the slope evens out, flattening time totally, and a patch of scorched stumps indicate trees, trees that might almost have been human. There in precisely that place five thousand years back, perhaps five thousand exactly for all I know, a shaman left behind his slaughtered son, wiped a reject of blood on his face and his tongue and walked the few hours up to the hanging glacier by whose edge he invoked geologies we can hardly conjure and ate some parts of the mushroom de magica right before immersing his body in the fissure's crevice, flaming with ice, from where he was carried down all these years to be deposited unambiguously and clinically at our moraine's edge flanked by trees that would be cut down and burnt. Whichever or all of these might have happened on this grass, there is an atmosphere here where the trees thin out to charred stumps, an aura that is strange to define …

3

What happened to us in those years? What happened in the interims that we have got to where we are now? What happened after we'd established the family tree in the house of Annibale? What happened to his son and his daughter who were well doing in school back then? What happened to his nephews who drove lorries across Europe and his nieces who waited in their kitchens and domains? How did it occur among the youth of those years that so many took to their veins dirty needles, that so many shared the communal fix from the goodness of their hearts, from the darkness of their bloods, from their urge to share and not to disdain each other. What happened to Annibale's son that his photograph got into the wall-niche of the snow cemetery before Annibale himself could get there. What white powders gave them succour in those bloated winters. Each snowless day Annibale walks up past Sankt Apollonia of the butters and cheese to his *baita* where once Luigi drove me in his four-wheel through ice flows and frozen speckled pastures in an astonishing scatter of driven skills. There is a photograph of me on the snow-path, grey-hair cropped, walking shorts, a glass in my hand, a smile on my face, a delight to have held history in my hands, to have held history back a short while and looked four-square into its poor face. Every written word is lost to time, it comes a second, a minute, a century after speech or act or the science of speech acts or the violence of friendship or the silence of snow. The last time I was in Annibale's house in Precasaglio, we had just come out of a little local harvest gala in Gadda's church and walked the thirty or so metres to Annibale's blue door. There he opened it and we went through into his living room and in a while back to the kitchen, the place where real conversations happen, and we were joined by many and no-one, and stories blossomed from the beams and dialect flowed and red wine and salami and breads. This was another gala, unrepeatable language in the backroom of an old house, beyond the power of speech, beyond the confines of politics. This is what can only be interrupted by time or assassination or white powder or the poverty of capitalism in the heart. All of us gathered in the small room, no-one on ceremony, no-one caring about pretence or appearance, all as we were with song and talk. But what happened in those years, that span between the appearance of the family tree in Annibale's front room and the gala of shared speech in the back one? What in the boredom of village winters, in the archive of repudiated histories, in the hands that throttle time, what in the parasitic visitations of the rich and infamous or the parabolas of war, what in all this drove the children to white powders and a sweet share-out of contaminated needles? What drove them to deal and fix in the brown sugars of glad time? The last I saw of Annibale he was walking fixedly in the summer sun, past the meadows beyond Precasaglio where old women in blue work-shifts and shawls still raked hay into tiny wains in the first years of the twenty-first century: Annibale on his way again to the *baite* and the storehouse of memory, lament maybe in his mind but more than that the sanguine knowledge of our lives and celebration of the galas of language and commune. My grandfather had walked there a century before arm in arm with his contemporary the Pezzo priest, and no doubt the same had flowered through their minds and hearts, for what changes in the micas of blood, or the flakes of sperm or of kissing eggs, or the white powders of contaminated time?

4

Nonno, didn't you love trees as much as I love trees? I'm sure you must have done. You must have walked up beyond Canè or up Gran Viso and gone through thinning trees until the last few remain stormed in late spring by white horses. Look, this is a matter of meditation, of meditation where time stands still and whole worlds can be sucked in or out of white and black holes! This is what history is, not the batter of commerce, not the mass murder of innocents by imbeciles, not the constraint of hope by injunction. Trees turn into people and people into trees, as surely as a sleeping man in his troubles becomes a cockroach. Haven't you seen high spruce bent slightly in the wind in the final meadows near the tree-line, how they sway and soak into bone and skin, how they moan and dance into blood and heart, how the bole is like a tower of blood and bone is meshed into the memory of bark. Dear heart, we destroy trees for our own peril. Or can I describe for you a circle of sycamores in St James's Park: how their great bowl of air swirls and dances, how their always-smaller-becoming arms and branches capillary themselves in the fortunate air. Here between the halls of a parliament and a banal regal house we can squeeze out a free space for breath! Or in the old oaks and blackthorn of Hyde Park, or a single lost tree beside the Thames. Or the superb deciduous woodlands on the borders of Easter Sutherland and Easter Ross, or the spring festival in Glen Lyon. I once stood up through the roof of a car moving slowly through an avenue of old larch in West Lothian. I once was mesmerised by a single white-thorn at a junction of the Ochill Hills. I once was unable to leave sight of a single stately holm oak not far from Stroud until my friends half-dragged me silent away. And I'm talking now just of the trees of one island! Think of the trees in the Alps. Or those trees by the railway in Satyajit Ray, in Tagore, or the flayed riverrine memory of Ghatak & others in places I've never been able to go. One time, Nonno, I lived three years on an island without trees! And it was so, so beautiful! An island and a moorland and a bandaged sun! Always a bandaged sun! And a moorland made from decayed trees, a shepherd's cloak of peat laid down on scoured ancient rock, across the scar-line of mountains, on schists cooled from the heat of magmas at great depths, on little protuberances amid the rocking seas. Our history, a seat beneath a bandaged sun: from galaxy to gaeltacht, from binary codes to *baita*, veins and capillaries mapped in the skies, models of life in the code of a leaf, the colours of butterflies' wings more complex than even our eyes. That is why, Nonno. That is why it all matters: your being born in the mountains and then your leaving the mountains and your life in a new city, with all the global tinynesses in between. If I write these things in both joy and despair, it may be because I've not eaten enough these past days, months and years, please forgive me.

5

If I were to try to describe Silvi's house, I would find it almost impossible, though in some ways it is not unlike my own home in London. But Silvi's is on the outskirts of the mountain town, really outside it on the main road that runs above the village of Pontagna, the cluster of houses where Silvi was born. It is a large house, not only the basement for storing cheese and salamis but two storeys and a loft in addition to the ground floor and all the rooms high-ceilinged. Moreover each floor has four rooms and to the side there is a yard and stables and hut-ments and enclosed chicken runs and covered corners. Silvi's father had it built in 1919, a strange time after the war and used it not only to house their family, including at times uncles and aunts and cousins, but also as the office and stage post for the carts and horse-trucks he ferried goods with between the rail-head at Edolo and the town of Ponte. Probably the war had served him quite well, with all the soldiering and trade that Gadda refers to in his *Giornale di Guerra*. There is a photograph from the workshop of Pino Veclani dating I imagine from the early 1920's, a sepia print of three shepherds leading a flock of sheep along the road away from Ponte. Silvi's house is in the near mid-distance, perhaps two hundred metres behind the sheep, standing on its own in the morning sunlight and its huge sloping outhouses in shadow and cool for storage. It stands there in wide isolation starkly but warmly and in total contrast to its present setting since the whole road on both sides is now crammed with modern and expensive houses. Indeed Silvi's house that must now be sold is also today expensive and in a way that would have dumbfounded Silvi and her father since the whole impoverished upper valley has been transformed by the tourisms of skiing. But it is not this makes Silvi's house so extraordinary, but rather the fact that it is almost wholly unchanged inside from the mid-1950's and in some ways totally unchanged from when it was first built over eighty years ago. Because Silvi after the death of her mother in 1964 never threw a single thing out: what couldn't be given to the pigs or chickens or manured for the vegetable garden or stored in the cool of the basement or burnt in the fireplaces, what couldn't be disposed of naturally or given away was, in its entirety and its complex quotidian variety, simply left in her home. In this way many rooms retained their ancient beds only one of which Silvi slept in and that in a room piled high with clothes and old clothes and furniture. The yard retained its ancient farm and garden implements, its harnesses and halters, its cheese packs and butter churns, its sheep bells and bum-shaped tractor's seats, its horse tackle and its horse, for Silvi lived on there with the animals. If an inventory were made – or the attempt at – of the contents of Silvi's house even now five years after her death and in its empty months before any final sale, if an inventory were to be made a whole domestic and social history of the past century would ravel and unwind and furl itself into openness of our faulty senses. But the house now must be sold, because Silvi in her years of abandoning her home and her self, in her years of sadness and her years of work, in her years of giving and giving and giving, forgot to leave her home to her nearest dearest and thus the house – far from being upkept in its most pristine disorder of abandoned disinterest – must be sold for the purpose of legal equality and with regard to long-left sisters in Vienna and Graz.

6

Nonno, I am walking behind you. You are walking down Frith Street. You are holding by the hand a young girl, perhaps six years old. She is your eldest daughter, my mother, and you go into the café at No 13. I follow you in. I am the young man in a woollen hat who looks across at you from time to time and who you are absently gazing over at. I remind you of a Polish or a Catalan anarchist, but more likely I am an Iranian revolutionary from the time of Mussadegh. For how long will anything last? It seems I am much older than my mother. It seems I see her across the café air and she is a brave little girl. I say to myself "there is my mother and she is hardly past six". Claustrophobic in the corner of the table. From time to time you look across at me and increasingly the shadow of a worry passes across your smile. Only some time later will it occur to you how appalled you were by my presence, fear at a politics you didn't really know, despite Malatesta. You are thinking how difficult it is to get good waiters these days, you are saying as much to Gaetano Crammeri who comes from the same village and almost the same house as your wife in Switzerland. "If you could find for me just two good waiters …" Nonno, I am walking behind you and you are perturbed. Because the blue bag slung across my back might not contain its wet fish and ginger, its ciabatta and fresh pasta that I am carrying for my mother eighty years later. I will cook it, pasta and fish with some tarragon when I get to her house. From the wine shop on Old Compton Street. God knows what fruits of the market may grow in our hearts. But I am interested only in you and in the girl who is going to be my mother. And for now, while I am intently observing the art and craft of your posture and conversation, you are drinking coffee with a finger of grappa and trying to fathom the credentials of possible waiters with your friend Crammeri. Your daughter is bored by all your business and talk. Dreadfully bored and she cannot stand cafés and moreover she cannot understand your Italian, much less the dialects you are trading with Gaetano. She is trapped by you against the café's walls, between the table and bench back without even a window to look out from and you have forgotten her existence there. "Papa" she is trying to say but cannot. Curt and rapid sentences splinter about her and you have misheard her caged voice. I from across the tables can smell hay and cow's breath and meadow flowers and I know that something will break inside her soon. Something from that array will wet her a very little, unexpectedly and she will whimper a few steps on the way home. Still young, from here will grow a great need to be alone, together with a yearning not to be when she is. Sewn tightly inside her and then petalling open. I am the anarchist from the year 1912. Nonno, you are going out again into Frith Street and I too will get up in a few minutes. You will buy pasta, some tagliatelle, wine, tarragon, tomatoes, mountain cheese. And a brown coat for my mother, just in time you remember Nina had told you to pick it up from Arturo's. And now she is sitting here in her eighty-sixth year with myself the anarchist at this other table. We are under a cherry tree in the mountain town, under the cherry tree planted in the front fork of the hotel garden, looking out into brown time, talking a little to the waitress who has brought us some tea and whose English is broken but not broken too far ...

7

Nonno, I had a dream. Fire destroys memory and memory is overwhelmed by flames. I dreamt that fires were raging across the whole of Europe. They were preceded by months of spring drought and at first there were isolated forest and scrubland fires in parched parts of Portugal and Italy and southern France. But then they spread and became more continuous, both in time and space. By the middle of August the whole continent seemed one fiery inferno: or black scorched on brown. Even the parched boglands of Tipperary and Cashel treeless as they were had scorched and burning mosses and top-peat. Even the northernmost treelines of Scandinavia and the high Alps and Pyrenees were reduced to stir-pots of ash and a dried grey scum. Cities were not spared at all. I thought as I dreamt this that there must have been signs or precedents, and I recalled fires in Sardinia and Corsica, fires on Majorca and in the wooded hinterlands of Lisbon, of trees struck down by lightning in the high Alps or the remote Scottish Highlands, of stark tree stumps in the midst of mild fields. I thought of the

National Library in Sarajevo bomb-burnt to rubble and of the
solitary cellist playing chords on huge lumps of stone. I thought
of all the times fires had been lit across Europe in desperate
attempts to keep warm. I thought of the dream some mind-
madman – maybe it had been Jung in his beatific calm – had had
in the months before war, of a great flood of yellow water ris-
ing up around the Alps and engulfing even them. And I thought
of the waters of the Vltava, Danube and Elbe-Labe – alter-egos
to fire, sisters in love and destruction – rising through their cities
of Praha and Dresden and Budapest and wreaking their havoc
and damage. Fire destroys memory, nonno, fire destroys every-
thing and of a sudden nothing is left. Even the superb and
ancient forests of Lithuania, their inland corals and seas were
reduced to a ravine of steaming stumps. Even the oak and elm
of Moravia, the spruce and larch of Sweden. Olive trees in
Sicilia and Campania, dry enough in their summer seasons, were
blackened scars on a violet sky. The beautiful trees of Swaledale
and Norfolk gone to blurry wind-scarred remnants. Even the
baite in the mountains, nonno, even their trees and their dwarf-
birch above the tree-lines. Mushrooms, wild strawberries,
snakes, many many birds, all that had accumulated in thousands
on thousands of years of balance and chance. Nothing was left,
nothing and no-one. In the face of such terror language loses all
relevance and ceases to matter and who is there left to speak or
to speak with? And yet what else can we hang on to? Or are we
such a small print and prick on life that earth will hardly notice
our going, and maybe celebrate as much as lament. Nonno, I
craved to have another dream ....

DAPHNE MARLATT
Journey

"Among the Aztecs dream interpretation &
divination by dreams were the prerogative
of the priestly class 'teopexqui', the Masters of
the Secret Things; and among the Maya of
'cocome', the Listeners."
Dreams: Visions of the Night

They had come from elsewhere, hundreds of them. Now they are stopped in a line that curves back down the road in the fading light. She can see his white truck glimmering behind her, and behind him, these cars, these trucks and jeeps and vans, sprawling into dark. Now they are here, now she sees the actual lineup, sees she is in it, she feels they have been pulled here, through a vast network of highways, roads, to this, this center (as if it were the heart of a continent, it isn't), this inspection center – yes, isn't that why they have come? the vehicles, their mechanism requiring inspection.

She takes her foot off the clutch and rolls down the window. After flying through the passes of those hills and then what seemed to be growing desert, though here, yes, there are trees, but stunted and far apart – it's hard to adjust to a crawl, her body, the car even, still canted forward in the impetus of speed, flying, it felt like flying, both windows down, hair streaming in the stream of air brushing her eyes trying to gauge, by feel, the lengths to leave according to their speed, his truck and her car juggling position in a kind of follow the leader or, since both love speed, a kind of dare, contingent on the bends, the turns, and then, after the tension of thrusting ahead letting her foot relax on the pedal, slipping back, feeling the slippage of air over the body of her car which responds like some animal alive to pavement its wheels mediate. Surrounding country, then, was just a blur.

And now she is here, is in it, rolls down the

window and night comes in, just the beginning edges of it dawning (how can that be? – but nothing seems to end here, sun glimmers horizontal and dusty behind those hills, as it has for the past hour, caught, on the verge of going – only not, only night bent on presence, invisibly growing.

And are they stopped? It seems to be something between first gear and none, or out of, slipping the clutch. Of course they're moving up a slight incline. Let the car ahead gain a few feet so at least she can *move* then, instead of slipping slipping the clutch. She misses their game and thinks he'll wonder what is holding them up. Glancing in the mirror for *him* now, and not the truck, she finds him a yard or so behind, arms crossed on the wheel and glancing out the side window. What's he looking at?

Rolls down hers, sees dust has stopped for the most part, just a light density in air, powder soft. Of course the earth here's sandy, or, she can't tell by colour, it's getting dark, it feels in the air, on the skin like a fine pulverized dirt, inland and old. The sea is beyond those hills, quite a long way beyond – was it yesterday? But there's a kind of freshness here she hasn't sensed before, not fresh, no, something out of night falling, some bush or herb that, freshened by the drop in temperature, releases an odour that is acrid and sweet.

She glances back at the truck, turning her head to look over her shoulder through the rear window. His window is dusty, he has the wipers going, squirting a clear arc to see through. She waves her hand to break his focus. He sees her and waves back and she turns forward, feeling a smile on her own face. Sees the car ahead has moved several yards. Shifts quickly into gear and follows. The smile, once she has felt it, begins to fade – it seems absurd to be smiling at a long line of cars – but she feels his presence warm behind her head like hair.

Near the top of the incline all the cars bear signs as if they had been numbered. She assumes she also has one and sees, glancing back, that he does too, but she doesn't remember seeing any men or feeling anyone approach the car. Maybe the signs have suction cups that would have been silently attached? Though she stares hard at the car ahead – actually it's a truck and, now that she stares intently, seems to be in some way official, a patrol truck, the kind a road construction crew uses to lead a line of cars through a restricted area – she cannot make out how the sign sticks. Each sign bears a number and a line or two of print too small to read. Not even the letters look recognizable and she thinks perhaps it's in some native language.

But now the truck in front, what is it doing? backs up a bit, turning, leaves the line and heads off down the road. Its brake lights flash on, pause, it is waiting – for her? Is she supposed to follow? If it's a patrol truck maybe it's starting a new lineup closer in to town, just to speed things up. She glances through the mirror, behind, to him, but can't make out whether he signals she should go or not. The patrol truck is still waiting, lights above and beside its sign flashing number seven. She's the next one, no one can move if she doesn't. She releases the clutch, steps on the pedal and veers out.

Her guide begins to pick up speed and she can see an unaccountable bend coming up. She glances back – is he following in the white truck? – but finds herself simultaneously at the bend before she can see – she *thought* she saw something white, but her attention is taken up with manoeuvering the turn at high speed. Out in the open, now they have left the avenue and moved into open country, the truck is streaking down the road. She presses hard on the pedal trying to catch up but the distance lengthens. Is it trying to lose her? Should she have followed? She remembers getting out of the car to look at her sign. Was it number six? (at least she thinks she remembers) was it number nine? Yes, she had to fix it with the print so she could tell – it was number six. If the truck is number seven she must obviously follow it. But was it really part of the line? She sees in the growing distance a number of tail-dragging black sedans, she can almost hear shouts, dogs barking, can almost see the sedans full of people, kids. So it's a native truck, it has nothing to do with the line. But it must know where to go, it must be going somewhere. The dust it leaves fills up the road. Impossible, impossible to see. She comes to a halt beside a ditch filled with dry weeds, fencepost above, a field. No one else on the road. A creeping stillness that is twilight glimmers down its length.

She gets out and stands alone for some time. No one, nothing comes. The pavement through the soles of her runners where heat is trapped around her feet, a sweat that is even now turning cold in the cool of evening, the pavement feels smooth, hardly tangible. She moves off toward the edge where weeds are and dirt. Her walking has slowed to an effort through air thick with smells of, what, some kind of dry grass smoke. Distance is charged with it. A faint magnetism runs between things, the fencepost and her feet, this stalk and that. No moon? She has turned, intending the full horizon, but finds herself looking west to the hills light still flares behind.

She will go in, there is a driveway further back, much overgrown, she will go in and ask.

Their faces hang in the dusk like fruit off a tree. She is standing on their land talking to them. On her left the man bends slightly over a stick or the handle of a pitchfork. To her right the two women and the girl – their faces float up towards her in the dusk, hardly aware, it seems, of what she sees as startling: daughter, mother, grandmother clustered together like so many berries on the one bush – all staring simply, at her own white face.

It was number seven, she says, the truck, where would a number seven truck be going? You see, I'm number six and I was supposed to be following ... and then she hesitates. If she is six, shouldn't the truck have been number five since it was ahead of her? She remembers the number seven, seven, flashing in the light. But how could that be?

In the stillness they watch her face. Something is gathering in the air, something she can't see. "Strange things ..." He seems reluctant to go on, and she turns to the woman she imagines might speak out of sympathy. What does he mean?

The woman doesn't answer. Or rather, behind her a fence post comes into view, bearing something nailed to it, some flayed animal. Its tawny hide flares up in the halflight. Matted fur. A warning? She thinks, that skin was nailed there for someone to see.

"I will tell you now is the time, now, when man's powers are coming to the full ..." It is pronounced, not spoken personally, not spoken to her at all. And yet she is allowed to overhear.

What do you mean? Is that all she can say? In the pressure of their silence she feels they feel she must know and is only pretending ignorance.

"The power of the sea and the power of dwarfs are acting together – that's what my mother would say." She turns her head to the old woman but the woman continues staring at her without expression, without understanding.

Go back to the line, he says, we can't help you.

Walking back to the car she is walking *toward* the hills light is still fading behind. Time seems to press in from there, like some tide rising like fear. He is right. They cannot help her.

Back in the car, she must turn around, but where? Drives on a little way, looking. There on the left, an abandoned garage, nailed shut, empty, and in front, a white truck. As she walks over to its window, she sees him in the passenger's seat, inert. For a second she thinks he is dead. What're you doing? Relief and fear sharpen her voice as he turns. He says quietly, I can't drive, and indicates the seat beside him. On it a parcel trussed up in rope sits in front of the driver's wheel, bulkily in front, leaving no room for him.

I followed you when you first left the line, he says, I trusted your sense of direction. I thought you were following the sea.

Here? But then she remem-
bers what was said. The parcel sits there, malevolent and unmov-
ing. It almost emanates its own presence, not a sign but, more
inexplicably, a knowledge of itself in front of them. She doesn't
ask him how it got there.

We must go back. Now.

She is driving
and he is in her car. She is trying to explain that there is no other way
out but the way they came, that the country surrounds them and
there is very little room – only the thread of their coming the way
they came. They are still looking for a place to turn. Up ahead, a
stone wall on the right, and beyond it, a driveway. As the wall
approaches and runs beside them, he leans forward and she hears
him say, they knew how to depict expression, certainly – almost real.
Looking, she sees them rise up from the ground, a few lopsided
crosses among them, huge iron heads like jack-o-lanterns with holes
for eyes and nose, but the mouths, the mouths have teeth, lips, some
with tongues even, myriad expressions of laughter, or scorn, or
knowing smiles. As the car begins to pick up speed, she sees, their
lips parted slightly, they are breathing, these mouths, as they them-
selves are turning into, a mistake, that driveway, carried by the
momentum of a plan, into the driveway of those others, those heads,
too late, onto *their* ground – No! – unwinds,

backward,

they are fly-
ing backward outside time in open country across fields, across
terrain that slips under them as they fly back in the slippage of
their own coming, down the road, through the house, wait, we
can't just fly through their house, through,

she sees him in a cor-
ner on a chair, unblinking, his stare which hasn't left her face since
she walked away, the man she asked directions of, she sees he has
known, he has always known, having just removed the pipe, it is in
his hand, it gleams in his eye which holds hers as they fly by, just
before and into the night, she realizes, looking back, how small he is.

Acknowledgements

Guy Birchard, "Tom Farr" and "Vicar of Distance", from *Further than the Blood* (Boston: Pressed Wafer, 2010). With permission of the author.

Paul Buck, extract from *skiP there is no story speaK to me*. Permission of the author.

Vahni Capildeo, "The Seven Dwarfs and Snow White", previously published in *Gather* (http://bit.ly/Jp7mSa). With permission of the author.

Johan de Wit, "A Dream" and eleven related texts (from *Blue Trumpet*), previously unpublished. With permission of the author.

Lawrence Fixel, "The Graduate", from *The Edge of Something* ([Berkeley?]: Cloud Marauder Press, 1977). With permission of Gerald Fleming, estate of Lawrence Fixel.

Giles Goodland, "Spring", previously unpublished. With permission of the author.

Barbara Guest, from *Seeking Air* (Santa Barbara, CA: Black Sparrow Press, 1978). With permission of Hadley Haden-Guest.

Paul Haines, "Unrecommended Lures", from *Secret Carnival Workers*, ed. Stuart Broomer with Emily Haines ([np]: H Pal Productions, 2007). With permission of Emily Haines, estate of Paul Haines.

Lee Harwood, "The Beginning of the Story", from *Collected Poems* (Exeter: Shearsman Books, 2004). With permission of the author.

Lyn Hejinian, "Lola", previously unpublished. With permission of the author.

Fanny Howe, "Even This Confined Landscape", from *The Lives of a Spirit* (included in *The Lives of a Spirit / Glasstown: Where Something Got Broken*, Callicoon, NY: Nightboat Books, 2005). With permission of the author.

Robert Lax, "21 pages", from *21 pages / 21 seiten*, with German translation by Alfred Kuoni (Zurich: pendo-verlag, 1984). With permission of the Robert Lax Literary Trust.

John Levy, "Goldilocks and the Five Bears", previously unpublished. With permission of the author.

Tom Lowenstein, from "Whale Hunt Journal", previously unpublished. With permission of the author.

Daphne Marlatt, "Journey", from *Zócalo* (Toronto: The Coach House Press, 1977). With permission of the author.

Brian Marley, "A Perigee Selection", previously unpublished. With permission of the author.

Bernadette Mayer, "Farmers Exchange" and "Nathaniel Hawthorne", from *Proper Name and Other Stories* (NY: New Directions, 1996). With permission of the author.

David Miller, "True Points", from *True Points: Eight Prose Texts 1981-1987* (Peterborough: Spectacular Diseases Press, 1992). With permission of the author.

bpNichol, three extracts from *Selected Organs: Parts of an Autobiography* (included in *The Alphabet Game: a bpNichol reader*, ed. Darren Wershler-Henry and Lori Emerson, Toronto: Coach House Books, 2007). With permission of Eleanor Nichol, estate of bpNichol.

Will Petersen, from "The Mask", previously published in *The Ear in a Wheatfield*. With permission of Cynthia Archer, estate of Will Petersen.

Kristin Prevallet, "Preface" and "Eulogy", from *I, Afterlife: [Essay in Mourning Time]* (Athens, OH: Essay Press, 2007). With permission of the author and Essay Press.

David Rattray, "The Spirit of St Louis", from *Opening the Eyelid* (Brooklyn, NY: diwan, 1990). With permission of the publisher, David Abel.

Ian Robinson, "Delayed Frames", from *Delayed Frames* (London: Oasis Books, 1985). With permission of Adelheid Robinson, estate of Ian Robinson.

Robert Sheppard, "The Given: Part I" (from *Out of Time*), from *The Given* (Newton-le-Willows: The Knives Forks and Spoons Press, 2010). With permission of the author.

Keith Waldrop, "Puberty", from *Hegel's Family* (Barrytown, NY: Station Hill, 1989. With permission of the author.

Rosmarie Waldrop, "A Form of Memory" (in an abridged version), from *A Form / of Taking / It All* (Barrytown, NY: Station Hill, 1990. With permission of the author.

Stephen Watts, "Nonno", previously published in *Modern Poetry in Translation*. With permission of the author.

M J Weller, "MySpace Opera – Twenty-Three Stories Slowed into a Fic-Blogosphere Microfiction During a Period of Thirty-Three Months", previously unpublished. With permission of the author.

Every effort has been made to trace the copyright holders of previously published material in this book and obtain permission to include it. In any case where we have failed to reach a copyright holder, we would be grateful if they'd contact the publisher so that their details can be included in the Acknowledgements in future printings of this publication.

In David Miller's "True Points", the phrase about the ways in which divine Being "is revealed in every being and yet always hidden in them" is taken from Ernesto Grassi's *Heidegger and the Question of Renaissance Humanism*.

REALITY STREET titles in print

Poetry series

Kelvin Corcoran: *Lyric Lyric* (1993)
Maggie O'Sullivan: *In the House of the Shaman* (1993)
Allen Fisher: *Dispossession and Cure* (1994)
Fanny Howe: *O'Clock* (1995)
Maggie O'Sullivan (ed.): *Out of Everywhere* (1996)
Cris Cheek/Sianed Jones: *Songs From Navigation* (1997)
Lisa Robertson: *Debbie: An Epic* (1997)
Maurice Scully: *Steps* (1997)
Denise Riley: *Selected Poems* (2000)
Lisa Robertson: *The Weather* (2001)
Robert Sheppard: *The Lores* (2003)
Lawrence Upton *Wire Sculptures* (2003)
Ken Edwards: *eight + six* (2003)
David Miller: *Spiritual Letters (I-II)* (2004)
Redell Olsen: *Secure Portable Space* (2004)
Peter Riley: *Excavations* (2004)
Allen Fisher: *Place* (2005)
Tony Baker: *In Transit* (2005)
Jeff Hilson: *stretchers* (2006)
Maurice Scully: *Sonata* (2006)
Maggie O'Sullivan: *Body of Work* (2006)
Sarah Riggs: *chain of minuscule decisions in the form of a feeling* (2007)
Carol Watts: *Wrack* (2007)
Jeff Hilson (ed.): *The Reality Street Book of Sonnets* (2008)
Peter Jaeger: *Rapid Eye Movement* (2009)
Wendy Mulford: *The Land Between* (2009)
Allan K Horwitz/Ken Edwards (ed.): *Botsotso* (2009)
Bill Griffiths: *Collected Earlier Poems* (2010)
Fanny Howe: *Emergence* (2010)
Jim Goar: *Seoul Bus Poems* (2010)
James Davies: *Plants* (2011)
Carol Watts: *Occasionals* (2011)
Paul Brown: *A Cabin in the Mountains* (2012)
Maggie O'Sullivan: *Waterfalls* (2012)

Narrative series

Ken Edwards: *Futures* (1998, reprinted 2010)
John Hall: *Apricot Pages* (2005)
David Miller: *The Dorothy and Benno Stories* (2005)
Douglas Oliver: *Whisper 'Louise'* (2005)
Ken Edwards: *Nostalgia for Unknown Cities* (2007)
Paul Griffiths: *let me tell you* (2008)
John Gilmore: *Head of a Man* (2011)
Richard Makin: *Dwelling* (2011)
Leopold Haas: *The Raft* (2011)
Johan de Wit: *Gero Nimo* (2011)
Sean Pemberton: *White* (2012)

For updates on titles in print, a listing of out-of-print titles, and to order Reality Street books, please go to www.realitystreet.co.uk. For any other enquiries, email info@realitystreet.co.uk or write to the address on the reverse of the title page.

REALITY STREET depends for its continuing existence on the Reality Street Supporters scheme. For details of how to become a Reality Street Supporter, or to be put on the mailing list for news of forthcoming publications, write to the address on the reverse of the title page, or email **info@realitystreet.co.uk**

Visit our website at: **www.realitystreet.co.uk/supporter-scheme.php**

Reality Street Supporters who have sponsored this book:

David Annwn	Romana Huk
Andrew Brewerton	Keith Jebb
Peter Brown	L Kiew
Paul Buck	Peter Larkin
Clive Bush	Sang-yeon Lee & Jim Goar
John Cayley	Richard Leigh
Adrian Clarke	Tony Lopez
Dane Cobain	Chris Lord
Mary Coghill	Michael Mann
Ian Davidson	Peter Manson
David Dowker	Ian Mcewen
Derek Eales	Ian McMillan
Carrie Etter	Geraldine Monk
Michael Finnissy	Camilla Nelson
Allen Fisher/Spanner	Maggie O'Sullivan
Sarah Gall	Marjorie Perloff
John Gilmore	Pete & Lyn
Harry Gilonis &	Tom Quale
Elizabeth James	Josh Robinson
Giles Goodland	Lou Rowan
Paul Griffiths	Will Rowe
Charles Hadfield	Robert Sheppard
Catherine Hales	Peterjon & Yasmin Skelt
John Hall	Hazel Smith
Alan Halsey	Valerie & Geoffrey Soar
Robert Hampson	Alan Teder
Randolph Healy	Philip Terry
Colin Herd	Sam Ward
Simon Howard	Susan Wheeler
Fanny Howe	John Wilkinson
Peter Hughes	Anonymous: 11

Lightning Source UK Ltd.
Milton Keynes UK
UKOW041140201112

202459UK00001B/4/P